ERIDANUS

Kim Idynne

for Sita

1: Strange Dreams

Dominic glanced nervously around the community room of the Phoenix veteran's home. Lively sounds floated from the hallway: conversation and laughter, billiard balls knocking together on a pool table. But here, in the near-empty room, Dominic sat wedged between two seemingly lifeless men. The one to his right had fallen asleep in a large motorized wheelchair, his head tipped back at a severe angle, silent and unmoving. Dominic strained to listen over the sound of the television, trying to detect the man's breath.

A young man, one of the nurses, approached and smiled at Dominic. "Do you need anything?"

"I was just wondering . . . is this guy okay?"

"Oh, he's fine. He's asleep most of the time."

"Okay. It just looks like his neck is bent too far back."

"It helps him breathe." The nurse approached the man who sat to Dominic's left—a figure who also sat immobile, but upright and with his eyes focused on the TV. "Has Ace said anything today?"

"No."

"That might be for the best." He gently set Ace's wheelchair upright and straightened his shirt where it had bunched up behind his back. "He doesn't know where he is or what's going on, and he's upset. He gets aggressive." The nurse gave Ace's arm a light squeeze. "Can't blame you, though, Ace. Wish there was something more we could do."

Ace Hale looked much older than his age of thirty-two. His skin was dry and thin, like a frail sheet of paper stretched over his bones, and his eyes looked cloudy and faded. Although Ace had shown no awareness of Dominic's presence, Dominic had given him the usual courtesies and an attempt at reassurance: *Your daughter can't come to visit for a while, but she wants you to know that she loves you. . . .* Then they sat silently, watching the evening news.

"How long has he been here?" Dominic asked. "At the home, I mean?"

"Well, I've been working here three years, and he was here before me. He was a military police officer. His unit ran into an IED." He eased the chair back again. "Do you have anyone serving in the military?"

"Just one—my cousin. He's stationed in Japan right now."

Dominic was surprised, suddenly, by the sight of Ace's daughter on the television screen. The photo of Hannah, wearing her hair in braids and forcing an awkward smile, popped up over the news desk. The anchor somberly announced: "Authorities have given up searching for Hannah Hale, who wandered off the designated trail at Wupatki National Monument and fell into one of the site's blowholes. . . ."

The nurse grabbed the remote. An old Clint Eastwood movie replaced Hannah's image.

He let out a long sigh. "Life can be a real disaster sometimes." He shot Dominic another smile, and Dominic saw that his eyes were glistening with tears. "Let us know if you need anything, okay?"

"Sure. Thanks."

The nurse wheeled the other man out of the room, and Dominic looked at Ace Hale, who sat gazing impassively at the screen. Dominic tried to speak confidently despite his own feeling of dread. "Not everyone has given up looking for Hannah," he said softly. "I'm going to find your daughter and bring her home. I promise."

"Why does she waste her time with this crap? No one cares about other people's dreams."

Chad stood beside the magazine rack at the record shop, paging through the latest issue of *Snapshots from the Dream World*. He slapped it onto the counter, where Dominic was closing the register for the day, and smirked. "You know, I'm just about done with this place. Working at a record shop for twelve bucks an hour has been fun, and I've made connections, but I have to keep *moving*. I don't want to be like these losers who just brag about meeting local musicians, or these pathetic cartoonists who spend their lives doing the same 'local zine' crap for a little attention and no pay. Surina has a dozen readers at the most. I mean, seriously, if I was standing here rambling about my dreams, wouldn't you just tune me out?"

Dominic browsed the copy of *Snapshots* as Chad continued his speech. Five of Surina's dreams were chronicled in varying detail on the pages, illustrated in black and white.

Surina was a year older than Dominic, a college student studying to be a music teacher. In person she gave the impression of being grounded and relaxed, but her cartoons indicated a neurotic disposition. She had dreamed that she tried to fly to work on a "magic pillow," only to realize that she was simply running down a public highway with a pillow between her legs. She dreamed that she accidentally broke her neighbor's souvenir necklace from Nigeria, and he chased her through town with a giant cleaver, swearing and screaming that he was going to kill her, until she jumped out of the bushes and sucker-punched him.

The last cartoon was called "Figure Out the Pizza or Die." Surina and her friends were stranded in the Andes

Mountains; they had missed their bus, and the local town had mysteriously vanished. As they sat on a rock, shivering and hungry, a young girl approached with a pizza.

"It's a take-and-bake," Surina complained. "How are we supposed to cook it?"

The final panel was illustrated in full color. The girl stood beside a large pizza, its round slices of meat and vegetables illustrated with symbols: glyphs, towers, jugs, and more. She gestured to it with a grave expression. "Eating isn't the problem," she said. "The real problem is that if we don't figure out the pizza, we're going to die here."

Dominic stiffened. "What the . . . ."

The girl, clad in a red vest and brown dress, her hair done in braids, was the very image of Hannah Hale.

And the pizza, with its array of strange symbols—he recognized that, too, from his own dreams. Dominic grabbed his backpack and dumped the contents onto the counter. He flipped through his notebook, paging back and forth, scrutinizing the images he'd drawn.

Chad leaned closer. "What's all this?"

Dominic slammed the notebook shut and re-stuffed his backpack, shoving Surina's booklet inside with everything else. "I'm done," he said quickly. "Have a good night." He slid his stepstool under the counter and hurried outside, pausing to think. Surina had just dropped off her cartoons and left. Where would she have gone?

He headed around the corner to the main street. Halfway down the block, at the nearest bus stop, a young woman in a yellow T-shirt and a cascade of dark hair was disappearing through the door of a city bus. Dominic swore under his breath and hurried toward it, waving frantically at the driver.

The bus started forward just as Dominic finished ascending the steps. He dug through his pockets and his backpack, trying to find enough change for the ride, panting from the run. He dropped his pack and grabbed the nearest pole as the bus rounded a corner.

The driver, a skinny, aged woman, gave Dominic a knowing look. "Haven't got the fare?"

"I've got it. Here." He dropped some change into the fare box and picked up his pack. Surina was a few seats back, watching him.

Dominic seated himself beside her. "Hi."

"Hi. Where are you headed?"

"I just wanted to catch up with you, actually." Dominic pulled out the crumpled copy of *Snapshots from the Dreamworld* and opened it to the last page. He paused, looking into Surina's eyes, detecting some unease in them. Surina had always been friendly; he had never seen any animosity or arrogance in her, but he suddenly felt certain that he had seen the last of her cordiality.

"I wanted to ask you about this drawing," he continued, smoothing out the page. "Do you know what these symbols are?"

"Um . . . ."

"Well, here's what I mean. You remember how I fell into that hole at Wupatki, and I breathed some cave fumes, and . . . ." He paused again. "Hang on a second." Dominic pulled his cell phone from his backpack. He tapped on a web browser and navigated to a news story about the incident at Wupatki. "That girl who fell in, Hannah Hale—do you know what she looks like?"

"No."

"Well, here's a photo of her." He handed the phone to Surina. "When she went missing, she was wearing a red vest."

The picture of Hannah, in a blue dress and braids, filled the screen. Surina frowned at it. "She looks familiar. Maybe . . . oh. That's weird."

"What is it?"

"Nothing. It's just, she looks like . . . ." Surina faltered.

"The girl from your dream?"

She eyed him cautiously, but didn't respond.

"Look." Dominic put the phone away and opened his notebook, flipping pages until he found a particular drawing. "Doesn't this look familiar, too?"

Quietly, Surina studied what Dominic had drawn: a large disc covered with a multitude of round medallions, each decorated with an image—a jug, a tower, and several other objects.

After some time she met his gaze. "What is that?"

"I don't know," he replied, "but it looks like we're trying to figure out the same pizza."

Thirteen days had passed since Hannah disappeared into the limestone tunnels at Wupatki. In that time, Dominic had dreamed of her every night—but he could only ever remember a few details. He would turn on the lamp and take notes, and then lay awake trying to make sense of them. Eventually he couldn't wake up to write; he was too exhausted. And so he made efforts to keep his other promises. He made attempts to find the family clan, found a few possible relatives and showed them Hannah's deer pendant, let them know that Ace Hale was lingering alone in the veterans' home. They had promised to ask around, maybe pay him a visit.

"You'll have to excuse the mess." Surina gave Dominic an apologetic look as she unlocked her apartment door. "I haven't spent much time at home lately."

The door opened to reveal a tiny studio apartment with a bathroom and compact kitchen at the back. Contrary to Surina's warning, it looked well-kept. To the right was a futon with fold-out trays on either side; Surina cleared books from the nearest tray and moved a cardboard carton from the seat. "Sit down," she said.

Dominic sat, leaning toward an open notebook that remained on the tray. A sudden clattering made him jump; Surina had toppled the carton, sending bottles of olive oil rolling across the carpet. She hurried to collect them.

"What's with all the olive oil?" Dominic asked.

"Oh—it's from my dad." She picked up the notebook and sat beside Dominic. "So, you know I take notes on my dreams. I've been dreaming about this girl a lot. Just, all of a sudden, she's been . . . ." She trailed off.

"Me too, ever since she disappeared."

"I named her Selena, because when I first started dreaming about her, she came down from the moon. She was telling me something, but I couldn't hear her voice, so she pointed at the moon—and it was covered with numbers and glyphs. I couldn't remember most of them, though."

"Look," Dominic said, "I know this is going to sound nuts, but I didn't hallucinate everything that happened in those tunnels. I was with Hannah. She told me all about her family, about things that have happened to her . . . things I couldn't know unless we had spent a substantial amount of time together. Something really strange is happening down there. I was supposed to help Hannah come home, but she's still in there, and I think she's trying to . . . ."

"Well, it does sound nuts. But I invited you in, didn't I?"

A long silence passed. Finally Surina slid the notebook onto Dominic's lap. "This is where it started. I wrote down as much as I could remember."

The entry, dated eleven days prior, featured a crude illustration of a girl's face next to a round circle covered with Roman numerals. Dominic paged through the journal; the name "Selena" was mentioned numerous times. The second entry began with an illustration of a fanged creature, standing upright and holding two ornate staffs in its claws.

Surina had written beneath it: *Jaguar temple, tunnels and off-limits area. Most of the tunnels haven't been excavated yet, so no one knows we're still alive in here. Selena is trying to draw the R. Stele. She says we can escape if someone figures it out. Our whole village is fading to nothing because we can't remember what the stele means (we are fading because we can't remember, but we can't remember because we are fading). Someone else will have to come and help us. Start at the outside and keep coming toward the axis (mandala), and they will end up underground, with us. They have to solve it from the inside.*

"What is this?" Dominic tapped his finger on the drawing. "I recognize this."

"It's part of the Raimondi Stele. It's a temple carving from Peru."

"And you don't know what it means?"

"No. No one will ever really know. The stele is three thousand years old, and the culture doesn't exist anymore."

"Okay, but I've been getting this same message: she wants me to go to a labyrinth and find *this* particular puzzle, and help her solve it."

"That's what I've been getting, too." Surina eyed him again and spoke hesitantly. "That's why I don't think you're nuts. She's been so . . . urgent. I was starting to feel like she was an actual person who needed my help."

"Do me a favor." Dominic opened his backpack. "Look through my notes, and tell me if you can make sense of anything."

They browsed quietly. Dominic felt himself flushing; he realized he was peeking into Surina's personal diary. Her dreams revealed someone who was worried about money, who fought with her brother and missed her dead grandparents, who was afraid of violence. Dominic only had a few pages of notes, but Surina murmured upon seeing them: she had seen some of the same symbols in her dreams, recognized Dominic's attempt at drawing the same fanged creature.

He flipped back to Surina's drawing of the stele. "Where in Peru is this?"

"Well, it's at the national museum now," Surina said, "but originally it was at Chavín de Huantar."

"And where is that?"

"In the Andes."

"Didn't your pizza dream take place in the Andes?"

"Yeah. That's where I usually see her—in Chavín. She keeps telling me to go back there, but . . . ."

"But what?"

"Once I get there, she wants me to help her get out. But we're always stuck." Surina pointed to one of Dominic's sketches: a labyrinth with a smiling, fanged creature at the center. Beside the sketch Dominic had written: *There's no way out but through the center?* "I'm not sure, but this might be the Lanzón. The Chavín complex is built like a labyrinth, with the Lanzón at the center. It has this same face carved on it."

Dominic mulled over that. He studied Surina's entry and read aloud: "'Start at the outside and keep coming toward the axis, and they will end up underground, with us. They have to solve it from the inside.' That sounds like the same thing I've been getting: If I go toward the center of this labyrinth, I'll end up back in . . . well, I'll end up with Hannah, and then we'll have to solve a riddle." He paused. "You've been to this place before?"

"Yeah. One of my dad's friends lives there. He wanted to open a retreat center across from the temple grounds, but it hasn't worked out. Chavín isn't very accessible to tourists. It's high up in the mountains, and the way there can be . . . unsafe."

"But, hypothetically, if I wanted to go there . . . how could I do it, and how much would it cost?"

"You could fly to Lima and take the bus. My plane ticket was eight hundred dollars, but my dad bought it months in advance."

"So if I absolutely have to go to Peru, I should buy the plane ticket now."

"You're really considering it?"

"I'm not considering. I'm going." Dominic tucked his notebook into his bag and stood up. "Thanks for letting me see your notes."

"Dominic . . . ."

He stopped and turned to her, his mind racing to make arrangements. *If I transfer my savings on the way home, I can buy the ticket tonight, and figure out the rest later.*

"Look . . . I know we barely know each other," Surina said, "but I want to get back to Chavín, too. If you're really going, I want to come with."

2: The Cosmic Wheel

Dominic woke to the smell of old carpet and bleach. A pair of unfamiliar brown curtains blocked out the mid-day light. Through the wall behind his bed came the sounds of conversation; he heard the exchange clearly, but couldn't understand a single word. Rolling over, he saw a young woman lying in a bed across from his, her dark hair covering most of her face. And he remembered: *I am in a foreign country with a stranger. I don't understand the language. I don't know my way around. I spent all of my money. And soon I'll be high in the mountains, in a strange temple, and then I might end up back in . . . .* He didn't know what to call it, but he was afraid to go back into that realm—the place where he had last seen Hannah.

After a full day and night spent in planes and airports, he and Surina had arrived in Lima, Peru, and began planning their route into the mountains. Surina insisted on renting a car; the fast, winding bus ride on the mountain roads would give her motion sickness. She persuaded Dominic with tales of vomit, pungent crowds, and urine-soaked bathrooms.

"The drivers are over-worked," she added, "and it's easy to drift off the roads. Just last week, one of the double-decker buses went over the cliff, and everyone died. It was on the local news because some tourists from Florida and Arkansas were on it. Besides, the drivers always play the worst radio stations. It'll be seven hours of high-speed Spanish polka."

"I'm convinced," Dominic replied.

Before they could drive, they needed sleep. Surina had suggested taking a taxi to another district. "We'll get a hotel closer to the mountains and rent a car out there. Driving through Lima is its own enigma."

And so Dominic was lying in a room far from the airport, overcome by dread and disbelief, as if waking from a trance. *I spent all my money*, he told himself again, *to come all the way here and go back into . . . that place.* His adventures in the stars rolled through his head— memories of sickness, toil, despair, even an unwitting murder.

A movement interrupted his thoughts: the deer pendant was sliding across his chest, falling toward the mattress. He thought of Hannah, then, and he even recalled bits of healing and revelation in the starry realm. Even so, the recollection of helpless suffering made him groan out loud.

Surina's eyes opened. She immediately sat up, still fully dressed in a purple T-shirt and blue jeans. She flashed a smile at Dominic. "All right, I'm rested. Let's go!"

"It's nine o'clock. We only slept for two hours."

"That's plenty," she insisted.

The rental place was within walking distance. Surina had reserved the cheapest car. She paid, threw her luggage into the back seat, and starting the engine. "Looks good," she said, checking the controls. "Now we just need . . . damn."

"What's the matter?"

Her hand hovered over the gear shift. "I forgot . . . there aren't any automatics here. They're all manual transmission."

"Is there a place that has automatics?"

"Maybe, but you have to be at least twenty-five to rent

at most places."

"Do you know how to drive a stick?"

"Um . . . ."

"I'll take that as a no. All right; let's find a bus."

"No, it's fine. I just need a refresher." Surina pulled out her phone.

"What are you doing?"

"YouTube," Surina replied. "I'll find a tutorial."

"Please don't."

"I've driven sticks before. We'll go around the block a few times just to make sure."

"Driving around a city block isn't the same as scaling a mountain pass hundreds of—"

"Relax," Surina said sharply. "I know what I'm doing."

He took a deep breath and settled back into the passenger seat. "Fine."

When Surina was done with the YouTube video, she made a slow circle around the lot, then around the block, circling a long plaza full of manicured shrubs and cobbled walkways.

"Piece of cake," she said.

She swung around onto the main street, passing shops and concrete sidewalks crowded with people. Surina deftly navigated the crowded lanes, avoiding most of the cars that darted in without warning and a few pedestrians making a brave dash across the street. "People don't always obey the stoplights," she explained, just as a car careened into their lane and banged into the rear door. "It's not really a law; it's more of a suggestion."

The other driver leaned on his horn.

"We got hit," Dominic said. "Shouldn't we pull over?"

"Not necessary." Surina turned a corner and headed for the highway.

The country roads, by contrast, presented a long

stretch of calm. Sunlight streamed through occasional wisps of clouds, illuminating snow-capped peaks in the distance and shimmering on the surrounding ponds and streams. Surina put an upbeat music mix into the CD player and began the slow ascent into the mountains. Dominic relaxed, glad that he was riding with her rather than an exhausted bus driver. He was impressed by how deftly she handled the chaotic city streets and curving mountain roads. She managed to seem relaxed and intense at the same time, lounging in her seat but instantly reacting to every obstacle. She would make a good partner in the otherworld. The two of them had spent the layover practicing enigmas and other puzzles, and she caught on quickly.

Surina saw him watching her, and gave him a smile—quick, but warm and genuine, so that her deep brown eyes and dark skin seemed to glow.

"Didn't you say your mom is from Peru?" he asked.

"Brazil. She worked at one of the tourist places that takes people into the rainforest. That's how my dad met her. He married her and convinced her to come back to the States . . . and then he left."

"Oh . . . ."

"He didn't leave right *away*," she added. "They were married for twenty years, and then my dad moved to Israel. My mom didn't want to go."

"Why Israel?"

"He was born there, and his sisters still live there. We keep in touch. We talk on Skype and play chess online, and I finally went to visit him last year. It was a strange experience. There were tanks and soldiers everywhere." Surina launched into a monologue about her dad, who spent a lot of time in places Dominic had never heard of, and who used to earn a lot of money as an IT specialist but now had to live on piece work. Dominic nodded his head a few times and said "Uh-huh" as if he understood what Surina was talking about.

"So, tell me again about the enigmas," she said at last.

"There isn't much else to say. They're just word puzzles. We had to solve one everywhere we went. It seems silly, but after a while you realize it's not about the puzzles. It's about what happens while you're solving them . . . but you *have* to solve them, or you'll get stuck. So I've been practicing. You know, I had never heard of enigmas before I ended up there, but I guess they're an actual thing—back home, I mean. People have enigma competitions at the University. Have you heard of this? They have enigmas and other word riddles, and math riddles. They even have science riddles that have no answer. People contribute their answers, and the judges try to decide on the best theory. They call the players Olympiads."

"Give me a riddle," Surina said.

"All right, here's one: I run, but I will never walk; I gurgle, but I never talk; I have a head and mouth, but no hands or feet; I'm always in bed, but I never sleep. What am I?"

"A river. That was too easy."

"Well, it's the only one I can think of right now." Dominic leaned closer to Surina and peered at the opposite side of the road, where the ground vanished just a few feet from the pavement. The space between the road and the drop-off seemed increasingly narrow as the car ascended higher into the mountains; the curves seemed sharper, the cliffs steeper. He'd been surprised to find little towns tucked into the side of the mountains. People hiked up and down the narrow roads, uncomfortably close to the car. Dominic decided to close his eyes for a while, hoping to forget the heights, but he drifted into sleep and ended up with nightmare visions of a crowded bus drifting off the road. The sounds of terrified screams mingled with a Spanish Oom-pah band that blared through the speakers.

He was jolted awake as the engine revved. The car surged forward, then slowed to a stop. Dominic opened his eyes just as it began to roll backwards. Through the windshield he saw nothing but mountain. To his right was the massive wall of rock, quickly receding as the car drifted away; and to his left, the edge of the curving road dropped away into nothing.

Surina swore and put on the brakes. Her voice was barely audible over the din of the radio.

"What are you doing?" Dominic asked.

"There's a problem with the car."

His heart pounded. He gripped the seat belt and twisted around to look through the windows. "What problem?"

"The road is getting steep, and the car won't go up. I have it in the lowest driving gear, but . . . ." Surina tried again. The car shot forward, then slowed and started a fast retreat. Surina hurriedly put on the brake.

"Please don't do that," Dominic begged as Surina came to a hard stop. "Slamming on the gas clearly isn't working."

"Well, you're right." Surina pulled out her phone. "Damn. No service. I could really use YouTube right now."

"Maybe you need it in first gear."

"First is just for idling."

"Okay. So, what's the plan?"

"We just passed a town. Let's roll backwards and ask—"

"No, no. No more rolling backwards, please. Someone will come around the curve and crash into us."

"It's just right there. Oh—some people are coming.

I'll ask them for help."

Dominic tried to look through the rear window, then gave up and scrutinized the radio display. "What are we listening to? I thought you hated Spanish polka."

Surina's eyes went wide. "This isn't polka. This is Victoria Santa Cruz! She's—"

Dominic switched the radio off. He rolled down the window as someone approached the passenger side—a man, middle aged, with a clear but weathered face and amused eyes that twinkled under his wide-brimmed hat. Surina leaned over and chatted with him. The man grinned at Dominic and headed back down the road.

"What did he say?" Dominic asked.

"He's finding someone who knows how to drive."

After a long wait, a younger man leaned into the opposite window and had an animated exchange with Surina. He gestured to the gear shift several times, then rolled his hands over each other to mimic the car rolling backwards. He seemed to find that hilarious.

"Gracias," Surina said, and closed the window. She gave Dominic a pointed look. "First gear. You were right."

"Maybe we can park in the village and take a bus the rest of the way."

"We're fine."

"You have to admit, though, that this was a bad idea. What if we'd gotten stuck half an hour ago, with no one around to help? What if we'd been sliding backwards at a tighter curve?"

"We would have figured it out."

"Maybe. Maybe you would have figured it out halfway down the long drop to our deaths."

Surina gazed at him quietly. "And what if our plan works, and we end up stuck in the Chavín labyrinth, with no one around to help . . . and we can't figure out the riddle? What then? Could we really die in there?”

He resisted a shudder. “We have to get there first.”

“Let’s get there, then.” She put the car in gear and started up the hill.

Around the bend, the incline was less extreme. Overhead, the cloud cover began to break, allowing a stream of light into the mountain valleys. A waterfall shimmered in the distance. Dominic began to relax—until he realized that the water was rushing onto the road.

Pedestrians leaned against the mountain on either side of the fall, waiting for the water to abate. Surina stopped the car and turned off the engine. “This happens sometimes,” she explained. “It’s been warm and sunny the past few days, so there’s snow melt coming down the mountain. We have to wait it out.”

“Shouldn’t we back up?” Dominic asked. “What if more water comes down?”

Surina turned the radio on and pushed her seat into a reclining position. “We’re fine.”

By the time they reached Chavín, Dominic had taken back all of the complimentary thoughts he’d had about Surina. She was not a skilled driver, nor was she prone to simple feats of logic. She had driven on the road while water was still rushing across it, and she insisted on listening to that awful radio station. And she said the words “We’re fine” far too often.

Dominic was about to criticize her for driving too close to a passing car when he was struck dumb by the sight at the opposite edge of the road: a dizzying drop into what appeared to be an endless mountain vortex, with no hint of a bottom. The details seemed to merge into a distant blur and vanish into darkness. Just beyond this narrow roadway was the town of Chavín, nestled in a scenic nook with views of nearby mountain peaks, some rocky and wild, others covered with a patchwork of agricultural plots in varying shades of green. Concrete homes lined the street, the front doors painted in bold colors. On the opposite side, a woman hiked along the road with a machete in one hand and a bundle of fresh green crops strapped to her back. A young girl in a felt hat walked ahead of her, leading a donkey with a large woolen pack. She turned and locked eyes with Dominic, and smiled. Just beyond her, two boys were urinating on the roadside.

"Let's eat first," Surina said.

"Where are we going to find food?"

"Um . . . first we'll have to rent a machete, and then we'll hike to the fields and find some wild edibles."

"I hope you're joking."

She laughed and turned left, toward the town's main thoroughfare. The street looked more metropolitan than Dominic expected. Surina parked at a restaurant tucked between a pharmacy and a dance club. "This is my favorite café," she insisted. "I used to go here with my dad."

The café, too, was not what Dominic anticipated upon seeing its small façade. The interior was designed around a central open-air courtyard with a cobbled floor; it stood two stories high, with ornate metal railings and lush, twining plants. The smell of fresh air and greenery complemented the scents from the kitchen. Dominic, still thinking of the long drop into nothingness, chose a table on the ground floor. "I'm kind of nauseous from the ride," he said. "Can you help me order something small? I need protein, but I don't want to eat much."

Surina helped him order a small meal of deviled eggs. He ended up with two raw eggs floating in warm water, served in a small glass bowl.

Dominic stared at it, then poked it with his spoon and watched the yolks rupture. "Surina, what the hell is this?"

"Huevos rellenos. Deviled eggs."

Dominic slid the dish across the table.

Surina peered at it and chuckled. "I don't know. Poached eggs? Send it back." She lifted a forkful of slimy-looking cactus paddles. "Want some of mine?"

The sight of wet green strips wobbling on the fork made Dominic's stomach go sour. "I'm not hungry after all," he muttered.

When the waiter returned, Surina was busy chewing her putrid-looking cactus, so Dominic tried to reject his meal with the few Spanish words he knew. "No gusto. I don't want it," he said, and then tried to apologize for his clumsy speech: "Lo siento, la España es muy pobre."

The waiter gave him a puzzled look and carried the eggs away. Surina, too, looked confused. "What were you trying to say?"

"My Spanish is bad."

She shook with laughter. "You just told him that Spain is full of poor people."

"What?"

"You said Spain has a bad economy. Spain is poor, very poor. That's what you said."

Dominic didn't laugh.

Not much was said between the two of them afterwards. They checked into a small hotel, where they showered and changed clothes, and then sat on opposite sides of the room while they waited for Surina's friends to show up. Surina browsed through a copy of *Scientific American* he'd picked up at the airport, while Dominic only pretended to read (he was actually preoccupied with various thoughts, such as how Surina had probably ordered raw eggs on purpose, and he couldn't look online to see what *huevos rellenos* really meant because he didn't have internet access, and so on).

Surina glanced at her watch and sighed. "It's already

six-thirty. Let's just go without them."

Voices sounded in the hallway, followed by a sharp knock on the door.

"That's them," she said. A smile lit her face; she hurried to the door and pulled it open. Two men stood in the hall, exclaiming with joy when they saw Surina. One of the men looked Peruvian—a small, thin man in an oversized button-down shirt. The other was just as petite, but light-skinned and bald, with frosty blue eyes. Surina immediately threw her arms around the Peruvian, and then hugged the other.

"Where's Pajarilla?" she asked.

The Peruvian answered in Spanish. Dominic stood awkwardly in the background until the bald man finally took notice of him. He nudged Surina. "Who's your friend?"

"Oh, that's Dominic," she replied, and made hurried introductions. "Dominic, this is Hank, and this is Nemcio. Nemcio doesn't speak English, but I can translate for you." She beckoned him eagerly. "Let's go before the temple closes."

The temple was a short walk away, past a row of small adobe homes with tiled roofs. Children peeked through the open windows to regard the group with shy, curious smiles, and little dogs wandered lazily past. Surina had warned of the possibility of altitude sickness, but despite the feral dogs urinating on the road a few feet away, the air here smelled supremely fresh. Dominic felt that he had never breathed so easily.

He walked quickly to keep up with Surina, who was impatient to get to the temple grounds. "Nemcio has worked at the site for years," she explained in a low voice, "and Hank knows plenty about it too. They should be able to answer any questions we have. Let's check out the Raimondi Stele and the Lanzón. The Lanzón is at the center of the labyrinth. The message I got is that we're supposed to go there. Maybe we'll find an entrance."

Hank hurried to match Surina's pace. "An entrance to what?"

"Um . . . I'm just wondering how much more of the labyrinth has been excavated since I was here last," she replied.

"They're still digging up tunnels all over. I'll show you all of that, but you should see the river first."

The site itself was unimposing. It was a small plot of land and seemed to contain little more than a few low stone walls and sculptures, mostly stylized jaguar heads with spiral eyes and fanged, grinning mouths. The main temple structure was a simple brick building. It stood at the western end of the complex, with a grassy plaza lying between it and a narrow river.

"Come this way." Hank waved the group onward, and they started across the plaza, toward the edge of the temple grounds. "No one understands the importance of the river. See that little shack on the other side? I own the property right there."

"Yes, I've been there," Surina reminded him.

"Have you seen the stones on that land? Those big ones—do you see them?"

Hank led the group to the riverside, pointing out various markers on the opposite side. "See, when people did ceremonies here, they didn't start in the courtyard. They started over *there*, on *my* property, because part of the ceremony involved crossing the river. The river is like the boundary between the mortal world and the spirit world. They would cross it, and then they'd crawl through that hole over here." Hank pointed at a circular opening in a stone wall, a few yards downriver. "This whole area was enclosed by a wall. That opening is the portal. The temple complex represents the spirit world that births you into the mortal world; and if you crawl through that hole, you know, it's like you're crawling back into, um . . . well, it's like you're going back where you came from."

"To the spirit world," Dominic said. "Got it."

"I could really make a profit off that patch of land if I can get the archaeologist to acknowledge it. I could charge people to cross the river like they're doing the actual ceremonies. The only problem is that the water is too high and fast after the snow melt. I wouldn't be able to do it year-round." Hank gave Surina a sly look. "Of course, I could just have everyone sign a disclaimer and cross at their own risk."

Nemcio had stepped into the river and was coaxing Surina to follow him. The water, though turbulent, only rose mid-thigh.

"Go ahead," Hank encouraged her. "You can sit on that big, flat rock in the middle of the river. You get really good acoustics there."

Surina began to remove her shoes. "Which river is this?"

"It's the Mosna. The Huachesca is back there." He jutted a thumb back toward the way they had come. "Farther down, they confluence into the Marañon. That empties into the Amazon River, and if you keep following it, it cuts all the way through Brazil into the Atlantic."

He kept talking, but Dominic was distracted by the sight of Nemcio, who stood in the river and very deliberately splashed water onto the front of Surina's pale yellow shirt. Dominic couldn't understand what he was saying, but Hank called out in encouragement: "That's right, you have to go all the way in. Immerse yourself."

Dominic rolled his eyes.

As they headed back to the temple, Surina tried to wring water from her soaked shirt. Dominic kept pace with her, falling behind the others. "Hank is quite a character," he said. "It's like, you know, someone gives birth to you, but if you crawl back through the hole, it's like, um—"

"Stop it." Surina slapped him lightly on the shoulder, but broke into a smile.

"I bet half his customers wash away down the river. But hey, he'll have a waiver, so who cares?"

Her smile broadened. Surina's face was radiant when she smiled—especially now, as the setting sunlight brought out the undertones in her dark skin. As they wandered against the vast, lush backdrop of rising green hills, Dominic felt his annoyance beginning to slip away.

"Nemcio won't be much help," he added. "He'll have all the girls dunking in year-round, just so he can see them in wet T-shirts."

She scoffed. "It's fine, I'm wearing a tank top underneath."

"Yes, I can see that."

Surina narrowed her eyes at him. "The rivers *are* important. Maybe . . . ." She frowned, then leaned close to Dominic and whispered: "I don't know what we're supposed to *do*. Should we just wander around until something happens?"

"Let's hit the important spots. Where are we headed now?"

"The Lanzón."

"All right. I'll trust your judgment on where we should wander. How many times have you been here?"

"Just twice. Once with my dad, and once with my husband."

Dominic gave her a startled look. "You're married?" He thought back to her tiny apartment, her seemingly solitary lifestyle.

"*Was* married. I've been divorced for nearly a year." She paused. "I got married here. Hank got a minister license through the Humanist church, and he performed our ceremony."

Nemcio and Hank had ascended the step to the temple entrance—a large stone block, white granite on one side and black limestone on the other. Nemcio explained, and Surina translated, that the builders worked hard to incorporate themes of duality. They traveled some distance to get the white granite, but had to go even deeper into the mountains to quarry the black limestone and bring it back. "The interior labyrinth winds around quite a bit," Surina added, gesturing through the doorway, "but now there's a path that goes straight into the central chamber. The Lanzón is that way."

Dominic was getting impatient. He hadn't come here to learn about Chavín. He had come to find Hannah. "Is that important?" he asked.

Hank pointed to a grassy area in front of the steps. "There are more tunnels down there, but they haven't finished excavating them. I think they lead pretty far—maybe all the way to the river." He paused. "Someone should go down there and take a look."

"They're off limits." Surina pointed to a sign that warned them not to enter the area.

"Oh, please. I go into the off-limits areas all the time. This is kind of a tight space, though." Hank stepped closer, peering into the cavity. Then he looked at Dominic, sizing him up. "Looks like you're the only one small enough to fit inside."

Dominic turned away. "I'm going to check out the Lanzón."

The doorway led into a series of enclosed hallways, brightened with rows of small light bulbs. Dominic found the central chamber easily. It, too, was off-limits, protected from intrusion by a barred metal gate. Behind the bars rose a stone column, engraved from top to bottom with a cartoonish figure whose large, clownish face was framed with spiraling serpents. The image stirred recognition. Dominic had seen photos of it on the internet, and he thought he recognized it from dreams. Its wide-lipped mouth, curved at the ends, bore two protruding fangs. The creature appeared to be rolling its eyes, reflecting Dominic's own feelings at the moment. He whispered: "Hannah, what am I doing here?" He closed his eyes, tried to will himself back into the zodiac realm—and opened his eyes to see that same ridiculous face. Nothing had changed.

Dominic gripped the bars and leaned his forehead gently against them, still staring at the stone column. "What the hell are you smiling at?" he muttered.

"Surina, you can probably fit," Hank said.

"You can fit, too, you little waif. Did you lose weight? You look like the wind might blow away."

Hank ignored the comment. "Wait until the guards aren't looking. If they catch you, just pretend you're a tourist who doesn't speak Spanish. I'll look the other way and pretend I didn't notice." He turned slightly aside, gazing out across the grounds. "This one's still looking. Wait . . . wait . . . ."

"You say all this as if I'm actually going to jump in," Surina said.

"Come on, when will you get another opportunity like this? In a year, this place will be packed with tourists and security and guard rails, and you won't be able to get within a foot of anything. Okay, he's . . . now! Go, go, go!"

Surina opened her mouth to utter a sarcastic reply, but the words didn't come. She felt overcome by a sudden, inexplicable urge.

She hurried across the grass and lowered herself into

the cavity.

Darkness swelled before her. A few yards ahead the tunnel ahead looked like a solid black mass, silent and imposing. Surina crouched low to the ground and lifted her face toward the sky.

Hank's voice floated to her, sounding strangely far away. "Great job. He didn't see you. I'll let you know when it's safe to come back up."

Surina's clothes were still dripping water. She quickly regretted having drenched herself. The tunnel was cold, and the dirt that brushed her hands and clothes turned to mud. She wiped her hands on her shorts and began to inch forward, keeping a crouching stance as she moved. Light faded behind her; the ground felt hard and cold beneath her feet. Surina reached for the tunnel walls, but quickly withdrew her hands, consumed by fears of creeping, stinging things that could not be seen. She stopped and waited for her eyes to adjust to the darkness.

At length she could see the outline of the tunnel. She ventured a bit farther, hearing nothing but her own breath—and then, the pulsing of her heart.

She stopped again, started again. The darkness disoriented her, made her feel as though she would fall through space. She reached out again, lightly touching the walls with her fingertips, comforted by their solidity. Somewhere up ahead the tunnel seemed to be vaguely lit, as though it opened to another hole in the ground. Surina made her way toward the light. She thought she heard a faint sound of running water, accompanied by a strange musical sound: a set of droning, harmonic tones. As the end of the tunnel neared, Surina began to relax—but she froze when that light was suddenly blocked by a moving figure.

Someone, or something, was approaching from the opposite end.

Surina began a slow retreat, trying to move without making a sound. The other figure also moved quietly, but she heard a footfall or two. And then a man's voice said: "Dominic? Surina?"

She jumped back, stumbling and falling onto her bottom. Her palms smacked against hard stone. She pulled herself back into a crouch, tried to collect her nerves. One of the guys had probably found another opening and jumped inside. "Hank?" she called. Surina moved forward again, eager to reach the light. The figure didn't sound like Nemcio. "Who is it? Hank?"

The voice spoke in a near whisper: "Come here."

"Where's that music coming from?" she asked.

"Shh. Not so loud."

Something looked wrong about the end of the tunnel. Rather than opening upward, to the ground, it seemed to open straight ahead. Perhaps she'd gone all the way across the plaza and reached the riverbank. She clearly heard the rushing of water up ahead, mingled with the musical droning.

Surina's breath caught. Something else was wrong. The man's face was becoming visible in the light, and she didn't recognize it at all. He was thin and gaunt, and there was something specter-like about his skin; it was so pale that it almost seemed to glow. A long white garment covered his body. It reminded her of a hospital gown and brought to her mind wild thoughts of escaped patients and dangerous lunatics. He pulled the garment up, over his head. Surina realized he was undressing.

She backed away, but stumbled again.

The figure drew near and extended the garment toward her, as though to catch her up in it. "Don't be alarmed," he said. "I'm a friend."

"Stay back."

"It's just a tunic. Cover yourself with it, quickly, before Tagua discovers you're here."

3: Achernar

Surina remembered the name Tagua: the underworld demon who had taken Hannah. She studied the ghastly figure in front of her, the blue-tinged skin and tired eyes. "Who are you?" she asked.

"My name is Wibben."

"Wibben . . . you're Bernhard Wibben? Dominic told me about you."

He paused, lowering his gaze; then he extended the tunic again. Surina decided to trust him, letting him slide it over her head.

"You're in the celestial plane, near Hydrus and the Eridanus," he said.

"What? No, we're at Chavín. This tunnel leads up to the temple. I was just there a minute ago."

He didn't acknowledge her words, but carefully arranged the material so that it covered her legs. "Hannah is looking for you—or rather, for Dominic. He isn't with you?"

"Is she here?" Surina peered toward the opening, then turned and scrutinized the darkness. "Really, this tunnel leads to Chavín. I can take Hannah through it. You can come with us."

"I can't," Wibben said quietly. "Neither can Hannah."

"Oh . . . that's right." Surina thought over all the stories Dominic had told her, but suddenly her mind blanked. She sat and stared into the dark.

"Are you all right?" Wibben asked.

"I'm just going to see if I can go back through this tunnel." She inched back the way she had come, sliding one foot carefully in front of the other. "I'll be right back, I promise."

"Surina . . . ."

Her legs trembled. She found herself unable to move.

"Here. Let me help you," Wibben offered.

"I can't get back, can I?" she asked.

"Not yet. I think you have a journey to go on before you can get back to your world. Come on, that's it. Get clear of this and then you can stand up straight. A little farther . . . ."

Surina clutched at his arm as they left the tunnel—not for balance, but out of fear. The landscape ahead of her was not what she imagined. It looked like a massive underground cave. Light blazed down through large openings in the rock ceiling, illuminating small streams that flowed from the rock walls and pooled together along the floor.

"We should leave this place quickly," Wibben said.

"Why?"

"Look behind you."

She turned, and then stepped back, tipping her head to take in the sight of a massive sculpture in the rock. The exterior of the tunnel she'd just traversed had been carved to look like a serpent's head; the tunnel comprised its open mouth. The lower jaw was mostly beige, streaked here and there with russet-colored lines, while the rest of its head was russet and gray. Its facets shone here and there where they reflected light—especially the eyes, two burnt umber spheres that bulged from the face, with black streaks that looked like narrow pupils. But the serpent barely caught her attention. It was surrounded by the even more imposing figure of a jaguar head, an enormous structure that reached from the floor to the top of the cave.

The beige and russet-hued figure was stylized, like the jaguar heads at Chavín, with flared nostrils and wide, concave eyes. Its mouth, fanged with stalagmites and stalactites, stood gaping, while the snake merely served as its tongue: a mouth within a mouth.

Two words were etched neatly into the rock below the tunnel: Alpha Hydri. Twin waterfalls trickled around both sides of it as water flowed from the jaguar's jaws, gentle and slow, as though the creature was drooling.

"Wow," she gasped. "This is under Chavín?"

"It's alive," Wibben said. "Sleeping right now. When the music stops, it wakes up."

"What wakes up?"

"Hydrus."

"Hydrus? This thing? It's a rock."

"So it is, at the moment. Such things have a way of transforming. See that fountain at the riverbank?"

Surina turned and followed his gaze. Small cave pools dipped into the rock, their stunning green bottoms lit up here and there by streams of light. Water flowed and trickled from above and below, dripping rhythmically from the stalactites that punctuated the ceiling, winding into and around the pools, flowing into a larger and faster stream of dark waters. Surina could see the point where countless rivulets joined to become an actual river with a discernible path. Along its bank were a few dozen tiny spurts of water shooting upward into the air, arcing over rock and descending into the river.

"A series of small tunnels runs through that rock," Wibben explained. "Once every cycle, the water rises high enough that water rushes through the tunnels. They operate like aquatic flutes. Right now most of the holes are blocked by sediment and other build-up, but the water will wash it away eventually. When all the holes in a rivulet are unblocked, or when the water gets too low, the music drops out."

"And the music keeps it asleep," Surina said slowly. "So you're telling me that this thing is alive, and it might wake up and . . . do what?"

"It will be very unhappy to see us, so let's move on. Hannah is waiting for you."

Surina stared up at the looming jaguar figure. Fear stirred in her being, but she couldn't heed Wibben's warning. The threat felt unreal—as if she was dreaming and didn't know how to wake up.

One of the tones suddenly stopped. Though it was probably her imagination, Surina thought she heard a soft sigh from the cave, and a flash of awareness in the eye of the serpent.

"Okay," she whispered.

As they approached the river, Surina was surprised by the darkness of the water. No longer did the light shine through clear liquid onto astonishing green and blue rocks. The river appeared muddy, almost black, and not even an inch of the rocky sides were visible beneath the surface.

"Most of the water comes from below," Wibben explained. "All the water you see flowing from up there . . . that's just a trickle."

Surina glanced at him and tried not to stare. Having given her his tunic, Wibben was scantily dressed. He wore nothing but a bulky cloth wrapped around his pelvis. The blue-gray shades of his flesh fascinated and repelled her; his figure was so thin that his ribs jutted beneath his skin, and though his coloring seemed sickly and even corpse-like, his flesh had some quality that made it almost luminescent in the dim cave.

"We're underground, right?" she asked, peering up at the cracks in the ceiling.

"We're in the celestial realm—very close to the

southern pole. Hydrus is guardian of the south, and Draco
guards the north. Both mark a boundary between earth
and the celestial realm. Hydrus brings you here, and
Draco brings you back to earth."

"So I can get home through Draco," Surina replied.

He laughed softly. "No. Draco is a portal of
reincarnation. You can't get through except by dying.
We'll get you back some other way."

Surina felt a small quiver of fear. She stopped
walking. Her gaze darted around the cave, at the shadows
lurking beyond beams of light. "How did I get here?
Hannah must have known there was a tunnel at Chavín
that led here. She kept telling me to come here."

"There are portals all over the earth that can lead to
the celestial realm. It's a matter of time and opportunity."

"But I can get back," she replied uncertainly.

"You can. Don't worry." He gazed at her wearily, but
with kindness in his eyes. "She didn't trap you here. The
temple you came from—it has markings that represent
constellations. The people who built it may have been
trying to map the celestial realm, and create portals
leading here."

"There was a portal," Surina said. "I just walked
through it."

"There is a portal that opens when Hydra sleeps.
When Hydra is awake, it guards the portal and prevents
anyone from crossing." Wibben paused. "The temple
builders may have known that. They could have predicted
the opening by watching the movements of the stars."

"They wanted to come here on purpose?" Surina
thought back over Dominic's stories. "Why? Dominic
made this place sound horrible. And if Tagua has been
here for thousands of years, trapping anyone who comes
through . . . ."

"He doesn't trap that many people. This is the realm

of the dead, but living people come here for different reasons. They come for power, or knowledge, or healing, or because they were called . . . or they come looking for someone who fell into the underworld."

"But this isn't the underworld—is it? Didn't you say it's the celestial realm?"

"They're the same. What's above reflects what's below. It's a mirrored reflection, but they're the same."

"But . . . are we above, or below?"

He stopped, gazing ahead at a long stone table that stood a few yards from the river. "We're at Phoenix," he replied.

The beige-and-gray slab sat across four stalagmites, and even in the dim light Surina could see that the stone legs had been carved into winged figures. Coming closer, she saw that the figures had human faces and cat-like paws that reached up to support the tabletop. The slab itself was six or seven feet long, its edges engraved with intertwining knots and spiral shapes. It stood low, only a few feet above the ground, so that Surina could easily see the carvings across the top. At one end of the table, facing the river, a bird's head and outstretched wings were engraved; this end had two edges that came to a point at the beak, making the whole table pentagonal rather than rectangular. At the opposite end, long plumage was carved in the shape of a widespread tail. The body thinned in the center; below and above it, the surface was etched with writing in neat cursive. "What's this?" Surina asked. "Is it an enigma?"

"A riddle." Wibben paused near the stone table, giving Surina time to look it over. She read the top passage:

> *Photoactive bird of prey*
> *enables life from tender ash.*
> *Ixion spins and never dies,*

the damned are stuck and can't come back.

And the bottom:

Three begin the lightning's rod,
two the begetting, two the god.
Combined, one is born not of soot,
but of a sage's changeless sooth.
What am I?

"I know the answer," Wibben said. "It's *phoenix*—but I don't know what to do with it. It's one thing to find an answer, and another to understand what it means." He looked sidelong at Surina. "Any ideas?"

"Not really," she said. "I just got here. I . . . I'll be able to get back home, won't I? Dominic got back, so . . . ."

"Keep hidden from Tagua, and you'll turn out all right." Wibben gave a light tug at the tunic. "Don't ever take this off."

She glanced down at his near-naked figure. "Do you have anything else to wear? I feel bad, making you walk around in your underwear."

"I've been through worse."

"How long have you been here?"

"A long time. I fell in at the Externsteine site in Germany. I was looking for . . . I'm not sure what I was looking for. I was a member of a secret society back then. We read a lot of mythology and performed a few vainglorious rituals. We struggled against fake adversaries and pretended to conquer them, and gave ourselves new names, as though we'd been reborn as stronger people— mostly the names of mythical figures or philosophers. Odin, Sigurd, Perseus, Proteus . . . those were popular ones."

"What was yours?"

"Ixion."

Surina glanced at the riddle. "Oh."

"He's a Greek king—a deity or half-deity, I think, who went mad with guilt after committing a murder. He slayed his own kin . . . ." Wibben trailed off, staring into the distance.

"Oh," Surina said again.

"Zeus took pity on him, but Ixion betrayed Zeus, too. He was bound to a fiery wheel, to spin across the heavens for eternity. Supposedly, his suffering stopped for a little while, when Orpheus played his lyre in the netherworld." Wibben pointed beyond the column. "Lyra is far across the ocean realms, near Cygnus. There's a riddle there, too, that I solved but haven't been able to understand—a musical riddle. It involves the circle of fifths. Do you know it?"

"The chromatic scale? Sure. I studied to be a music teacher."

"So did I. Do you play the violin?"

"No."

"It was my favorite. My friends always asked me to play for them. There was something sensual about that instrument . . . but I don't really remember that, either. It's a memory of an impression—like knowing that food was delicious, but not remembering how it tasted." Wibben folded his arms and looked up at the stone bird, a large figure with a long neck and curved wings half-spread, its face looking up at an invisible sky. "There isn't much music here. Sometimes I sing; it helps me feel like I'm still connected to my old world. It gives me a sense of comfort. I don't remember many songs, but I hum. I try to make the sound of a violin, but I can't re-create that sound, or the feeling of making it."

Surina looked across the landscape. Rocky walls rose

close on the opposite side of the river, but beyond the Phoenix table was a massive tunnel, brightly lit in the distance. Perhaps it opened to the surface—and if she followed it, she might find herself back at the temple grounds. "Wibben, what am I supposed to be doing here?" she asked. "Where's Hannah?"

"Hannah is nearby. She's waiting for us at Piscis Austrinus."

"I don't think Dominic got through. What if he's not here? I know Hannah wanted him . . . well, both of us, to help figure something out."

"Yes. Hannah has been trying to solve Orion."

"How? Is it an enigma?"

"It's a puzzle—a tiling puzzle, with missing pieces." Wibben turned toward the river and gestured downstream. "Orion is fairly easy to get to. It's at the end of the river. The trouble is that in order to solve the puzzle, you have to go through Aquarius. He's the one who has the pieces."

"How can we get them?"

"You can get them by solving his enigmas . . . and his riddles, and whatever else he wants to challenge you with. I can't go with you," he added pointedly.

"So, Aquarius is a person," Surina said.

"Sort of."

"And he gives challenges, like this one?" Surina scrutinized the table. "How do you know the answer is 'phoenix'?"

He pointed to the first word. "Three begin the lightning's rod: three letters begin 'photoactive.' Two begin 'enable,' and two begin the deity Ixion. Together they spell phoenix."

"Oh . . . okay, I get it. How many of these would I have to solve?"

"It depends on the mood he's in," Wibben replied. "If he's friendly, you might stand a chance. Offend him, and he'll keep giving you riddles until your brain explodes."

Surina frowned. "Okay. So, how do I put him in a friendly mood?"

4: Aquarius

The sanctuary at Aquarius was ethereally beautiful. The river widened here, and the water rose for some distance upon the bank, so that the pale stone temple appeared to float in the midst of it. A lone walkway provided a path to the entrance. Above the pillared anterior, the entablature was carved with geometric shapes and other symbols: waveforms spiraling into each other, animal figures and merfolk.

In the foreground, someone was seated by the riverbank. This figure also wore a white tunic and had two dark braids trailing down her back. As soon as Surina spotted the girl, Wibben leaned close and whispered in her ear. "I can't accompany you any farther. Don't ever remove the tunic—and please don't mention me. Tagua mustn't discover that I helped you."

He slipped away quietly.

Surina stood still for some time, anxious about what might happen next. Then she began to walk toward the figure sitting on the bank.

Hannah turned her head. Her eyes focused on Surina—dark eyes that nevertheless seemed to shine in the low light. Surina stopped, taken aback by the girl's face. Hannah's skin had paled from brown to a sort of beige-gray. She seemed sallow and weary.

Hannah stood up quickly and looked beyond Surina. "You're here? Where's Dominic?"

"He's . . . I don't think he got through."

The girl's face fell. Surina saw despair in the dark eyes.

"I'll help you, Hannah," Surina said hastily. "Dominic tried to teach me everything he learned. I know you don't know me, but I'll try just as hard as he would."

Hannah looked at her mutely.

"What were you trying to tell us? I kept getting your messages. We figured out where we should go, but I don't know what we're supposed to do now."

"I . . . right now, I have to solve Orion. It's like a chain: Orion will help me solve Ophiuchus, and if I solve Ophiuchus, then I can open the sun gate."

"How do you know that?"

Hannah gestured widely. "The realms said so. They keep leading me from one place to another. I thought Dominic was supposed to come back. It seemed like there was something he was supposed to do. The queen said—" She hesitated. "I don't know. Maybe I misunderstood. I used to be able to spend time on earth, for a few hours at a time, but now I'm too sick to go back. I never got to Arizona; I always ended up at other places. I usually tried to get to a library, so I could do research, but I didn't find everything I needed. But I found out that Chavín is a real place. One of the riddles said that there's a philosopher's stone at Chavín, and that once I have the keys from Sagittarius, I can use the stone to solve Ophiuchus. The riddle said . . . ." She trailed off, and the despair returned to her face. "I can't remember."

"It's all right. Wib—I mean, I think we can get the Sagittarius pieces from Aquarius and then head down the river to Orion. It shouldn't be too hard."

Hannah gazed up at her for some time. She said quietly: "You met Wibben?"

Surina lowered her voice to a whisper. "He asked me not to mention him. He doesn't want to upset Tagua."

Hannah nodded. "Let's go in. Aquarius is probably expecting us." She took a few steps, and then stopped and stared into the water. "Thanks for coming to help me," she said quietly. "You didn't have to do that. So, thank you."

"Yeah. No problem. I'm not sure how you were able to find me, though. Did you know that I knew Dominic?"

Hannah looked at her with those dark, shining eyes—a look of curiosity and wonder. "I saw him on you," she said. "I saw his impression, I mean. You knew him, and you knew Chavín, and I was drawn to those things. Chavín and Dominic were in your dreams."

The revelation surprised Surina. She didn't recall ever dreaming about Dominic.

They had just started on the path to the temple when something emerged in the water to their left. Surina jumped back, narrowly avoiding falling from the path.

She caught herself and stared at the creature that bobbed in the water only a few feet away. Surina supposed it was a merman. It had the torso and arms of a man, though its flesh was a mottled shade of gray. Its head, by contrast, looked entirely alien. The face was narrow and elongated in front, like a fish face, with a mouth at the tip and lidless, bulging eyes on either side. The creature's wide, fish-like lips curved into a smile at the edges.

"Hello! I am Piscis, steward of Aquarius," it said. "You are both very welcome here."

Surina grabbed Hannah's arm.

Hannah seemed unfazed. "We're here to see Aquarius," she replied.

"Of course. You are welcome, and so is your friend who entered through the jaguar gate." The creature gestured toward the temple. "Please, come in."

The thing vanished below the water. Hannah and Surina exchanged glances, and then Hannah led the way into the temple. They passed through the pillared promenade and into a rectangular doorway. Inside, the walkway continued; the interior of the temple was surrounded by a moat, so that the central court stood like an island in its midst. Two of its four sides were lined with long banquet tables, though they were mostly barren; only a few plates of bread and cakes were there, along with a number of pitchers and smaller drinking vessels. Another table, covered with a floor-length cloth, was situated in the center of the court. On the far side, another walkway led to the rear of the temple.

Piscis popped up on the right-hand side of the moat, very close to Surina's feet. She startled and nearly fell into the water again.

"Make yourselves comfortable!" the creature entreated them. "Aquarius is always happy to have guests, so please put yourselves at ease. Help yourselves to some butter cake; it's the finest in the region." Piscis swam toward the table and rose higher in the water, exposing a fish-like tail beneath the humanesque torso. It reached one gray arm toward a stone pitcher. "I'll pour each of you a mug of our best beer."

"No thanks," Surina said. "I don't want . . . ."

She trailed off, alarmed by the sight of Piscis' head. It was rotating upon the neck, slowly, but enough that Surina caught a glimpse of another face on the rear side: a slightly wider and flatter face, with a sneering mouth full of long, razor-sharp teeth. Piscis' two eyes, though lidless, seemed somehow to narrow with displeasure; the wide lips at the back of the head curled downward. As Piscis half-turned toward her, both faces were profiled—one still smiling, the other a frightening mass of saber-like teeth.

Hannah didn't seem to notice. She stood on the walkway, peering at the table. "Is that pound cake? I can't eat that stuff. It sticks in my throat."

"I'm allergic," Surina stammered, staring down at Piscis. "I'm horribly allergic to gluten. I really can't. I don't want to go into anaphylactic shock."

The strange, fanged face slowly revolved away from her. The calm countenance reappeared. "Very well," Piscis said. "And you, my dear? We have the best butter cake in the realm, with milk from the heifers of the starry fields—and plenty of cool, refreshing water to wash it down with." The rubbery fish-lips smiled at Hannah.

Surina spoke quickly: "Is it all right if we wait for Aquarius? I'm not familiar with your customs, but where I'm from, it's rude to start eating without the host."

Piscis bowed its head ever so slightly. "Very well. Come in and have a seat at the table. My master will present himself shortly."

The creature submerged again, leaving Surina and Hannah to step tentatively into the court. "Have you been here before?" Surina asked.

"I've been to Aquarius before," Hannah replied, "but the temple wasn't here until now. It changes all the time."

She fell silent as a man approached from the rear of the temple. Surina had seen depictions of the sea-gods Poseidon and Atlas, and anticipated that Aquarius would look much the same: tall, muscled, bearded, clad in a loincloth. But the man who entered the opposite walkway was modest in stature, with just a hint of a beard. His aged, weathered flesh was a deep brown, and the close-cut hair on his head was a mottled black and gray. Instead of a loincloth he wore loose gray pants and a long sapphire-blue shirt.

"Hello, my guests," he said mildly. "Make yourselves comfortable. Help yourself to some cakes. I will pour the beer."

He approached the right-hand table and reached for one of the tall pitchers. "This is the finest brew in the region; it was crafted by the field-maids in Capricornus, where the best barley grows." He poured the brew into a clay mug. "It's made from malt and flour mixed with honey, twice-baked and fermented, with a hint—"

"I'm sorry," Surina said, before he could fill a second mug, "But neither of us can have barley."

"We're allergic to glusen," Hannah said.

"Gluten," Surina corrected her. "But please, don't abstain on our account."

Aquarius stood with the pitcher half-raised.

"We can still drink with you," Surina added. "We both love water."

"Ah." He lowered the pitcher. "Of course." He reached for another pitcher, and poured the contents into two small glasses. "This is fresh water from my purest springs," he said. "The glasses are of crystal from the Hydra cave. Drinking this will help you feel refreshed. Both of you, I know, are on a long journey." He brought the glasses to the central table and gestured for Hannah and Surina to sit across from him.

A book lay on the table where Surina sat. Aquarius began to move it out of her way, but when she saw the cover, she jumped at the opportunity it provided. "Oh, is that a book of enigmas?" she asked. She leaned forward to examine the cover. It was a red hardcover, imprinted with a solitary word: *ENIGMAS*.

"It is," Aquarius said, returning to the banquet table and selecting a large beer mug. "It is a book of *my* enigmas."

"I love word puzzles," Surina said. "Back at home, we actually have riddle tournaments—all kinds of them. Math riddles, word riddles, science riddles that don't have a definite answer . . . we call the players Olympiads."

The water-lord approached them slowly, walking in a slow, slightly stooped way. He set his mug on the table.

"And you've participated in these tournaments?"

She hesitated. "Not yet, but I'm always looking for an opportunity."

"Really."

"Maybe you can solve one of mine," Surina suggested.

"What, a riddle? Go ahead."

"All right, here goes. I run, but I can never walk; I gurgle, but I never talk. I . . . ." Surina struggled to remember the rest. "I'm always in bed, but I never sleep. What am I?"

"A river."

"Yes."

"That's very unoriginal," Aquarius said.

"I suppose so, but it's one of my favorites."

He stood at the table, gazing steadily into Surina's eyes. His own eyes were a strange hue—possibly shades of gray and black, or clear with black flecks, like a flawed crystal. "See if you can solve this riddle," he said. "When water makes its light arrests, I stay behind to wash the crests and scatter at a faster pace to stain the heaven's inward face. What am I?"

Surina hesitated. "The color blue?"

A glint of surprise flashed in his eyes. "Correct."

She tried to look confident, but the riddle filled her with unease. It was through sheer luck that she'd guessed the answer. Dominic's copy of *Scientific American* had featured an article on light and color wavelengths. Blue, being in the mid-range, was most visible in the sky because of the speed at which it scattered air molecules, and was most visible in bodies of water because it was the least absorbed . . . or something like that.

Aquarius seated himself and took a small sip of beer. "The two of you must have a long journey ahead, and other enigmas along the way. Do you really want to stay and pass the time with useless word puzzles? My riddles won't unlock any gates or reveal any profound truths. They're just for fun."

"We could use some fun. There's nothing I would like better." Surina eyed the beer mug. She wouldn't have much luck solving the puzzles; she would have to rely on plan B.

"Tell you what," Aquarius said. "I have seven new puzzles: an acrostic, an enigma, an acrostical enigma, a jumble, a cryptogram, a riddle, and a mesostic. They're all fairly simple. If you can solve those, I'll let you test your skills with a difficult one."

Surina refused to look downcast. "Let's play," she said, and lifted a glass of water toward Aquarius. "And let's have a drink—to word puzzles."

The acrostic, inked onto a thick sheet of paper, was time-consuming but simple. Surina and Hannah had to guess the answers to two questions and use the letters to complete the rest of the puzzle. When they had solved it, Surina took the water-lord's mug, saying: "Here, let me refill your cup."

The second puzzle, an enigma, offered a greater challenge:

Cymbals clash, strike all the gongs;
Have pity and drown out these songs.

Enchanting us with siren tones,
A young dame sings of skulls and bones.

Hannah looked up at Aquarius. "Is it a regular enigma?"

"It is."

Surina pretended to look for the answer, but at the

moment she couldn't remember how to solve any type of enigma. She leaned over and whispered: "How do we start?"

Hannah whispered back: "Each couplet has a one-word answer. Some of the letters should be at the front of each one. So, we could use C-Y-M . . . or C-Y . . . probably C-Y. That's the end of the word. So, it could be *lacy*, or *spicy*, or something like that. The second line gives us a hint. The hint could be . . . pity, or drowning, or songs. Or something that drowns out noise, like earplugs . . . but it's not that. What's a word that ends with C-Y, that's another word for pity, or drowning, or singing—or music?"

Surina's mind seemed to be shutting down. She thought for a while, and whispered: "This is not 'fairly simple.'"

Hannah nodded in agreement. But after a while she beckoned Surina closer, and whispered: "*Mercy*. It's like pity; I can't think of anything else that fits." She pointed to the second couplet. "E-N . . . or E-N-C-H. It's probably one of those. Trench, bench . . . or something that ends with E-N. Young, dame . . . singing . . . bones."

Surina felt useless. Hannah looked up at her expectantly, so she tried again. "The hint is in the second line? Um . . . *wench*?"

"Well . . . you have to put the unused letters together, so that would give us M-E-R and W. It's probably something that ends with E-N."

"Young dame . . . maiden?"

"M-E-R . . . M-A-I-D. *Oh*." Hannah met Aquarius' gaze. "Is it *mermaid*?"

He nodded. "Fairly simple, isn't it?"

Surina let out a long, quiet sigh. She took a gulp of water, and then checked the beer mug. "Let's have the next puzzle. Here—I'll fill our cups."

Wibben had filled her in on the water-lord's peculiarities: *Aquarius is formal and elegant, but he's also a pitiful nerd. He loves to create word puzzles that no one is interested in solving. Show interest in his puzzles; that should put him in a friendly mood.* He'd smiled and added: *He also loves barley beer. If you're not good at enigmas, you can try getting him drunk.*

He was joking, but Surina thought it the more promising strategy—and so she filled the water-lord's mug again, and again.

Together, Hannah and Surina solved the first five puzzles. By the sixth puzzle, Aquarius had started helping them. He gave generous hints about the riddle, and then he taught Surina how to solve mesostics, in which the whole riddle hinted at the answer and the letters were arranged in a column.

> *Sceptics may open the sun's bright gate after*
> *trying the snake-bearer's scion,*
> *but the problem is that the*
> *exam can be tried only after unlocking Orion.*

"Is that supposed to say 'skeptics'?" Surina asked. "'Skeptics' is spelled with a *k*."

For the first time, Aquarius looked unsure of himself. He leaned worriedly over the paper. "What?"

"You spelled 'skeptics' wrong. It's S-K, not S-C."

"Is it? I think you're right." He rubbed at the word with his thumb, uselessly. "I'll have to use a different word; the second letter has to be *C.* I'll change it to 'Schemers.'"

Hannah perked up. "It *has* to be *C*?"

The water-lord went still, but Hannah fidgeted excitedly.

"You just told us where to find the answer!" she

exclaimed. "C-R-U-X. What's that?"

"It's like . . . the most important part of something, or the most challenging part," Surina replied. "The crux of a problem, the crux of an investigation."

Aquarius raised his eyebrows. His lips curled upward in amusement. "And what is the crux of the *current* investigation? I'll tell you: Before you know how to get out, you have to realize how you got in. Solve that one first."

"How we got in where?" Surina asked. "You mean, we have to figure out how we got into this place?"

"Exactly! Think of it as the Eridanus mystery." Aquarius was already getting drunk; he was slouching, leaning with his forearm against the table, slurring a few words here and there. "You can find the answer at Orion—but to enter Orion, you must be properly attired."

"With what?"

"Well, for starters . . . you'll need . . . an armpit!" From the pit of his arm he pulled a flat, round object. He leaned it forward, waving the small disc between Hannah and Surina. "This puzzle piece represents Betelgeuse, one of Orion's brightest stars—and one of the brightest in the Earth sky. Some say it designated Orion's armpit; others say it represents his raised arm, or his raised sword, or staff, or what have you."

The disc was a thin bronze plate stamped with the word BETELGUESE in block letters. Above the letters was a single image: an open hand, the fingers and thumb pressed close together. The disc was nearly as large as Aquarius' palm, the back unmarked but discolored with splotches of red and olive green.

"There are seven keys to Orion," Aquarius continued. "Solve seven puzzles, and in the name of my realm, I will give them to you."

Surina felt a surge of excitement. She had already

helped solve seven puzzles; surely she and Hannah could solve seven more.

"We're game," she said. "Right, Hannah?"

Hannah looked back at her. It seemed to Surina that her eyes were less dull, and her face slightly less gaunt than when they'd arrived. "Right," Hannah said, quietly but firmly.

"Good!" Aquarius closed the book of riddles and tucked it somewhere under the table. He pulled out another volume—an enormous text with a green cover. The title read: *ENIGMAS. Level of Difficulty: Advanced.*

Surina restrained a groan, but Hannah gasped out loud and cried: "Why are you giving us the advanced enigmas?"

"Because only a true Olympiad can be trusted with the keys to Orion." Aquarius opened the book and flipped pages, and paused to look up at his guests. "Are you still game?"

"Yes," Surina said.

"Very well. Here's the first puzzle." Aquarius turned the book so they could read it. He tapped his finger on the right-hand page.

A shove from elder brother Cain
leads to death from bitter hate,
while shoves from elder sister saint
break through to gains which must elate.
Link ends of first three ends to sense
how heart affects the consequence.

After only a little effort, Hannah figured out that the answer was *intent*. The next puzzle was a mesostic that turned up the word *peace*. In return for their answers Aquarius gifted them two discs: the one representing the star Betelgeuse, and another representing Rigel.

Hannah took the discs and clasped them tightly in her lap.

"You're doing well," Aquarius assured them. "Solve five more, and you can have the keys; in the name of my own realm, I will give them to you." He pulled another disc from beneath the table and held it up. On its surface was stamped the image of a full breastplate, adorned along the front with a bird whose wings spread up toward the shoulders. Below this image was the word BELLATRIX. "Here is the symbol of Bellatrix, the warrior woman who came to these depths. I'll gift this token to you if you can finish this rhyme." Aquarius enunciated carefully: "Students seeking special trades are trained and taught in college; wisdom applies generally, but craft requires . . . ?"

"Knowledge." Surina reached out before he could confirm the answer.

Aquarius placed the token in her hand and spoke gruffly. "That was too easy."

"Give us a harder one, then," Hannah replied.

Surina elbowed her.

"Very well." Aquarius' crystalline eyes appeared to gleam with sudden intensity. "In the tunnels of Wupatki you'll find an enigma: a vast sea in the middle of the desert."

Surina thought back to her conversations with Dominic. He had spoken of such a thing; he'd said the subterranean rock at Wupatki was made of sand and fossils from an ancient sea. She struggled to remember what it was called—something that reminded her of kabobs. "Do you mean the . . . Ka . . . Kaibab limestone?"

"Exactly! Kaibab limestone. Far in the past, long before the dinosaurs roamed, that rock was formed from the skeletons of sea creatures. But when stone is hundreds of millions of years old, it has time to change. The Kaibab is transforming—too slowly for a human being to notice, but transforming nevertheless."

"How so?"

"The tunnels have become like so many temples. Take the Khufu pyramid in Giza, for instance. The builders used Mokattam limestone on the inside, and Tura limestone on the outside. Do you know the difference between the two?"

"No."

"Of course you don't, but do you see how the places are similar? In a pyramid you have a wide base and a narrow, central top. At the Chavín labyrinth you have a wide base of closed tunnels and a narrow, central opening. In the Wupatki underworld you have a wide base of tunnels, and at the top you've got a blowhole—and all that air, all that energy blowing around inside the tunnels. How is it going to get out?" Aquarius spread his hands, then leaned forward and slapped his palms loudly on the table. "How is it going to get *in*? It has to *squish* through the blowhole!" He leaned back with an air of satisfaction. "By the way, those passages used to be nothing but a bunch of puny cracks. Do you know what transformed them into tunnels?"

"No, I don't."

"Well, figure it out, because that's your riddle."

"That's not a riddle," Hannah said. "It's just a question."

Aquarius raised his eyebrows. "Well, look who's become precocious again. You've been losing that quality since you fell into this realm. Feeling better, are you?"

Hannah looked at him somberly.

"Do you know what made the tunnels?" Surina whispered.

"I don't remember."

"Water!" Aquarius tapped his index finger on his

chest. "My very own water did that. I'm giving you that one for free."

"You're very generous," Surina said.

"Don't patronize me."

"All right."

He pulled another metal disc from beneath the table. In its center was stamped a large image of a human foot, and below that, the word SAIPH.

Hannah took the disc and scrutinized it. "It's a foot."

"Not just any foot! This is the *supporting* foot. When one foot steps forward into the unknown, the other must support it. They complement each other while they're doing opposite things—but really, they're doing the *same* thing."

Surina tried to sound interested. "Brilliant."

"Same as Chavín. The white granite and black limestone have contrash, contrashting . . . *contrasting* but complementary quallies. *Qualities*—and I'm not referring to their colors. Together they help create the doorway. D'you believe me?" Aquarius leaned forward and slapped his hands lightly on the table. "Or d'you think I'm a drunk?"

"I don't mind if you're drunk, as long as you'll help us," Surina replied.

Aquarius took some time to present the next riddle. He rambled on for a while, talking about the role of water in purification rites such as baptism and so forth, while Hannah fidgeted in her seat.

"You look tired," Surina said. "We don't want to keep you too long. Do you want to give us the next question?"

"There is no next question. There's a story." Aquarius reached out and flipped another page. "Solve this'un."

Finally a girl forged a shield with which to
deter the arrows of the underworld, but the

*craft took time. It required intent and
knowledge; it required forces such as heat and
the answer to this puzzle, and substance such
as metal, and most significantly it took a hard-
earned path toward Righteousness. Eventually
she found that the solving of puzzles was of
little consequence, but virtue was capital in
the solution.*

"I don't get it," Hannah muttered. "Solving the puzzle
is of little consequence, but seeking virtue is capital . . .
what virtues are mentioned? Intent? Knowledge . . .
righteousness." She glanced up. "Is righteousness the only
one that counts as a virtue?"

Aquarius gave her a lazy wave. "I'm not helping with
this one."

Hannah and Surina mulled for some time. Then Surina
said, "Is it *fire*?"

He nodded. "It is."

Hannah scrutinized the words. "Where do you see
that?"

"You just look at all the capital letters. F, I, R, E."

"Oh." Hannah looked dejected. "Capital . . . I should
have figured that one. But why does it talk about virtue?"

"Turn the page." Aquarius handed them another disc
and gestured impatiently. "Do the next one."

Frowning, Hannah turned to the next puzzle.

Magi, come lord, stele rise!
What meter would proud Paris prize?
The weak half-feet, in premier line,
Each letter pair a third of thine,
Where all above the belt is fair
And nigh the breastplate one might wear.

Silence endured. Surina read the words over and over again. No matter how many times she read it, it didn't make any sense. She began to guess anyway: "Is it the Raimondi Stele? Is it a stomach? Is it a boxer?"

"Is it Achilles? Or an Achilles heel?" Hannah asked.

"No."

She frowned. "But Paris killed Achilles, didn't he? He shot him in the foot, at the only weak spot."

"It was a good guess," Aquarius replied. "There's a lushion . . . an *allusion* to Paris and Achilles, but thass not the answer."

"Premier line . . . each letter pair," Hannah muttered. "The letters must be in pairs, at the front of each line. Ma-wha-the . . . maw . . . okay, maybe not. Oh—are they all in the first line? M-A . . . C-O . . . macolostri . . . gimerd. I think that's not it."

"Can you give us a hint?" Surina asked.

"No."

As time dragged on, though, the water-lord began to lose his patience. He swallowed two pints in the time that Hannah and Surina mulled over the words. "Come, Surina, you should know this," he said at last. "Don't you study poetry and music?"

She lifted her gaze from the page. "Not this kind of poetry."

"But you study rhythm—the rhythm of poeshry."

She read the enigma again. Her mind felt sluggish— but suddenly she saw it. "Oh," she said. "Is it *rhythmic* meter and feet?" Surina studied the lines again. "*Magi, come* lord, *stele rise.*"

"What are you doing?" Hannah asked.

"Well . . . in poetry, there's a rhythmic pattern called an iambic meter, and it's measured in feet. Each foot has two syllables: one strong and one weak. In the word *magi*, the emphasis is on the first syllable, so that's the strong one. The second syllable isn't stressed, so it's weak. The weak half-feet . . . could refer to all of the weak syllables. Each weak syllable is half a foot."

"*Ma*gi," Hannah murmured. "G-I is a letter pair."

"Gi . . . lord . . . le. Those are the weak syllables."

"Use those. We only need pairs from the first line."

"Gilordle."

"No, they have to be pairs," Hannah said. "And we only need three pairs. Each pair makes a third of thine . . . so, two times three, six letters total."

"Where are you seeing two times three?"

"Just guess!" Aquarius demanded, slumping sideways with his head resting on his hand. "Guess. There are three letter pairs. You have two of them: G-I, something-something, L-E. What fits? What two letters can you fit in there to deshribe sumph . . . *describe* something that goes above the belt and near the breastplate?"

"Well, it's either L-O or R-D," Hannah replied.

"Yes, it's *R-D*. It's *girdle*, for crying out loud." Aquarius lowered his head until his eyes were hidden behind his hand.

"What's a girdle?" Hannah asked.

Surina slid her hands from her back to her own belly, to indicate where a girdle would fit. "It's like a corset."

"I don't know what that is either."

"Well it's a good thing there are three of us," Aquarius said, sitting up. He produced another bronze disc and gave it to Hannah. "Tell you what: I'll give you an easy one. Surina! What does Wibben miss most about your dimension'?"

Surina was taken aback by the question. She exchanged glances with Hannah, then thought over her earlier conversation with Bernhard. "Music."

"What does he do to comfort himself, to stay connected to his own world?"

"He sings."

"And that's your answer." He tossed the final plate onto the table. On its surface was the figure of a woman kneeling with a long string of beads, perhaps a rosary or a mala. Above the image was the word ALNILAM.

"Now go." The water-lord waved them away. "Piscis will give you a boat to take downriver. It will bring you all the way to Orion. Here—take this satchel, too." He pulled a brown rucksack from beneath the tablecloth and extended it to Hannah, holding it open so that she could drop the discs into it. "Put the stars inside, and keep them close to you."

Surina picked up the last disc and slowly slid it into the bag. Something about his final questions nagged at her. *What does Wibben miss most . . . .*

"Here—I'll give you a bonus," he said. Before either of his guests could protest, he dropped a large handful of bronze plates into the sack along with the Orion tokens. "You can have these keys as well."

Hannah gasped. "Hey! I don't want those. I'll get them mixed up with the Orion keys."

"Nevertheless, I'm giving them to you. Take all of them or none."

"That's not fair," Hannah said.

"I'm sure you're mistaken," Aquarius mumbled drowsily.

Surina watched as he slumped forward in his chair. He folded his arms on the table and slowly lowered his head onto them.

Hannah had grabbed the satchel and stood waiting for Surina, but Surina went around the table instead, moving close to the water-lord. She glanced down at the tablecloth that draped over his legs and onto the floor, hiding the books and other objects that he kept beneath the table. As she approached, he murmured: "I think I overindulged."

"Aquarius?"

"Mm."

"How did you know that I study music?"

"Oh, that. I heard you talking about it with Mister Wibben."

"Did you hear our entire conversation?"

The water-lord was silent. He didn't move. As Surina stood over him, he began to snore.

5: Acamar

As Hannah and Surina headed for the walkway, Piscis emerged in the moat. It smiled at them with its rubbery lips. Surina looked into the wide, lidless eyes and tried not to shudder.

"Please, leave through the back way and head downriver," it said. "I will escort you to the port at Acamar, where you will find the boat of the celestial waters."

They did as Piscis asked. Outside, the realm was dark and enclosed. As Surina walked along the riverbank she could see wider gaps in the rock ceiling up ahead, some large enough that she could see patches of blue sky. The sight gave her some comfort; it made her feel that she was really just underground, and still very much in her own world.

But as Piscis emerged in the river nearby, her sense of comfort fled. The strange, hideous face made it undeniable that she was in some otherworldly realm.

They walked for some time along the rocky bank. Neither Surina nor Hannah spoke. Whenever Surina had the urge to say something, the sight of Piscis kept her in silence. It bobbed alongside them in the water, swimming sideways, staring at them so that the sabered mouth was kept hidden at the back of its head. The relentless gaze made Surina feel that she was being spied upon.

Piscis was more talkative. The creature called out from the water, providing a few key details about the journey ahead. It sounded simple enough. They would be riding with the current; the boat would practically carry them to Orion, which was at the river's end.

The river passed beneath bright patches of open sky, and then began to darken again. Rocky cliffs pressed close on either side. Along the floor were mounds of flowstone that transitioned from pale beige to deep reds and browns, sometimes shaped like recognizable figures: a seated human figure with a large belly, a horse with flowing mane. Tiered mineral columns rose among them, some so high that they nearly reached the formations that hung from the ceiling—draping, curving shapes, and spiked forms that looked like stone icicles. The figures became shadowed as the rock ceiling arched overhead, blocking out the light. Suddenly Surina stopped. "Wait," she said. "What's that? Are we at the end of the river?"

Ahead of her, the cavern ended in a flat wall of rock. The river appeared to stop there, though she could still hear it rushing.

"No," Piscis said, "but that's a common misconception. This is the port of Acamar. The river doesn't end here; it bends and flows onward."

"It doesn't bend," Hannah said. "It just stops."

"Look again. Around the bend is a gate. The river flows through it. Open the gate, and your journey will begin."

"Let me guess," Hannah said dryly. "We have to open it by solving a puzzle."

"The puzzles along Eridanus are simple. I'm sure that you, Hannah, will solve this one in a matter of seconds."

Surina was unconcerned about the puzzles. A small dock was visible in the water ahead, with a solitary boat beside it. The sight of it filled her with worry.

Piscis stopped near the dock and made a grand gesture. "And here we have the celestial boat!"

Hannah and Surina peered into the water. The "celestial boat" was a small rowboat. It had a pair of front-facing oars and a pair of rear-facing oars held in place with oarlocks, so that the rowers had to sit facing each other. It was plain and rough-looking, low and wide in the middle. Surina guessed that the middle of the boat only rose a foot above the water.

"Journey well, and take care to stay out of the water," Piscis said. "Getting splashed by a few drops probably won't do any harm, but more than that may thwart your plans."

"How?" Hannah asked.

"Oh, in a lot of ways. Celestial rivers aren't like Earthly rivers. Have you heard of the river Lethe?"

"The one that makes you forget everything?" Surina asked.

"Exactly. Human souls, having traveled to the celestial plane, dip into the Lethe before reincarnation. It helps them to forget the details of their past lives, so that they can begin new ones."

Hannah's shoulders slumped. Surina saw the sudden dejection in her eyes and wanted to comfort her, but found herself unable to. "We're supposed to avoid the river in *this*?" Surina gestured to the low-riding boat. "It will barely hold us above water."

"This boat has everything you need to traverse the celestial river," Piscis said. "Any other boat would fail you. Good luck with your travels."

The creature vanished beneath the dark waters.

Surina stepped onto the dock and took a closer look at the rowboat. It had a box-like appendage attached to one end—a motor, she supposed, though it didn't look like any motor she'd ever seen. It had a bulbous disc on the back, with a few rings radiating around it.

She looked up at the wall of rock across from her.

Through a number of gaps in the wall, she could see that the river did flow onward; light was visible on the other side, shining here and there on the rushing waters.

"Let me get in first," she said, as she looked down at Hannah's weary figure. Surina sat on the dock and swung her legs into the boat, and slid into it with utmost caution. She offered her hand to Hannah. "Go slow, okay?"

Hannah descended into the boat, her eyes fixed on the dark water beyond it. "I didn't see any puzzles on the dock, or on the boat," she said. "It's probably written on the gate. We can row closer and see if we can find it."

"All right. Is it okay if I sit in the back? You won't be able to see where we're going, but you won't have to row as hard, and you can keep an eye on what's behind us."

"Sure."

Surina sat sideways on the rear bench, twisting around to inspect the box-like object behind her. "Do you know what this is? I think it's a motor. There's a lever here that lowers it into the water."

"It doesn't look like a motor."

"But there's something on the back . . . ." Surina started to lean over the edge of the boat, but thought better of it. "I saw something on the back that might be a propeller. Maybe it rotates when we put it in the water." She pulled the lever, gently, so that the box was gradually lowered into the dark river.

"There's a button here, underneath the lever. I bet it starts the motor."

She pressed the button.

A muffled boom shook the waters beneath them. The boat lurched away from the riverbank, and the rocky shore cracked apart. Chunks of stone fell into the river, splashing water at the edge of the boat, so that Surina scrambled backward to avoid being doused. The dock broke away with a loud crack. Hannah and Surina watched in silence as it sunk beneath the dark waves.

"Oops," Surina said. "Okay, it's not a motor. Is it a sound cannon?"

Hannah picked up her oars. "Let's just row."

The river ran for a short distance before curving sharply to the right. As Piscis had promised, a tall, barred gate blocked the way—and as Hannah had predicted, a word puzzle was inscribed across a metal plate on the steel doors. Surina reached out and eased the boat up against the gate, peering hard, trying to make out the text in the dim light.

Kibbeh was the final meal,
extra onion, lamb, and veal.
Reverse the tails of onsets, the alpha of the vessel's
bend.
If I am the beginning, how can I also be the end?

"Reverse the tails of onsets," Hannah murmured. Several seconds passed, and then she said, "It's 'heart.'"

The gates opened with a loud groaning of metal against metal. Hannah took the oars and began to row.

"Wait, how did you know the answer?" Surina asked.

"I've been doing this a long time. A lot of the puzzles are kind of the same."

"Okay, but how did you find the answer to this one?"

Hannah spoke wearily. "It said to reverse the tails of the onsets. The onset is the beginning of something; the tail is the end. So, it means you have to reverse the letters at the end of the first words. And the rhyme gives a hint: the heart is the beginning of a system of blood vessels. But it's not really the beginning, because the cycle doesn't end when blood returns to the heart. It just keeps going."

"Huh?"

"And I knew some of the letters were in the word 'kibbeh.' Whenever there's a weird word like that, it's probably part of the answer. The puzzle needed a word that ended with e-h. How many words do you know of that end with e-h?"

"Um . . . one. 'Meh.'"

"Exactly."

"But, how did the gate open? It hears you?"

"*Something* hears me," Hannah muttered. She turned and glanced downriver. The gaps in the rock ceiling had suddenly decreased, so that a stretch of the river beyond them was shrouded in darkness. Beyond the darkness, though, was another steam of light that exposed another bend in the river; it veered to the right, disappearing from view.

Eventually they rounded the bend, and Surina felt a small sense of disappointment. The rock ceiling gave way again, and the river was bathed in streams of light—but it stretched onward for such a long distance that she couldn't see the end of it. It looked miles long.

Hannah let out a tired sigh. "Eridanus is a long river," she said.

"We'll still get there fast. Piscis made it sound easy."

"If someone made it sound easy, it's probably because it isn't easy at all. Anyway, I'm more worried about what will happen after we get there. I'm afraid I won't remember which keys are the Orion keys. I didn't look at all of them when Aquarius gave them to us. I only remember Betelgeuse, Bellatrix, Saiph . . . ."

"Rigel," Surina said.

"So, that's four." Hannah released the oars and picked up the sack. She removed bronze plate and examined the imprint. "Nah-sij," she pronounced uncertainly, "with a picture of a basket." She dropped the plate and pulled out another one. "Tahara, with water pouring from a pitcher. I don't think either of those are Orion stars." Hannah tossed the disc in with the others. "There must be fifty plates in here, at least! Aquarius did that on purpose, to make it harder for us." She set the rucksack next to her feet. "It doesn't matter. Once I see them, I'll probably remember . . . ." She trailed off doubtfully as she took the oars.

Some distance behind the boat, a voice called out: "My lady!"

Surina turned around. Piscis was treading water upriver, waving an arm urgently. For a moment she saw a ghoulish outline of both faces—but the creature quickly turned its placid face in their direction. Polite and smiling, Piscis called again. "My lady Hannah!"

Hannah paused in mid-stroke. "What?"

"Hannah, I'm afraid I have been sent to you with grave instructions."

"What instructions?"

"You and your attendant may continue onward, but I must return the boat to its dock immediately."

Hannah turned and gazed down the river, at the looming rock walls and the patched sections of light and dark. She looked at Piscis. "But . . . how are we supposed to get to Orion?"

"My master is also demanding the tokens. I'm afraid he was rather inebriated when he gifted them to you, and he wants them back in their proper place."

"No way!" Hannah drew the oars tightly across her chest and gathered the rucksack behind her feet, as though Piscis might come and snatch them from her.

"My master's orders must be obeyed. Kindly step out of the boat."

"That's not fair! We *earned* the tokens and the boat, and he *said* we could use them. What a cheat! This is the second time he cheated us!"

"We sat and talked to him for hours," Surina

protested.

Piscis' voice became stern. "Dock the boat and step out immediately."

"No," Hannah replied. "You can—"

The other face turned on them suddenly, its ghoulish lips twisted in a sneer, the long teeth jutting like sabers. Piscis' voice came loud and strong: "*Do as I command, or upon my word, all the priests of the underworld will set their spells against you! They will thrash the boat and toss you into the deep waters!*" The fish-like figure rose even higher above the water. The surface began to churn beneath it.

"Row!" Surina cried.

The two pulled the oars frantically, hurrying away from the swirling water.

"*Upon my word you will be lost forever!*"

Hannah shrieked: "I don't care! That's going to happen to me anyway!"

Piscis vanished again into the river. In its place, other figures began to rise from the water. Surina caught a frightening glimpse of them as they passed beneath beams of light: mermaids and mermen with ghastly salamander-like faces, dripping with river water, sleek green-and-gray creatures with large, unblinking eyes. A dozen sprang up, and then a dozen more, and still more. They moved steadily down the stream, closing the distance between themselves and the boat. The wide mouths opened as they began to chant in unison, a strange gibberish that resounded through the cavern. The water churned more severely.

"We're going to tip over!" Hannah cried.

The creatures were nearly upon them. Surina gave up rowing as the boat rocked and spun out of control. She let go of the oars and reached back, jabbing the button on the sound cannon.

A muted *boom* stilled the waters. At once, the merfolk writhed and fell into the river; the surface calmed, the waves becoming smaller and smaller until at last the river resumed its gently flowing course. Around the boat, a few large fish leapt from the water and flopped in again.

Hannah resumed rowing.

"Well . . . that was horrifying," Surina said.

Hannah made a half-hearted sound of agreement.

"What happened?"

"Sound yields form," Hannah muttered. "That's what the riddles say. In this place, sound can change things. If it's a sound cannon, you might have turned them into something else—or just knocked them out."

"I wonder what else is down there." Surina paused. "I wonder if Piscis got hurt. I feel like I just did something really bad. Are you sure I didn't kill those things?"

Hannah paused and leaned over, looking into the water. "No . . . I think you turned them into fish."

"I hope so. Still . . . Aquarius will be pissed."

"I doubt it," Hannah murmured.

Surina paused, musing over the fate of the merfolk. "When I was taking classes on sound sciences, we talked a lot about sonic weapons. They can blast a certain frequency at you and cause damage, or loss of control. My classmates used to make jokes about the weapons we could create. People did research on the different things they could do. Like, they found out about a frequency that's called 'the brown note.' Can you guess what it does?"

Hannah looked at her blankly.

"It causes something unpleasant to happen to your body. Something that's brown."

"I've been here for a long time," Hannah replied, "and I'm tired of riddles."

"Sorry. It's not a real thing, anyway. Supposedly

there's a frequency that makes you lose control of your bowels."

Hannah remained expressionless.

"It makes you poop your pants," Surina clarified.

"Yeah, I know what bowels are."

"Okay. Well, I thought it was hilarious."

Hannah sat stone-faced as they continued down the river. Surina broke the silence by asking questions about her adventures—the things that had happened since being separated from Dominic. Hannah talked about her journey through the constellations in a subdued tone. She described visiting the same places again and again, but finding a different realm every time, always with a new puzzle to solve.

"I'm starting to feel trapped," she said. "I thought the puzzles were leading somewhere, but maybe they're just going in circles. The zodiac is like that. There's no beginning and no end to it. It's just a ring that keeps on cycling around."

"What about that demon guy? The one who kidnapped you?"

Hannah tensed. "Tagua isn't a demon."

"Where is he? Dominic made it sound like he hangs out somewhere near Libra. Does he move around in the stars?"

"He . . . has people who roam around the constellations," Hannah replied. "If they find someone new, they go back and tell him. Tagua has some way of watching people from inside his temple. I'm not sure how he does it. He can focus on certain constellations and watch what people are doing there, and he can even see some things that happen back on Earth, when a portal is open . . . kind of like he's watching TV." She paused. "At least, that's what it sounds like."

Surina spoke with sudden alarm: "So, he might see

us?"

"He won't look unless one of his . . . ." Hannah hesitated. "Unless one of his assistants tells him to."

"You mean, one of the people he trapped here. The demon-kids, or whatever they are."

"They're not demons," Hannah replied softly. She gazed at the floor of the boat rather than look Surina in the eye. "They're just confused."

"Because Tagua drains them, right? Isn't that what happens?"

Again, Hannah paused. "Tagua has reasons for what he does. If it wasn't for him, all those people would be dead."

"Is that what he told you? Wow, what a hero. People who abuse other humans always want to seem like they're doing something noble."

Hannah finally looked up at her, but her face was set in a frown.

"I hope you're not excusing him. You would be safe at home if he hadn't kidnapped you," Surina reminded her.

Hannah shrugged. "Home wasn't that great anyway."

"Wasn't it? I thought you liked your foster parents. What are their names . . . Carmine? Carmina?"

Hannah's gaze became distant. Her eyes looked wet, as though she was suddenly on the verge of tears. "Carmina. That's right. Carmina and Andy." She looked up then, at the rock wall to her right. The ceiling had completely given way, and the river was once again bathed in light. "That's better," she murmured. "Now I can see."

"There must be a gate up ahead," Surina said. "I *hope* it's a gate. It's blocking the way."

From where she sat, the obstruction looked like a dead end. A tall barrier of rock appeared to stretch from one wall to another, completely blocking out any view of the landscape beyond.

Hannah turned around to look at it. The oars went slack in her hands. "It's opening," she said.

She was right. Surina could see the wall of rock coming apart at the center. Slowly, but steadily, the massive doorway drew open, wide enough for the boat to pass through, enough for even two or three boats to pass through side by side—and then the rocks slammed shut, sending a massive spray upriver. Surina heard the loud slosh of water, the sound of clashing stone.

"Damn," she said.

Hannah stared mutely.

On the left-hand bank, a gray statue stood in sharp contrast to the russet-colored rock. The humanesque figure held a torch in one hand, and on its head was a spiked crown.

Surina nodded toward the shore. "Look over there. It's a miniature Statue of Liberty."

Hannah looked, but didn't respond.

"Maybe she'll free us," Hannah said. "Should we dock and take a look?"

"Yeah."

Surina dipped the left-hand oar into the water, turning the boat toward the bank. As they drew closer, she caught sight of another stone figure standing beside the first, and yet another one behind them.

On the bank they found a grouping of three statues standing on a pedestal, close together in a tight circle, facing outward. They depicted the same woman, but in different poses. Each had the same broad nose and stern brow, and featureless eyes. Only the one holding the torch was crowned. She looked nearly identical to New York's Statue of Liberty. Her tiara had seven points, and she wore a flowing tunic. But the torch-bearing arm was

extended outward rather than raised above her head—and
the torch was made not of metal or stone, but of wood,
and the wick burned with real flame. She faced upriver,
while the right-hand statue faced the gate. That one held a
small stone bird in the palm of her outstretched hand.
Below her feet, etched into the pedestal, was the word
COLUMBA.

The third statue faced the rocky cliff beyond the bank.
In her hand she held a piece of white chalk.

"Here's the puzzle," Hannah said, crouching beside
the chalk-bearing figure. Between that and the statue
wielding the torch was a stone tabula, standing upright, so
that the tunics appeared to drape along its sides. Surina
squatted beside Hannah and read the inscription.

Choose one of three schemes to cross this gate:

A changed perspective may seem odd
but can be key for everyone.
Flip last first two, then give a prod
to turn the wood, soar toward the sun.

A limestone ferrule marks a notch
on oblate stones where people walk.
Join ends of ends and check your watch
four times to gauge the shifting rock.

Hidden in the crags you'll find
the tension snaps; the burn relieves.
Start ends, two pair, seek what binds
and scorch the strands within the sheaves.

"Start ends, two pair," Hannah murmured, and
repeated slowly: "Start ends, two pair . . . ." She put a
hand over her eyes and rubbed her eyelids. "I can't think."

Surina studied the moving rocks. From where she

stood, she could see the far side of the gate sliding into a crevice on the opposite bank. It moved slowly, and then withdrew from the crevice at a much faster pace. As the gates came together they sent another surge of water upriver, though this time the surge was a large wave rather than a spray.

"Chalk is made of limestone," she said. "Do you think the answer to the second one is 'chalk'?"

"Yeah, but I don't know what we're supposed to do with it."

"Right," Surina mused. "It's one thing to figure out the answer, but another to know what it *means*."

"The first one says to turn the wood . . . I haven't seen any wood, out here or in the riddle. Do you know what a crag is?"

"A crag, I think, is . . . a stone edge. It's something to do with stone."

Hannah gazed at the vast expanse of rock.

"I'll try this, if you want to try figuring out the other riddles." Surina lifted the chalk from the statue's grasp. "It says we have to use it to gauge the shifting rock, four times. So . . . I'll count the seconds that pass in between the rocks opening and closing, and I'll mark it with the chalk. If we're lucky, there's a pattern, and we can row through during the longest opening. I'm guessing there are four different times in the pattern."

Hannah looked at her silently.

Surina crouched over a flat stone, the chalk poised and ready. "I'll count when they start to open again. Here goes . . . *one*, one thousand. *Two*, one thousand. *Three*, one thousand. . . ."

She counted until the rocks had completely opened and closed again; she quickly marked "84/4" and began again. "*One*, one thousand. . . ."

The next count turned up 56 seconds, and then only

35, and then 120, and 84 again. Surina kept measuring the seconds to make sure the cycle was repeating itself.

Hannah wandered while she counted, and returned with a frown. "I didn't find any wood, or anything in the crags."

"There's a pattern," Surina replied excitedly. "There's a part where the rocks spend exactly two minutes opening and ten seconds closing. That's our only chance. I know it isn't long," she added hastily, seeing Hannah's anxious face, "but we can make it. It looks like we only have a few feet of rock to pass through. We can get a head start and row through as soon as it's wide enough."

"But the rocks will spray water at us!"

"We'll stay at a distance until that happens. Then we'll start rowing hard. The rocks need time to separate anyway; we'll probably get there by the time it's wide enough to let us pass." Surina studied the numbers again. "It's on the eighty-four count right now. It'll close fast, in four seconds, and then the fifty-six second count will start. Let's try to make the next two-minute opening."

She hurried toward the canoe, with Hannah trailing reluctantly behind her. Surina reached for the bow and realized she still had the chalk in her hand. She dropped it into the bottom of the boat. "Get in, quick. Sit down." Surina pushed the boat into the water and jumped inside after Hannah. "Let's row out to the middle of the river!"

They tried to situate the boat in the middle, not too near or too far from the gate—but the currents threw them. As they waited through the next count, the rocks opened quickly, then slammed shut. The force of the closing rocks sent a torrent of water toward the boat, sending it into a sideways curve. Hannah and Surina struggled to straighten their course and heaved toward the opening rocks, but the shifting waters turned the boat this way and that.

"We won't make it," Hannah said. "Let's—"

She froze, her mouth still open but unable to speak. Her gaze was fixed on something beyond Surina.

Nearby, a voice cried: "My lady!"

Piscis had risen in the water a few yards behind them. When Surina turned, it bowed his head cordially. "My lady, I've been sent with instructions—"

"Go!" Surina said, and rowed hard.

"My lord Aquarius has sent me to you. His words cannot be ignored! You must return the boat immediately!"

Hannah and Surina ignored the creature.

As they struggled into the shifting gap, Piscis began to shout. "*I will set the cluster of fifty stars upon you, and they will appear minuscule no more! I will send the giants of Columba!*"

The boat stayed on course, and had nearly passed through the gate. "We're going to make it!" Surina said.

She had barely uttered the words when the boat lurched backwards. Surina struggled to propel it forward again, and as she looked anxiously at the shifting rock walls, she realized that the water level had lowered—as though the river was draining beneath them.

She dared to glance back, and for a moment she was unable to row. Surina stared at the spectacle taking place upriver as the boat slipped backwards through the gate.

Huge salamander-like creatures rose from the river. They stood four dozen feet tall, at least, with thick bodies and long limbs. Their deep red flesh was mottled with black. As they rose higher in the water, the river sunk lower, emptied of the space that had been taken up by the giants.

Surina began to row frantically, her eyes fixed on the nearest creature as it extended one water-slicked arm toward the boat. "Keep going! We won't get another chance!"

Hannah pulled at the oars, but yelled: "It's going to crush us!"

"It hasn't been two minutes," Surina said, though she wasn't sure how much time had passed.

As they brought the boat between the rocks, Surina's heart began to race. The gates had drawn wide. Surely they would close soon. She rowed with all her might. *Ten seconds. Once the gates start to close, we only have a few seconds to get out.*

And then the rocks changed direction, and began to close in.

The boat was not quite clear of the gates. Surina gave a last desperate attempt. She pushed the oar against the oarlock so that the lock cracked and broke from the boat. She pushed the oar against the oncoming wall to propel the boat forward, but she was not quite fast enough: the rocks closed on the stern of the boat. With a loud crack, the black box was crushed. The tip of the stern was caught, so that the boat became stuck. It dipped forward as the wave swell receded below them.

"Surina!" Hannah cried, as the bow began to dip into the river.

Surina jabbed at the broken stern with the oar, until the wood broke away completely and the boat was free. She clutched the sides of the boat as it bobbed in the water.

"It's leaking!" Hannah cried.

Surina looked into the bottom of the boat. A thin line of water was growing between her feet. The pressure of the crash had cracked the wood along nearly a third of the hull's length.

"We're fine," Surina assured her. "Put your feet up and row faster. We can make it to shore."

Hannah grabbed the sack and set it beside her, and

braced her feet against the side of the boat.

The bank rose gradually from the water, making it easy to land. Surina coaxed the boat as far onto the rocky land as she could, trying to land it sideways. Hannah jumped out, carrying the rucksack, and held the edge of the boat while Surina leapt out. They pulled the craft some distance onto the bank, and then stood and caught their breath.

Surina surveyed the damage and grimaced. "Well," she said, "at least Piscis will stop nagging us to get out of the boat."

"I *need* that boat!" Hannah's eyes burned with exasperation. "How am I supposed to get to Orion? I don't know any other way there!"

Surina gestured to the path beyond. "There's a trail and a sign. Let's see what it says."

6: Fornax

Surina gazed up at the sandstone walls that lined the riverbank. The mishmash of giant stones obscured the landscape, making it near impossible to see what might lie behind them—but, mere yards from the ruined boat, two towering boulders leaned against each other, leaving a triangular opening between them. Beside the opening was something that looked like a map stand. Surina looked from the stand to the path beyond and felt a twinge of anxiety. Though she tried to maintain a calm expression, inwardly she was thinking: *What am I doing here? Why do I do things like this?* The twinge became a wave of fear. *Where am I? Is it another dimension? What if I can't get out?*

She thought over her past impulses, her habit of jumping into situations merely because they "felt" right. Coming here had seemed insensible, yet somehow inevitable. The circumstances had lined up too perfectly: Hannah appearing in her dreams, Dominic's plea for help, her chance to return to Peru. At first glance it seemed that Surina had been granted an opportunity to help someone in need and to resolve her own problems, but as she gazed into the oppressive-looking stone passageway, she wondered if she was being drawn into another trap.

She tried to shove her doubts aside and led the way forward. On approaching the stand, Surina saw that its surface was etched not with a map, but with a riddle:

Ahead is the tree that will give you a lift;
solve one of three schemes to enable the gift.
Each couplet's first letters, bound, giveth a clue;
the first two give one, while the third giveth two.

Fleetly shall the dead one gift
celestial arts to heal the rift.

Work a new and older ark,
odd but firm within the bark.

Lili for the arriving warrior
turning toward her home at last.
An owl and griffin act as couriers;
zucchini cannot fly as fast.

Surina stood with her hands on her hips. "We're really at a disadvantage. We spent hours listening to Aquarius' riddles, and I never want to see another one—but now we're getting three or four at a time."

"Try putting up with it for hundreds of years, like Wibben has," Hannah replied quietly. "I've only been here a year or so, and . . . ."

Surina started to interrupt: "You've been here a couple—" She cut herself off. Surina didn't want Hannah to know that she had been underground, without food or water, for two whole weeks. "A couple days, or maybe three," she lied.

Hannah looked up at her with somber eyes. "It may have been a few days on Earth, but this is a different space-time." She read over the words again. "Each couplet's first letters. Flee . . . Flec . . . ." A long pause ensued; Hannah looked at the words with consternation. "I found *fleece*, and *wood*, and . . . I'm not sure about the last one."

"That's okay." Surina glanced beyond the boulders. The path ahead was walled on either side by more lopsided stones, the rocky landscape dotted with tiny green shrubs. "It says we have to keep going, and find a tree—right? 'Ahead is a tree that will give you a lift.'"

"Yeah. But it says we have to use wood, or fleece, or something else to enable it. That's what I *think*, anyway." Hannah tried the last passage again. "Lilt? Lil . . . ."

"We only have to choose one, right? We have wood and fleece. Let's find the tree and see what we can do with those words." Surina started forward, through the sandstone archway.

The path continued for a short distance, and then branched off into a series of irregular, narrow passages. Surina and Hannah peered through the openings in the stone walls and tried to decide the best course. Any way they looked, the landscape was daunting; smooth rock walls towered high above them, striped with dizzying patterns of tan and red. Misshapen openings in the walls offered glimpses of tall stone ramps and castle-like turrets, some with boulders balancing precariously on top.

"This reminds me of the Fiery Furnace," Surina said. "Have you ever been there?"

"What?"

"The Fiery Furnace. It's at Arches National Park in Utah. I went there a couple years ago with . . . ." Surina hesitated. "With my ex-husband. It's basically a sandstone maze. It's so easy to get lost that no one is allowed inside without a ranger or a special permit." Surina ran her fingers along a chasm in the right-hand wall. "Hey . . . stay here, okay? I'll be right back." She hurried back toward the entrance.

"Wait!" Hannah started after her.

"I'll just be a minute. I'm getting the chalk from the boat."

Surina sprinted to retrieve the chalk, and returned to find Hannah trailing after her, her face drawn with worry. "Got it," Surina said, holding up the stick. "I'll use this to mark our way, so we can follow the line back to the river. I can make little arrow heads so we know which way we came from." She held the tip against the right-hand wall, tracing a white line as she walked, pausing every so often to draw an arrow.

Hannah stopped as the path came to a dead end. "Which way?"

Surina peered through one of the three openings near the end of the path. None looked more traversable than the others; each sloped and curved away, its destination hidden from view.

They chose the path with the largest opening. The stone passage angled left, and then right, and then sloped downward, the walls rising higher around it. The air in the stone labyrinth was hot and dry, and not even the smallest breeze reached inside. Surina's throat already felt parched. The dry air made her skin feel taut around her bones.

"That's another thing about the Fiery Furnace," she said, raising her hand in a useless effort to fan her face. "Not only can you get lost, you can easily get heat stroke."

As they rounded another bend, they stopped in shock at the change in the landscape. The misshapen walls spread wide, curving around a large space filled with boulders. Each boulder had been carved into a human figure—some crouching, some standing straight, some lying on the stone floor. Each was etched in full detail, down to the buttons on their clothes and the retinas in their eyes, with the exception of a few statues whose heads were missing.

Surina's gaze became riveted on a male figure in

sneakers, shorts, and a T-shirt. His face was expressively formed with furrowed eyebrows and an open mouth. He stood with one arm lifted, as if caught in mid-movement. In his raised hand he gripped a single object: a ridged bottle with a small, round cap.

Surina took a breath. "*That's* creepy," she murmured.

Hannah stepped closer to one of the decapitated figures. "Yeah. It looks like they had heads, and someone cut them off."

"No . . . I meant . . . this statue looks like my ex-husband." Surina gazed at the smooth stone eyes and felt a slight shudder. "This place is bringing back some unpleasant memories. The Fiery Furnace was the last place I went with my husband. We split up after we got home."

"This place can do that. Bring up memories, I mean." Hannah's tone was quiet, morose. "Sometimes, this place shows me things I'd forgotten about. A lot of them are bad memories."

"Well, these memories are definitely bad ones." Surina thought back to that day: Victor holding a plastic water bottle and smirking. *You're no fun today*, he'd said. *I'm doing all the talking, and you're just standing there like a statue.* She had looked at him without responding. Less than an hour beforehand, she'd found his secret stash of cocaine in the car. Victor had always referred to himself as a recovering addict; he had put all that behind him, or so he said, and was committed to making a good life with Surina. But over the past year he'd become increasingly dependent on various substances: caffeine pills, then nicotine, then hard liquor, and then the street drugs he tried to keep hidden. The more he used, the meaner he became. *What does it take to get some life out of you?* he'd demanded—and then he lifted the water bottle and lightly smacked her in the head with it.

A woman standing nearby had given Surina a knowing look, a look of compassion and pity.

Victor smacked her with the bottle again, harder this time. Up to that point, Surina had always reassured herself that *Victor isn't the kind of guy who hits; he prefers to use words.* It struck her, then, that she didn't really know what he was capable of. She went home and quietly began to file for divorce.

"That was a really tough time," she told Hannah. "We had only been married for a year. My mom was still trying to pay off our wedding, and I loved my in-laws. My husband had certain problems and refused to get help, and I hated seeing what was happening to him. I felt really pressured to fix things. But . . . you can't force the other person to work things out. Sometimes they just refuse." Surina felt a sudden pang of despair, remembering how Victor's words and gestures had changed in that short time. In the beginning it was *I love you so much. You're worth so much more than any of that meaningless, self-destructive crap I'm leaving behind. We're going to make a great life together*, and then it was *Yes I'm using drugs, because I'm bored out of my mind living with you. What do you expect?*

"Let's keep going," she sighed. "This heat is really getting to me."

The opposite side of the chamber opened to another walled pathway. Surina felt warmth emanating from the sandstone as she scraped the chalk against it. She raised her other hand in a useless effort to catch a breeze. Overhead, the tunnel became enclosed by a series of arches—but their shadows gave no relief from the oppressive heat. A tiny pool of water gleamed beside the stone wall, and some prickly-looking shrubs even grew through the cracks. Surina paused beside the pool. "I need water," she said. "Do you think it's safe to drink this?"

"I wouldn't. If it comes from the river, it might make you forget everything."

"Right." Surina continued onward, toward a bend in the path. "I'm tempted anyway. My throat is . . . ."

Her words trailed off as she rounded the bend. She and Hannah had come to a bridge; the stone floor ended abruptly, and a cavernous drop stretched below, its shadowy bottom a jumble of jagged rock. A single beam of stone traversed the pit. It was wide enough for Surina and Hannah to walk side by side, and looked sturdy enough at the ends, but as Surina peered at it from different angles she noticed that the base thinned in the middle—enough that she worried it might not hold their weight. A gap had opened near the middle of the beam, right down the center, possibly wide enough for someone to fall through.

"Walk behind me," Hannah said.

"Are you sure? If we hold hands, it will help us keep steady."

Hannah shook her head vehemently.

"All right," Surina said, "but we should walk side by side in the middle. See that gap?"

"I see it," Hannah replied, and started walking. Surina followed close. She watched as Hannah walked unsteadily across the stone bridge, her arms stretched out at her sides, the rucksack gripped tightly in one hand. Near the center Hannah stumbled; she leaned to one side, gasping with sudden fear.

Surina laid a firm hand on her shoulder, helping to steady her. "You're fine," she assured her. "Walk beside me now. Let's hold hands. You can walk on the right side of the gap, and I'll walk on the left."

Hannah stepped carefully aside, grasping Surina's arm as they maneuvered beside each other.

"Just walk," Surina said. "Relax and keep walking."

Surina's heartbeat quickened as they walked past the opening. It was not quite as wide as it had appeared, but Surina remembered how thin the stone was becoming beneath her feet, and she struggled not to show her nervousness. Hannah's hand began to sweat in hers.

They passed the gap without incident. To Surina's surprise, Hannah stayed beside her, lightly clutching her arm.

At the opposite end Surina paused to draw an arrow on the ground. She stood and observed the path ahead: an enclosed tunnel with light streaming through openings in the roof. The path angled upward and led them around another bend, and then opened into a wide plateau. Once again, Hannah and Surina stopped in surprise.

To their right stood a small shack, a rickety structure of warped planks and shrub-thatched roof. A sign above the open doorway bore the words "Sculptor's Studio" in large letters, and a dozen or so tools covered an off-kilter wooden bench: a hatchet, mallet, several chisels, and hammers of varying size.

Surina was still staring when a man emerged from the hut. He was tall and bronzed, with plastic goggles over his eyes and a dusty bandana over his nose and mouth. He stopped and gaped at the visitors, and then yanked the bandana down around his neck. "Hi there! Looking for a sculptor?"

Surina leaned closer to Hannah and whispered: "Who is he?"

Hannah shrugged and shook her head.

The man put his hands on his hips and squinted. "Not looking for a sculptor?"

"No," Surina said. "Um . . . this is going to sound strange, but we're looking for a tree."

He raised his eyebrows. "Oh, the *tree*. Good luck. I've tried a hundred times to find that tree, but I always end up going in circles—or worse. Supposedly it's at the center of the labyrinth. I've nearly died a dozen times, wandering around in there."

Hannah and Surina exchanged glances.

"Why were *you* looking for the tree?" Hannah asked.

"Well, I've heard things about it. That's where the anzu is hiding."

"What's that?"

"The anzu? It's a creature who stole the Tablets of Destiny—a frightening half-bird, half-human thing . . . really more of a demon than anything. It took the tablets from Aquarius and nested somewhere in the labyrinth, where no one can find it."

Surina couldn't resist a smile. "Aquarius has had a bad run of luck lately."

"What are the Tablets of Destiny?" Hannah asked.

"You haven't heard of them? I thought everyone in these parts knew about it. It's said that whoever holds the tablets has power over the universe."

Surina nodded. "So . . . a demon bird is controlling the universe."

"Well, I don't really know the details." The sculptor's brow furrowed. "Why are *you* looking for the tree?"

"We need it," Hannah said. "Our boat is broken, and we're supposed to find wood or fleece to . . . ." She hesitated. "I'm not sure. We just need to find it."

Something stirred in the man's eyes. He eyed Surina, then Hannah, with quiet scrutiny. "So . . . you're looking for the golden fleece."

"I don't know if it's golden."

"The tree supposedly holds the golden fleece of Chrysomallos, the winged ram. It's said to have incredible healing powers." His gaze flicked toward the rising sandstone. "This is a place where people come to get lost. Even if you find the tree, you're not likely to find your way out."

Surina held up the piece of chalk. "We've been marking the way. We'll just follow the line back to the beginning."

Again, he regarded them for some time with quiet contemplation. "Tell you what: I'll help you find the tree. I don't know where it is, but I know where it's *not*. If we find it, you can have the wood and the fleece. I'm only interested in the tablets."

Hannah looked aghast. "You want to control the universe?"

"No! That's too big a responsibility. I want to return them to Aquarius. I'm sure he'll reward me—maybe with a lifetime's worth of beer, or some other fine product that's lacking in these parts." He nodded to Hannah. "What've you got in the bag?"

Hannah glanced down at the sack in her hand. "Oh. Just . . . stuff. Nothing that would be useful here."

"Fair enough. So, are you with me or not?"

Surina looked down at Hannah, who shrugged. "Sure," Surina said.

Excitement played on the sculptor's face. "I'll be ready in a minute." He disappeared inside the hut, but quickly emerged again, pausing beside the bench and swiping the hatchet. He tucked it into a loop in his belt.

Hannah eyed it uneasily. "Why are you bringing that?"

"You gave me an idea," he replied. "Your chalk is small, and the labyrinth is enormous. When the chalk runs out, I'll carve a line in the sandstone with this." The sculptor clutched the head of the hatchet and gave it a light shake. "Let's go. The heat will only get worse if we wait."

As the trio ascended back into the sandstone mountain, the sculptor rambled on about the legends and myths surrounding the labyrinth and its mysterious tree. "I don't know much about the ram itself, except that it was created to rescue Phrixos and Helle, two children who were about to be devoured by the celestial guardians. The ram carried the boy, Phrixos, to safety—and then the ram was sacrificed, and its fleece removed. I'm not sure what happened to the girl. I think she fell into the sea and was swallowed by Cetus." He quickened his steps, calling over his shoulder: "Come on, let's pick up the pace!"

"It's too hot," Hannah complained. "I feel like I'm dying in the desert."

"Oh, it isn't that bad." The sculptor burst into an eager sprint, clambering onto a rocky slope ahead of them.

"I didn't expect to see another person here," Surina said. "Dominic made it sound like there wasn't anyone else, except Wibben."

"I'm not sure he's a person," Hannah whispered. "He might be a constellation. The Sculptor constellation is next to Fornax, the furnace." She crouched as she made her way up the small slope. "I think we're in Fornax now. It *feels* like a furnace."

"Oh. I should have studied the constellations better. I thought I would end up in the zodiac, so I just . . . ." She trailed off as the next length of the path came into view. Relief sculptures covered the beige-and-tan walls— figures of birds, fish, sea creatures, a magnificent horse, and an androgynous human form that seemed to peer out at them from the stone. At the base of the wall, a few boulders had been carved into frogs and a large owl.

"Wow," Surina mused, stopping to admire the intricate figure of a giant turtle. She glanced up at the sculptor. "Did you carve these?"

"No, not me. They were like this when I got here. It's good work, isn't it? You can find a lot of these carvings in the labyrinth, even statues. Of course, I had to lop the heads from a few of those."

"You did that?" Hannah asked. "Why?"

"They were . . . unpleasant."

"How?"

"They were statues of cursed beings. You know—Medusa, the snake-headed woman, and other monsters like that. Who wants those creatures standing around and leering at you whenever you pass by? They're bad luck. I don't know who made them, or why. The studio isn't mine either. It was just sitting empty, with all the tools lying around. I waited there, thinking the sculptor who lived there would come home, but nobody ever came—so I settled in. Seemed like a waste of space if someone didn't use it."

They followed a narrow path between two massive boulders. The sculptor's knife hadn't cut there, but Serena saw clearly defined faces in the beige lines streaking against the lighter tan background. She started to point them out, but the sculptor couldn't be interrupted. He had launched into a long speech about the enigmatic tree: a majestic, ancient timber with high, thick branches. In those branches lived not only the anzu, but also the demon-woman Lilitu. "And a huge serpent guards its base," he added, "so, getting the tablets won't be an easy task."

"It sounds crowded," Surina replied. "Do you think that's actually true, though? I doubt there's anyone living in the middle of this furnace. Maybe we'll get there and find their skeletons."

He shrugged. "Let's hope we find out soon."

"Is that why you live out here?" Hannah asked. "You've been looking for the tablets and the golden fleece?"

"No! There's an abundance of sandstone here. Sandstone is hard on my tools, but it's the best rock for carving. You can see that for yourself." He gestured to his surroundings, adding: "Even without all this fancy work, it proves itself suitable. There isn't much of a breeze in these parts, but on the outskirts there are amazing sandstone figures carved by the wind."

Surina had stopped admiring the landscape. Its elegant forms and colors no longer impressed her. The heat made her skin feel taut around her bones. Her throat was painfully parched, so that her steps were often interrupted by a dry cough. As the journey wore on with no end in sight, she remembered that Dominic had felt a year passing for him in this place—and Hannah was still trapped here, fading away like Wibben.

"We've already been in this spot," Surina said, pointing to a white line that ran along one of the sandstone boulders. "We're starting to go in circles."

The sculptor's spirits were finally beginning to fade. He sighed and looked at the opposite archway as though viewing a heavy burden. "All right. Let's go the other way."

The "other way" was an imposing slope leading to three small openings in the tall rock—two large circular holes and a smaller one below, their arrangement resembling the eye and nose cavities of a skull. Surina helped to heave Hannah up the incline, and then scrambled up herself. They passed easily through one of the larger openings. When the sculptor had finished climbing through, he stood beside his companions and stared.

A bare sandstone arena spread before them, with a sole figure rising from the center: a large juniper tree, twisted and bare, its gray branches radiating near the top like the arms of a warped skeleton. No demon-lady or demon-bird rested there; the tree appeared unoccupied except for a large owl, its chestnut-hued chest mottled with dark brown. Two feather tufts came to points on its head like the ears of a cat. It peered at the intruders from a nest of gray twigs, partly obscured by thick branches.

As Surina moved closer, she saw that the grooves in the tree bark made up a distinct pattern, as though someone had deliberately carved into it. The pattern resembled the image on the Lanzón: a figure standing upright, with two long, protruding fangs and stylized eyes—and from its head, instead of hair, several small snakes sprouted. It stood with one clawed hand raised up beside its head. From where Surina stood, the other hand wasn't visible, but she assumed it was resting at the figure's side.

"Wow," she said. "It looks like the Lanzón. Hannah, isn't this what you were showing me in my dreams?"

"It is," Hannah replied, with the same note of wonder. "Sort of. It's the same carving. Except . . . this doesn't look carved. It looks like the bark just grew that way."

As the trio moved closer, Surina saw that the base of the tree was thin and wide rather than round; its edges curved inward while the center depressed outward. "That's it," Hannah said excitedly. "This is our boat." She turned anxiously to the sculptor. "You can cut it down, can't you?"

"You're right," Surina said. "It's a tree shaped like a boat. We could use the hatchet to hack off the branches, but there's an—"

"Look!" Sculptor pointed to the upper branches with a fearful expression. "It's the anzu!"

Surina glanced up and saw nothing but the owl, still peering at her from the nest. She looked at the other branches and saw nothing. She let out a soft chuckle. "That's an owl."

"We have to get rid of it somehow," Hannah said. "We need that tree."

The sculptor persisted: "That is the anzu! It has the body of a lion and the wings of a bird!"

Surina tried to restrain her laughter. She noticed, with some admiration, that the fluff of tiny golden feathers along the owl's feet did make them look more like paws than bird feet. "No, it's a great horned owl," she said. "We have them in Arizona, where I live. They're . . . ." Surina was about to say *They're harmless*, but then the base of the tree began to move, and the words caught in her throat.

Hannah grabbed her arm. "It's a snake!"

It seemed to Surina that the trunk was unfurling, but after a moment she saw it: the head of a large serpent, streaked with shades of gray, its two large yellow eyes scanning the chamber. One of those wide, unblinking eyes seemed to fix on Surina.

"You see?" Sculptor's voice was high and frantic. He raised the hatchet.

"Wait!" Hannah said, but the sculptor lurched forward, hacking at the snake in a frenzy. The massive body thrashed at the first chop, which struck very near the head; it thrashed and heaved as the blade struck again and again, so that Surina was sure the sculptor would be knocked from his feet—but he kept hacking until the serpent was in pieces. Its blood, a dark reddish-gray, sprayed the sculptor's tattered pants; it stained the rock floor and seeped into cracks.

The owl fluttered its wings. Two tiny heads peeped over the edge of the nest, brown-and-white balls of fluff with golden eyes like their mother. Surina, trying to overcome her shock at the sudden violence, began to point them out—but another face appeared then, a human-like face with blue-tinged skin and impossibly dark eyes. The creature was poised on the opposite side of the tree, up in the branches not far from the nest. It looked down at the mess of blood and snake flesh, at the decapitated head with its mouth wide open in pain. The creature's eyes were two black voids in a ghoulish face, but Surina could nevertheless see the look of utter horror in those eyes. In an agonized voice, it cried "No!"

The owl, too, made sounds of distress. It beat its wings and nudged its young, pushing them from the nest. They dipped clumsily, struggling toward flight.

"Catch it!" the sculptor said. He raised his arms and jumped, reaching uselessly for the owl, then for the chicks. They got their bearings and followed their parent over the labyrinth walls.

The demon's face twisted with rage; the dark eyes burned with fury. "Idiots!" it shrieked. It moved to the front of the tree and spread its wings wide, so that for a moment a foreboding shadow was cast over Hannah and Surina. A bundle of items fell from its lap as it moved, bouncing along the branches—and then one strong leg lashed out, striking the tree with one clawed foot, and the creature flew away.

The sculptor ran back to the tunnels. He peered through one opening, and then another, then gave up and returned. "Blast it! After all this, I missed it again. Did it come back this way?"

Hannah didn't pay him any attention. She stood gazing at the ruined tree. Several of the smaller branches had crashed to the ground, along with a bundle of sticks that had been the owl's nest. Her shoulders slumped. "Now this one is cracked, too."

"I'll fix it," the sculptor said. "It can be patched up easily. All I need is some epoxy and silicone caulk, and I have plenty of that."

"Wait, are you serious?" Surina looked at him in disbelief. "You have tools to fix a cracked boat? Why didn't you just offer to fix our old boat?"

"I . . . didn't think of it." He rummaged in the fallen branches with his foot. With his toe he pulled a long cloth from the pile—a length of wool, worn and discolored with dirt. The sculptor made a sound of disgust and kicked it aside. Suddenly he crouched. A moment later he was holding a drum frame in his hands, a round juniper frame with a crossbar at the back. "Well . . . this is nothing, but I'll hang onto it. What's this?" He plucked a light brown stick from the mass of gray. This, too, he turned this way and that, scrutinizing its surface. From where she stood, Surina could see that it had been carved with small figures.

Hannah turned on the sculptor with sudden fury. "Why did you *do* that? We could have *asked* the snake for what we wanted, and it probably would have *given* it to us."

"You told me to get rid of it," he retorted, standing. "Anyway, what we wanted isn't here. There's just a dead tree and a dirty old frock. And these things," he added, clutching the stick and drum to his chest, "but they're nothing special."

Hannah stepped forward and retrieved the fallen garment. She stared down at it for some time. "It's mine," she said at last. "This is my nightgown. I lost it . . . a long time ago."

"You lost it *here*?"

"No. At Lupus. That demon girl must have taken it."

"Will you fix our boat?" Surina asked, but Hannah gave her an urgent look and shook her head. "We don't need him," she said quietly.

"Yes we do, we need a boat."

"We can't ask him to fix the boat," Hannah said, louder. "It's against the rules. We'll have to use one of the other enigmas."

Surina frowned at the shattered tree.

"I'll leave you to it, then," the sculptor said, and waved. "Good luck."

He disappeared into the labyrinth. Surina watched him go, and then asked, "How is that against the rules? We still would have been using wood. Not that I want to drag this thing through the labyrinth in this heat, but we didn't find fleece, and we never solved—"

"This *is* fleece," Hannah mumbled, so quietly that Surina barely heard her.

"What?"

"I have the fleece. I didn't want Sculptor to know, because he would have taken it." She lifted the worn garment in her hands. It was mottled and discolored, but in several places it remained a soft, golden brown. "It's my nightgown. It was made from the fleece of the Aries ram. He died so that I could get through the next realms."

Surina looked at it doubtfully. "Well . . . that's good, right? Maybe it does have some kind of healing aspect, and it can . . . fix the boat, or something."

"Maybe," Hannah murmured.

"Let's head back. I can't stand much more of this heat." Surina started away. "But, there's a bright side to being here. At least Piscis can't come after us."

"I'd rather deal with Piscis than bake alive in an oven," Hannah muttered, walking beside her.

From somewhere in the labyrinth a voice rang out, near and perfectly clear: "My lady!"

Hannah froze.

"My lady Hannah! A word, please!"

Hannah turned to look at Surina, her eyes wide with dread.

"A moment of your time, if I may."

Surina quietly approached the far edge of the arena. She poked her head through an opening, into a stone passageway, and caught a disturbing glimpse of Piscis' fish-like head peering at her from a small pool of water. Greenery from a shrub brushed against his face as he tried to keep his head above the surface.

"The water-lord Aquarius has commanded that you repair his boat and return it immediately. I'm afraid you have been quite careless in your handling of it. Additionally—"

Surina ran back to Hannah and grabbed her hand, pulling her back the way they had come.

They clambered through the hole and followed the chalk arrows backwards through the labyrinth, stopping at a place where the lines converged. "Which way was it?" Hannah asked. "This is where we started going in a circle. What if we just follow the line back into the same circle?"

"I should have fixed it," Surina said apologetically. "Let's try this way first."

The moment she started down the path, the gray-green head popped up ahead of them. Water splashed across the hot stone. "*I will rouse the fifty lahama!*"

"Other way," Surina decided. They hurried off, while Piscis called after them: "*Run fast, then! Your livelihood depends upon it!*"

The route led them back across the beam, where the two held hands and crossed side by side. At the opposite end they started to run again, but Hannah stopped at the sight of a small bundle of feathers on the stone floor. On closer inspection Surina saw that it was a tiny owl—likely one of the owl chicks that had fled from the sculptor.

"Is it alive?" she asked.

Hannah crouched beside it. Her fingertips probed the fluffy white feathers. "I don't know." She picked the little creature up in both hands, moving carefully—but the head slipped between her fingers and hung there at a severe angle. The eyelids were nearly closed, but in that small glimpse of the eyes Surina saw a dull lifelessness. "I think its neck is broken."

Hannah wrapped the bird in her fleece gown. She looked anxiously at Surina. "It might help. Probably not, but . . . maybe."

Surina nodded. "Come on, let's keep going."

They made their way back to the riverbank. The chalk lines led them back to the two towering boulders at the sandstone entrance. The horned owl was perched there, intently watching their approach. Beside it, Surina could see bits of fluff—probably the tops of the chicks' heads.

Hannah stopped and looked down at the bundle in her arms. Sweat gleamed on her palms as she unfolded the wool gown. The chick was still lying limp and still—but Hannah lifted the bundle, as though to encourage the animal to fly away, and the mother owl let out a low *hoot-hoot*, and suddenly the chick moved. Its eyes blinked; it stumbled to its feet, flapping its wings until they carried it up and out of the tattered wool.

Surina watched as it landed on the boulder beside its mother. It disappeared from view, but Surina could see the mother dipping its head and stretching its wing, as if to shelter the chick beneath it.

"There's hope," Surina said.

Hannah nodded. Her eyes gleamed with sudden tears.

"Come on." Surina started toward the boat. It lay cracked and useless on the bank, where they'd left it. Pools of water still shone in the bottom. "Let's flip it over first, and get the water out," Surina suggested. "We can do it without touching the water. If we tip it sideways, the water will pool in the middle, where it's wide."

They maneuvered into place at either end of the boat, slowly turning it onto its side. One of the oars wedged itself against the rock, propping the boat at an angle and keeping it from flipping completely over.

"That's good enough," Surina said. "I was about to

drop it anyway. It's . . . ."

"It's a bird," Hannah said.

The bottom of the boat bore a large carving, the lines of which took up the entire area that had been submerged in water. It was the image of a bird, its wings folded, its short beak pointing toward the prow. The carving itself was simply done, and nothing about it was unusual—except that, at the site of the break, the bird's figure dripped a red liquid, as though it was a living thing that could tear and bleed.

Hannah laid the fleece across the wound and stood back, waiting.

"It might take a few minutes," Surina said. "It seemed to take a while with—"

She broke off as the carved lines snapped into sudden action. Impossibly, the wooden bird had flapped its wings.

The boat rose suddenly from its place on the ground, standing on all four oars. The upper rim of the boat folded in on itself, forming the creature's belly, while the rearward oars mutated with a few snaps into a pair of legs, and the other pair disappeared beneath it with a loud *whack*. The bird stood up, shaking itself, and then seemed to look at Surina and Hannah with one of its blank wooden eyes.

Surina stood back, swearing under her breath. "What the hell do we do now?" she asked.

"We fly," Hannah said. She went to the creature and knelt beside it, picking up the fallen rucksack from between its legs.

"No way. How?"

Hannah petted the smooth wooden neck. "Is it okay if I get on?" she asked.

The giant bird made a slight movement, bending its legs and lowering its body. Hannah moved the fleece so that it lay closer to the head; then she hoisted herself onto the creature's back, tucked the fleece under her bottom, and wrapped her arms around the neck. "Sit behind me," she said to Surina.

"I prefer the boat," Surina replied.

"But we have a bird now, and birds are faster."

Surina felt her pulse racing as she climbed up behind Hannah. "There's nowhere to put my feet," she said. "The wings are in the way."

"Sit on them," Hannah suggested. "Fold your legs, and put your feet behind you."

Surina tried the position. She fit well enough, but she felt precariously perched, and not the least bit secure.

"Hang on tight to me," Hannah said.

Suring wrapped her arms around the girl's waist, clutching her firmly. "I don't feel good about this at all," she said, and as the bird stretched out its wings, she added: "We're going to die."

Hannah didn't say anything in response, but as the bird lifted into flight, Surina thought she heard her laughing.

7: Azha and Rana

When the bird reached the fourth gate, Surina was still alive—so much so that she could feel her heart pounding wildly in her chest.

After soaring over the third gate, the crew found themselves unable to pass over the fourth. The rocks on either side of the river rose higher and higher, eventually forming an enclosed ceiling, with the only light streaming through crevices in the rock. The bird flew into the tunnel and stopped just short of the metal-barred gate.

It landed on the rocky bank and sat down, allowing Hannah and Surina to slide from its back.

"Let's not do that again," Surina said breathlessly. She walked toward the rocky wall, where she saw the next riddle posted, and felt her legs trembling as she went. "I think I see our next path," she said, pointing to the rocks.

Several yards above, a large hole opened in the rock wall, large enough to pass through. A staircase had been cut into the dark gray stone, leading from the ground to the base of the opening. Surina eyed the steps with concern. Not only did they make for a steep climb, but there was also a stream of water trickling down beside them, spouting from numerous holes in the rock, and the ceiling overhead cast the area in shadow.

Surina stopped, leaning over with her hands on her knees. "Can you read the riddle?" she asked Hannah. "I'm shaking all over."

Hannah went to the wooden placard and read aloud:

"A tributary leads you toward the sea and shows you a . . . ." She paused. "A confluence of three. Do . . . ." Again she hesitated, and spoke the remaining words slowly. "Do fortify friends, rather than forsake, and once again the larger river take."

"A tributary leads you," Surina said aloud. She came to stand beside Hannah.

"A tributary," Hannah repeated, "like an ode to someone?"

"No, a tributary is a stream that flows into a larger body of water. So . . . ." Surina pointed to the thin waterfall beside the stone steps. "That's our most obvious path. The water is coming down and flowing into the river."

"What about there? Isn't that a tributary?" Hannah pointed to a small stream that broke away from the river, flowing toward the rock wall and disappearing into a hole.

Surina went to the stream and crouched beside it. "No. It's a . . . distributary. The water is flowing out of the river, not into it." She went back to the placard and studied the riddle. "So, the waterfall supposedly leads toward the sea. There's going to be some kind of joining of three things, maybe three different streams combining into one. We need to strengthen our friends—each other, probably—rather than forsake them, and then we come back to the river." Surina took a few steps back, looking at the steep path above. "Well, let's get climbing." She gestured to the sack in Hannah's hand. "Are you bringing that with?"

Hannah clutched the sack close to her chest. "I'm not letting it out of my sight."

"All right. But, be really careful on the way up, okay? The water might have splashed on the steps. I'll go up behind you."

The climb was easier than Surina anticipated; she

reached the top in little more than a minute, in spite of her unsteady limbs. Near the opening she heard the rush of water and caught the briny smell of saltwater in the air— but instead of the sea, she saw a wide, rocky plateau, bordered on both sides by rock walls, with a large pool of water in the center.

Surina was about to step through the opening when a movement caught her eye. Someone was standing on the far side of the plateau, near the wall that rose on the left. Surina felt a moment of panic, remembering the sinister figure who supposedly lurked in this realm, but then she recognized the pale, skinny man who stood there in little more than underwear and a pair of foot wrappings.

"It's Wibben," she said, stepping out onto the plateau. "What's he doing here?"

Hannah shrugged and started across the plateau.

Wibben stood looking at a riddle etched into the rock wall. Surina only glanced at it as she passed; her attention was caught by the horizon, and by the cool waves of salty air that came from beyond the cliff. She walked to the cliff's edge and stood looking down at the sea below, watching the waves crash rhythmically against the dark stone. Water spouted from the cliff wall, spurting through the air and falling to mingle with the great waters.

"Well," she said, "we found the sea." Surina went to join the others at the wall, where the riddle was carved into the rock and inked in yellow. "What are you doing here? Trying to solve something?"

"I'm looking for the cauldron of Dagda." Wibben gestured to the writing. "There's a reference to a cauldron here, but I can't figure out the riddle."

"What's Dagda?" Hannah asked.

"I don't know yet. But I've been looking for it for a long time."

The group fell silent as Surina and Hannah read:

While bound above the darkest sea, a needling beak will agitate
to push my hope toward misery, to pick at anger, flesh out hate.
Still loath am I to know the one who teaches metamorphosis
within the ocean's cauldron where the lost soul in the darkness sits.
The faithful children of the deep in their affinity remain
until the day when hard-wrought friendship and forgiveness crush my chains.
The man from Media am I, who took right actions for mankind
and learned beforehand what the rest shall fulfill at a later time.

Who am I?

"It doesn't have any word clues," Hannah said uncertainly. "I think it's just about Andromeda. She was chained above the sea and sacrificed to the sea monster, but Perseus cut her chains. The man from Media . . . ."

"No, isn't it what's-his-name?" Surina asked. "It starts with a P. Prometheus? Look: it says a needling beak was pecking at him, picking at his anger."

Hannah hesitated. "I don't know who Prometheus is."

"He was a demi-god who helped humans. Zeus punished him by having him chained to a rock, where a bird pecked at his liver every day for . . . I don't know, thousands of years. Then they made a pact, and Zeus freed him." Surina scrutinized the passage. "I wouldn't say they were friends, though. Zeus was just being selfish."

Wibben pointed to the fourth line. "What's the

reference to a cauldron?"

"I'm not sure. The sea-god, Oceanus, offered to teach him metamorphosis and self-knowledge, but . . . ." She gave Wibben an apologetic look. "We studied *Prometheus Bound* in one of my literature classes, but I didn't read all of it. I mostly read the Sparknotes."

"I know what it is," Hannah said softly. "It's Cetus' belly. When you're inside of it, in the dark, you learn how to transform."

"Was Prometheus swallowed by Cetus?" Wibben asked.

"No, but I was. I think Cetus and Oceanus are the same thing."

"Cetus is the gorgon who tried to eat Andromeda," Surina said. "She was sacrificed to him."

"That's what I thought, too," Hannah said, "but I was wrong." She looked toward the opposite side of the plateau. "What's that?"

Near the other wall was an apparatus that looked rather like a swing-set, with a single fancy swing suspended high in the air. Wibben didn't reply to Hannah's question, but beckoned her to follow.

On closer observance, the "swing" appeared to be an elaborate throne with an attached foot rest, positioned much too high for anyone to sit on; its lowest point was at the same level as the top of Wibben's head. The gilded throne was replete with interweaving designs, with arm rests that ended in a pair of lion heads and a golden griffin above the head rest, but its fabric resembled cheap vinyl. An extra rope, this one of braided golden fibers, trailed across its seat and down to the ground.

The shape of the chair reminded Surina of something she'd seen in one of her constellation charts. The seat was positioned at an angle, so that its occupant would be at a half-standing position rather than a full sit. With its

attached footrest, the throne looked somewhat like a
crooked letter *M*.

"Is it supposed to be the Cassiopeia constellation?"
Surina asked. "That's what it's shaped like. The
constellation is supposed to represent her throne.
Cassiopeia is next to Perseus and Andromeda, so it would
make sense."

Directly below the suspended chair, etched in stone,
was a rhyme:

In vanity one clings to dreams of royal primacy,
avoiding the great cauldron and the children of the
sea,
loath to upend one's throne; but how can wisdom truly
grow
if one refuses to pursue the art of letting go?
Overturn the boastful throne, let modesty wash down
and open up the gate that leads unto the starry crown.

On the throne itself, along the tilted seat, a single
word was etched in large letters. To Surina, it appeared to
say "jatiom."

"It's about Cassiopeia," Surina confirmed.
"Andromeda's mother. She was condemned to ride a
revolving throne in the stars. It circles around Polaris and
turns completely upside-down, and then it goes upright
again. She has to cling to it to keep from falling into the
sea. The children of the sea are there, waiting for her. The
Nereids . . . or, the Oceanids. Cassiopeia said that her
beauty was superior to theirs, and that her daughter was
superior. That was the whole reason for Andromeda being
sacrificed to the sea, and Cassiopeia being banished to the
stars." She paused, looking down at Hannah. "That's a
lame way to spend eternity—hovering under someone's
chair, because you're mad that they said they were prettier

than you.”

“It’s not about the Nereids,” Wibben said quietly.

“J-A-T-B-M. Jat-bem,” Hannah pronounced, peering at the throne. “What is that supposed to mean?”

“I don’t think that’s a *b*,” Surina replied. “It looks like an *i* and an *o* close together.”

“Jatiom? Maybe it’s a cryptogram. We probably have to find the cipher.”

“No . . . .” Surina moved closer, studying the rhyme again. “It says to overturn the boastful throne. Look: there’s a rope. It looks like it could overturn the chair, if we—”

Before she could finish, Hannah hurried forward and yanked hard on the rope. The *M* upended, emptying a cascade of water from the seat. The liquid sloshed over Hannah’s head, dousing her hair and clothes.

She gasped and stumbled backward. Hannah stood with her arms held out at her sides, and for a few moments she stood like a stone, watching the water run from her braids and down her soaked tunic. Then she shrieked: “The river water got me!”

Surina quickly reassured her: “It’s just rainwater.”

“It’s going to make me forget everything!”

“No, no, it’s not from the Eridanus. The river up here is a tributary. It flows *into* the Eridanus, not from it.” Surina stepped forward, taking Hannah by the shoulders. “I’m touching it too. See? We’re fine. Just relax.”

Hannah gasped for air, still staring down at her body. Water dripped from the rucksack that she clutched in one hand.

“Hannah, look,” Wibben said. “Look up at the throne.”

Still panting, Hannah raised her head. Her gaze fixed on the writing in the middle of the chair. The word “jatbm,” with its double-storey “a” and short-stemmed "b," when viewed upside-down, appeared to say "water."

"It says 'water.' It's just the answer to the riddle." Wibben stepped closer to her, stooping a bit to look into her eyes. "Let's make sure. What's my name?"

"Wibben," she said shakily.

"What city are you from?"

"Flagstaff."

"And how are you going to free us from this realm?"

"I'm going to figure out the riddle on the sun dial," Hannah said.

"You're fine," Surina assured her again. "Come on. Let's go back. We can probably use the word *water* to get through the next gate."

She started around the edge of the lake with Hannah by her side. The ground in front of her was uneven, full of sharp points and side crevices to throw her off balance. To her surprise, Hannah reached out and gripped her hand. The small gesture gave Surina a sense of solidarity, of being wanted—feelings she hadn't realized she'd been longing for.

Hannah stopped suddenly, looking behind her. Surina turned and saw Wibben lagging behind. Rather than following them, he was going the opposite way around the lake, toward the cliff.

"Wibben!" Surina called.

Even from a distance, she could see the grim look in his eyes. "I'm not going," he said, just loud enough for her to hear. "This riddle is for me. I'm going into the ocean."

Surina looked at him in confusion, and he added: "Hannah will explain." Then he turned and leapt from the cliff, throwing himself into the sea.

"Wibben!" Surina cried. She let go of Hannah and hurried to the edge of the rocks, kneeling and clutching the cliff's edge. Hannah stood close beside her, looking down at the turbulent waters where Wibben must have landed. Together they looked from one frothing wave to another, waiting to see if he emerged.

"Well," Hannah said, "I guess we helped a friend."

A figure rose above the waves—just a head at first, quickly followed by shoulders. Surina felt a momentary relief. Then the figure turned slightly, and Surina saw that the head was impossibly narrow.

"My lady!" the strange figure called. "A word with you, please!"

"Are you *kidding*," Surina whispered.

Piscis rose higher as a wave swelled beneath it. "My lady Hannah, I have been seeking you from the aqua realms! My master commands that you return the boat of the heavens at once!"

Hannah leaned over the precipice and screamed: "Your master is a cheat! He said we could take it to Orion!"

She stepped back and gasped as another figure appeared from beneath the ocean swells—a massive figure, more massive than the largest whale, smooth and gray against the blue ocean waves. It swam about a quarter-mile out to sea, but moved in the direction of the cliffs. Surina only caught a glimpse of its rounded back as it rose above the waves, and then the creature descended again.

"It's Cetus!" Hannah said.

Surina grabbed her arm. "Let's run," Surina said, as Piscis' face began to rotate away from them.

"*May the sea-beast Cetus devour you whole!*" Piscis cried.

They fled back toward the stone steps as he continued to shout: "*Keep the boat, and flee Cetus, but all the little fish will flee after you!*"

Surina went through the opening first, carefully

clambering down the stone steps toward the river, making sure Hannah kept a safe pace behind her. At the bottom, she rushed toward the wooden bird—but the creature thrust out one wooden leg, flipping itself over, and Surina stopped in surprise. The belly unfolded, and the oars snapped straight in the oarlocks.

"We have a boat," she said with relief. "Hurry, let's get it into the water."

"Look!" Hannah cried, pointing.

The metal gate was already open.

"Good," Surina said. She grabbed the fleece gown and tossed it into the boat, and then pulled at the prow of the boat. "Here, take the back. Try to lift it."

As they eased the boat into the water, a sudden commotion sounded behind them. Surina looked back to see a silver fish emerging from one of the lowest holes in the rock, splashing with the waterfall into the tributary below—followed by another, smaller fish, and then a multitude of fish bursting from the openings at the base of the rock.

Piscis' angry faced popped up in the distributary, still spewing his warnings: *"All the little fish will flee after you! Row fast, or they will upend the boat of the heavens and hurl you into the dark waters!"*

"Thanks for the warning," Surina muttered as she began to row.

She and Hannah maneuvered the boat through the gate as the river became gorged with fish. Aside from making a lot of noise, the fish created no interruption; the boat drifted through the gate, and the metal bars slowly drew to a close behind it.

Surina pulled her oar in as the current drew the boat steadily downstream. She could see the end of the tunnel, and then as the boat passed out of it, she looked up to see a solid expanse of blue-tinted sky. The bank became less rocky, hosting sand bars here and there, along with a few tough-looking shrubs that seemed to be growing through cracks in the ground—and then, in the distance, Surina could see some scraggly gray trees that reminded her of the juniper tree at Fornax. She gazed at them thoughtfully. Something about that tree nagged at her; the demon, the snake, and the owl remind her of something.

"You should be careful about solving too many riddles," Hannah said suddenly. "If Tagua finds out, he'll catch you and make you stay."

"I'll be careful," Surina replied. "But, tell me about this Tagua. Do you still have contact with him?"

"Sometimes. He's usually at Lupus. That's where his . . . temple is."

"But he lets you walk around, and go wherever you want?"

Hannah hesitated. "He wants me to practice solving the puzzles. They might help me unlock the sun gate. So, I can go wherever I want in this place."

Surina's voice dripped sarcasm: "How kind of him."

"He just wants to go home," Hannah replied.

"So do I, but I wouldn't trap anyone here to increase my chances."

"Maybe," Hannah said softly. "But this place does things to you. If I'd been here thousands of years, I think it would affect me."

Surina didn't reply. The boat was nearing the next gate, close enough that she could see its details. Engraved across the top were the words *Delta Eridani.*

"Now what?" Hannah muttered.

On the left-hand bank stood three humanesque statues, sculpted from a solid gray stone, grouped close together in a tight circle. The bank was sandy and the river bed was low, so that Surina and Hannah could push the boat up onto the sand and disembark without stepping into the water. They climbed carefully over the bow and stood side-by-side, pulling the boat farther ashore so that it wouldn't drift away.

The stone figures of three women faced outward, each looking in a different direction. The smallest, a young figure with long hair arranged in a pair of braids, looked barely out of childhood; another appeared middle-aged, and the other's face creased and sagged with the guise of old age. Below the feet of each was a stone base inscribed with a riddle.

The younger woman's riddle read:

Seaward subsurface streams will flow
as we slight souls for Earthly goals.
From each, construe a one-word key.
Vexed is third sonant of the first;
Omit next second phone, and verse!

"Omit next second phone?" Hannah repeated, sounding perplexed.

"I think it means 'phone' as in a speech sound," Surina said. "Sonants and phones are both speech sounds. They could be letter sounds, or syllables."

Hannah's frown deepened. "I don't know these things. These riddles all seem like they're directed at you, or at Wibben. It's like I'm not important anymore. I'm just . . . fading."

"No, Hannah! You won't fade. Let's try the other ones." Surina read the oldest woman's riddle aloud:

Stars glowing shall provide a clue;
a circumbinary has two;
light seems to rise up and go down;
a pair of mutts comprise a crown.

The other contained a heading. Hannah breathed a small sigh of relief, grateful that it presented a clear key to its solving.

AN ACROSTICAL ENIGMA:

Red flames light up the dry frontier
as wet drops leave the atmosphere;
ne'er will this antonym be closed
as yellow nuggets are exposed.

"The acrostic looks easiest," Hannah said. "Tell me again how to solve it."

"Each line describes a word. Figure out the word, and then use the first letters of all four words to spell the answer. The first line is *F*, fire, or maybe *W* for wildfire. The second is *R*, rain."

A voice interrupted Hannah's musings, calling out from somewhere behind them: "My lady Hannah, I have come to reclaim the boat of Aquarius!"

"Keep going," Surina said. "Never will this antonym—"

"My master's instructions cannot be disobeyed!" Piscis was swimming some distance upriver, slowly moving closer. "Cease now, or I will have to take the boat by force, though it sorely disobliges me to do so!"

"Never closed," Surina finished. "Open! The antonym of closed is *open*. It's never closed. Yellow nuggets . . . ." She glanced anxiously upriver, saw Piscis rising higher out of the water, his pleasant face beginning to turn aside. "Let's get in the boat. We can solve this last line."

They pushed the boat back toward the water, muttering to themselves as they climbed back inside.

"*Desist, or I will bring the guardians of this realm from their posts! All creatures who traverse the land and waters I will set against you!"*

"As yellow nuggets are exposed," Surina recited, grasping the sides of the boat as it rocked in the waters. She picked up her oars and pushed hard against the sand. "Hurry, let's get close to the gate."

"Boogers!" Hannah cried. "F-R-O-B. Or, W-R-O . . . ."

"It can't be W-R-O," Surina said, straining against the oars. "No fourth letter will make that into a word."

"They will rise from the waters to overwhelm you! Your bearings shall be lost to the river!"

"Chicken nuggets," Surina said as she rowed. "Cheese curds . . . damn."

"Something's coming toward us!" Hannah cried.

"Yellow nuggets . . . frob, froc, frod—"

Her guesses were interrupted by a loud thud. Surina froze at the sight of a slimy webbed hand gripping the side of the boat. The hand was quickly followed by another hand, and then a pair of bulging red eyes with black slits running down the centers, rising slowly over the boat's edge. It looked at her, unblinking, as it raised itself up.

Hannah shouted: *"Frog!"* With the flat of her foot, she shoved the creature back into the water.

The gate creaked open.

"It's opening! Go, go!" Surina shook a pair of giant frogs from her oars and rowed frantically. The creatures splashed into the river and disappeared in the murky water.

As soon as the boat passed through, the metal gate closed behind it. The river became calm again. Hannah and Surina rowed in silence.

After some time, Hannah asked: "How come the gate opened?"

"Who knows."

Surina listened to the gentle murmuring of the water against the banks. Suddenly she let out a low chuckle. "It was *frog*."

"What?"

"The answer to the enigma: it must have been *frog*. It was F-R-O-something. Fire, rain, open."

"But . . . what's a yellow nugget that starts with *G*?"

"Doesn't matter now."

"Oh!" Hannah said. "It's *gold*."

"Ha! I bet it is. See, together we're genius."

Hannah's smile faded; her eyes clouded over. Even as the river carried them closer and closer to their goal, she seemed remarkably subdued.

8: Zaurak and Cursa

The next gate was a short distance away; they had hardly passed the last one when they saw it up ahead. Hannah gasped and pointed to the right-hand bank, where in the distance they could see a large shape with two curving spires at the top, which Hannah insisted was a statue of a bull. "We're almost there," Hannah said excitedly. "Orion is next to Taurus."

The way was barred by an iron gate that descended beneath the water. Its lock was a placard that bore the riddle:

> *Perched midstream a hero waits, firm unto her last breath;*
> *rearward creeps a fearful one, to slay the haunt of death.*
> *Set against the daunting tau, one holds a shining sword;*
> *users of mean arms may cut a friend to gain award.*
> *Beginnings, when teamed up, will find the sire of Mycenae.*
> *When you board the boat again, which hero will you play?*
> *Sodden paths will be traversed by stag or ternion;*
> *seek you solidarity, or pine for a paean?*

"Beginnings, teamed up," Hannah murmured. "The beginnings will find the sire of Mycenae—the sire of the Mycenaeans. Oh, I know this. Wasn't it . . . P-E . . . ." She paused for some time. "Perseus!" Hannah looked at Surina with relief, her eyes lively and shining. "My brain is working again."

"Good work. I wonder if—"

Surina's question was interrupted as the gate creaked open. She glanced upriver, saw serene waters behind and heard nothing but gently flowing water and the drawn-out groan of the opening gate. "Piscis didn't come after us. Maybe we out-rowed him."

"Just watch," Hannah muttered.

As if on cue, Piscis sprang up from the waters not far behind. Hannah rowed hard, her eyes fixed on his half-submerged figure as he made his way toward the gate. She heard the usual polite greeting, followed by requests and demands, and saw the turn of his head as he began to spew threats: "*I will set the guardians of the canal against you!*"

Surina had become accustomed to his inconsequential warnings; even his strange, saber-toothed face no longer provoked her. She satisfied herself that she no longer felt intimidated by him, only mildly annoyed.

As usual, the gate closed before he could pass through. Hannah continued to row mightily, but faltered when Surina dropped her oars and pointed to the riverbank. "Look!"

Hannah paused, turning to follow Surina's gaze. A man stood on the bank, scantily clad in a loincloth, waving at the boat and shouting.

"Isn't that Wibben?" Surina asked. "Let's stop. It looks like he needs help."

Hannah protested: "But we're almost at Orion!"

"Yes, but he's calling us."

"So what?" Hannah's dark eyes fixed on Surina with intense anxiety. "Wibben might seem nice, but he's done horrible things. He doesn't deserve our help."

Surina regarded her with quiet puzzlement. After a moment she dipped her right-hand oar into the water, causing the boat to veer aside. "Hannah, let's stop," she said gently. "Just to see what he wants. He helped us before, remember? He even let me wear his clothes."

Hannah complied silently, and helped row toward the riverbank.

"What's the matter?" Surina called as they came close.

An object lay beside Wibben's feet, something long and thick and lustrous. He gestured to it. "I'm supposed to lift this, but it's too heavy. Maybe if the two of you give me a hand . . . ."

"Sure." Surina reached for the riverbank and pulled herself up onto the dry ground. She turned and grabbed the rim of the boat. "Hannah, will you just hold the boat here? I'll see if the two of us can get it."

Hannah moved to the middle of the boat, mooring it in place by grasping onto a rock on the bank.

The object at Wibben's feet was a statue—a human figure encased in a close-fitting sarcophagus, its black-lined eyes open and staring at the sky, hands folded across its chest. An eight-petaled rosette had been stamped into the gleaming metal just above the resting hands.

Surina stared at it with a strange sense of déjà vu. She had seen a statue like this before, on a different riverbank, during a canoe trip with Victor. They had stopped for a picnic lunch, and on the bank they discovered a finely crafted sand sculpture that looked like a pharaoh in a sarcophagus. The casket was formed to the shape of the body, and the figure itself was adorned in an Egyptian headdress, with its hands folded on its chest. Surina and Victor had kept a safe distance as they admired the sculpture and voiced their praise. It was one of her better memories of him.

Surina could have sworn that the two figures were identical. They had the same rosette on the chest area and the same headdress. "What the hell," she whispered.

Wibben knelt down, reciting the riddle on the side of the casket. "'Two form a pair, there you will go: one half above, one half below.' The riddles I've seen lately have all involved flipping things over, so I'm guessing this is the same: half of the riddle in on the top, and the other half is on the bottom." He crouched beside the figure and tried to slide his hands beneath it. Surina noticed again the thinness of his arms, the meager muscles that seemed to be wasting away beneath his flesh.

She knelt beside him, and together they strained to lift the statue. Surina's knees slid in the sand; she tried to brace herself with one foot, pulling upward, and then pushing as the statue tilted upward from the ground.

Sand sprayed in a short burst as the heavy statue landed on its other side. It appeared almost identical to its opposite; it had the same body encased in the same close-fitting casket, and the same shades of red, blue, black, and golden-hued metal, with one small difference. Wibben took a few seconds to catch his breath, and then he pointed at T-shaped symbol on the figure's chest.

"It's the Tau symbol," he said. "Tau plus the rosette. Tau-ros. I've seen it before in this realm: a tau symbol with a rosette on top, to symbolize Taurus. It's the . . . ." Wibben trailed off as he glanced back toward the river. "Is she leaving without you?"

Surina looked behind her. The boat was drifting away.

"Hannah!" she cried, and started along the bank—but she stopped and stared. The boat, she realized, was not drifting. Hannah had the rear set of oars in hand and was rowing steadily away.

"Hannah, stop!" she shouted again.

Her cries went unheeded. In a matter of seconds, the

boat vanished around a bend.

Hannah tried to forget the sound of Surina calling after her. Surina would be fine, she reasoned. Wibben was with her, and Hannah no longer needed her anyway. The Orion puzzle was about to be solved, and after that, surely, Hannah would be on the verge of solving the final riddle—the one that would free so many trapped souls from this dimension.

The last gate bore the word "Cursa" across its doors—the name of the last star in the Eridanus constellation. As Hannah came closer, she could see the metal plate in the center that bore the riddle. She rushed to the front of the boat, grabbing at the metal bars to keep the prow from ramming them.

As she reached, the boat seemed to dip under her. Hannah gasped as her balance was lost; her fingers caught the metal bars and clung fast, saving her from falling into the river—but the current was pulling the boat aside, and Hannah felt herself starting to slip out of it. She strained, pulling the boat back to the center with her legs, until she had it in a safe position.

Hannah took a few seconds to recover from her sudden terror. Her heart beat so hard in her chest that it almost hurt—but she was glad to still have a heartbeat. It likely meant that she was still alive.

The metal plate was close to her face. When her heart had slowed a little, Hannah turned her head and whispered the words aloud:

Angels circling Karphi
make gold rings with their halos;
for fables told by Aesop,
a crowd of children gathers;
but for a sacred catalyst,

a mage must strive alone.
The tails of tongue communicate
a path of heat and stone.
What am I?

"Okay, it's easy," Hannah whispered. "Tails of tongue. Hilos . . . philos . . . philosophers . . . ." She was quiet for a few moments, and then spoke aloud: "Philosopher's stone."

The gate began to open.

"My lady Hannah!" called a voice behind her.

She ignored the call and pulled on the metal bars, trying to maneuver the boat between the gates. Hannah assumed it would be a simple task; surely the current would carry her through, and she would have an easy journey the rest of the way to Orion. Instead she found that the boat was stuck against the opening gate. It began to pull her away from the center; the boat teetered at the door's edge, almost free one moment, but swinging behind the next. Hannah struggled to get around the edge of it, rowing with one hand and pushing against the bars with the other.

Just as she managed to break free of the doorway, Hannah found herself stuck again. She turned around in confusion and saw Piscis' face very close to hers. Its gray-green hands grasped the stern of the boat.

"Let go!" she demanded.

"My lady Hannah, I must warn you that my lord Aquarius is not as amiable as he may have seemed. Kindly return the boat of the heavens at once."

Hannah grabbed the rucksack and walloped Piscis' face—directly on one round, unblinking eye. The creature's hands slipped from the boat.

As she rowed through the gate, Hannah glanced over her shoulder. Piscis kept one hand over its eye as the head began to turn upon the shoulders. *"Such behavior is an outrage!"* Piscis boomed. *"The great princely scion shall bestow curses on you!"*

The waters churned, and some dark figure began to rise behind Piscis—but the gate closed, and Hannah fixed her gaze on the statue ahead of her.

Orion was a mere two minutes downriver from the last gate. The current had eased, and the boat drifted straight ahead, toward the statue that Hannah had already become so familiar with: the stone figure of Orion, a young warrior bearing a club and shield, standing thigh-deep in the midst of the river.

Hannah released the oars and dumped the contents of the sack into the bottom of the boat, sending coins rolling across the wood floor. She rifled through the closest ones. Eadawa, with the image of a knife engraved into it: not one of the Orion stars. Tashhir, with an arrowhead—most definitely not. She tossed the irrelevant tokens back into the sack.

She'd found five of the stars by the time she reached the statue. Hannah steadied the boat as it bumped against the stone legs and drew it lengthwise beside the figure. She pulled the drawstring from the sack and tethered the oarlock to Orion's knee. For a moment she sat gazing up at the gray stone sculpture; she had only ever seen it from the river bank, and now its details were clear and immediate. The eyes were blank, but the face bore a stoic expression. A small wing was carved into the side of the helmet, and Hannah saw a braid trailing from the head, behind the shoulder and down the figure's back.

Hannah fancied that the statue resembled her.

Looking up, she detected a shimmering around the tip of Orion's club—and she saw that it wasn't a club, but rather a thin, ornate staff. Serpentine figures twined from base to head, and the top was carved with feathered wings. In this section of the river Hannah could also see the sky streaked with what appeared to be a haze of stars, tiny lights twinkling high above, visible even in the bold light of day. Orion stood with the shield grasped in one hand and the staff raised high in the other, with the tip aiming for that mass of stars. Sitting there with the keys of Orion in her hand, and gazing at the backdrop of majestic sky beyond Orion's noble face, Hannah felt a sense of magic and destiny.

The shield was the same gray stone as the rest. Like the armor, it was inscribed with zodiac symbols: the lion, the bull, a crowned feminine figure that probably represented Virgo, and more. The shield bore a circular depression on the lower half—just the right size for one of the tokens to fit into. Above it was a riddle:

The key in which Orion stands,
the gateways that the river spans
lead to the shadow you must face;
put each star in its destined place
to sail aloft or brave the pangs,
the cusps in which the balance hangs.
If one would seek, and traverse there,
with deference must one prepare.

"The key in which Orion stands," Hannah muttered, and read the poem over again. "Put each star in its destined place . . . ."

Her gaze moved over the stone figure. She stood up in the boat, scrutinizing, running her fingers over the stone. Hannah counted five circular pits in the statue, but she'd thought that Orion had seven major stars—and hadn't Aquarius given her seven keys? Hannah thumbed through the tokens she'd found so far, naming them off: "Bellatrix, Betelgeuse, Rigel . . . ."

She sorted through the rest of the pile. Hannah was sure that Aquarius had given her seven—but then her certainty wavered. *If Surina was here, she would remember . . . .*

A mixture of guilt and irritation crept through her. Hannah shook it off and kept sorting until she found the last two tokens. When she saw the seven laid out before her, she felt sure.

Some of the placings were simple: Bellatrix, with its engraving of a breastplate, became an insignia upon Orion's breastplate. Alnitak, with its image of a sword, she placed into the scabbard that held the sheathed sword. Betelgeuse was placed into the raised arm, and Mintaka, with its image of a cup, onto the small canteen that hung from Orion's belt. Hannah was unsure about Alnilam, with its image of beads—but Alnilam was the last belt star, so she placed it into the remaining slot on the belt. The tokens slid easily into place and stayed fast.

Rigel and Saiph were more difficult. Hannah had untied the boat and maneuvered around the statue, looking for more slots, but found none. "Where are they?" she muttered. The stars belonged somewhere near Orion's feet, but how could she find the slots without dunking her arm into the river?

"There has to be a way," she assured herself. "Think, think . . . ."

A voice shouted from upriver: "My lady!"

Hannah jerked her hand away from the statue, but she grabbed Orion's leg again as the current pulled at the boat. She peered around the stone leg to see Piscis floating waist-deep in the river, just a few yards away. Its rubbery lips were set in a smile. It was close enough that Hannah could see the scales beginning to form near its navel, dark gray marks against the lighter tones of its torso.

She shouted: "You're not taking my Orion tokens!"

"My lady Hannah, you have my deepest admiration! You have brought the Orion keys to their proper berth; may you place them with a spirit of peace and righteousness! May Orion gift you with knowledge and truth, and may the waters of the Eridanus bestow blessings upon you!"

Hannah regarded the creature with suspicion, but it only continued to smile at her. "If you're so happy for me," she said, "then tell me how to put the tokens in without touching the water."

Piscis began to reply, but faltered. Consternation played on its face. "Touching the water is quite necessary."

"But . . . the water will make me forget everything!"

"It will not! Why would water make you forget?"

"Because it's the river Lethe."

"No, no. This is the Eridanus River. Look: Orion is touching it, and she's fine."

Hannah glanced at the statue. "But you said . . . ." She pursed her lips, thinking back. "You said that we shouldn't touch the water, because it would . . . it would ruin our journey. And then you said that this was the river Lethe, and that it makes people forget their old lives before they get reincarnated."

"I did not."

"You did!"

"I merely suggested that getting wet would thwart your mission. The river is quite chilly to humans. You might have caught cold. Who wants to travel the whole Eridanus in soaking wet clothes?"

Hannah's eyes narrowed. "You little liar! You talked about the Lethe! If you didn't want us to think this was the Lethe, then why did you *say* that?"

"I simply explained that celestial rivers can have

otherworldly properties. The Eridanus, for instance, is full of creatures I'm sure you would rather not meet."

"Yes, creatures like you!" Hannah peered into the murky water. It was possible that Piscis was lying—that it was trying to trick her into touching the water and forgetting everything. But how else could she place the tokens? She didn't have anything to grab them with except her own hands.

"Now Hannah, that isn't the attitude you should take with you to Orion," Piscis admonished her. "Please know that I wish you the best of luck, despite your earlier act of violence. If opened *properly*, Orion is a gate of joy. May you be peaceful and balanced in your—"

With a splash, Hannah thrust her arm into the river. Her fingers slid against wet stone, seeking the keyholes. Orion's front knee was raised, as though the figure was stepping onto a pedestal; she found the circular depression on the foremost shin, just below the river's surface.

"Not the supporting foot," she murmured. "Rigel is the front foot. Right?" She picked up the Rigel coin doubtfully.

"Yes, Rigel is the front foot," Piscis replied.

Hannah shot an annoyed glance at the creature. "I wasn't asking you," she started to say—but she checked herself. The scaly gray-green flesh around Piscis' right eye was discolored. Hues of black and blue accented the tender, puffy skin. Hannah felt mortified.

"I'm sorry I hit you," she said.

"Are you? You seemed satisfied with the result."

"I just wanted you to let go of the boat!" Hannah said. "I *need* this boat, and I *earned* it from Aquarius, and you keep trying to cheat me out of it!"

"I seem to recall that someone else did most of the earning. Where is she now, and who is cheating whom?"

The question caught Hannah off guard. She felt her

face flushing. Piscis regarded her with a cool expression, but Hannah was acutely aware of the silent accusation in that gaze. She tried to shake off her disconcertment; she needed to focus. Hannah slid Rigel into place and began groping around in the water.

"You'll have to go much deeper than this," Piscis said calmly. "Tie up the boat and get into the water. You have to go all the way in for this one."

Hannah paused to scrutinize Piscis. There was something soothing, even hypnotic about its voice—and she didn't trust that hypnotic quality. Yet, even if she didn't trust Piscis, she couldn't think of an alternative to the creature's suggestion.

Hannah tethered the boat again. Holding fast to the statue, she began to climb into the water, pressing her bare feet against Orion's rear leg. The stone was slippery; she felt herself sliding down, and as the boat dipped away and her own legs sank into the cool river, Hannah felt a moment of panic.

But her feet touched the bottom, and the boat stayed tethered in place. The water rose just above Hannah's knees. She felt around with her toes. Just below the tip of the sheathed sword, and just above Orion's foot, she felt the last keyhole.

Hannah lowered the token into the water—but the stones along the river bottom were slick, and she slipped. Water splashed around her chin as she tried to steady herself. Her right hand kept a desperate grip on the Saiph token. Fear gripped her as she realized how close she was to success, and how many things could go wrong before she achieved it. The token could be washed away; Piscis could take it from her; the river, or any other strange and unpredictable force of the constellations, might weaken and confuse her.

Hannah steadied herself and pushed Saiph firmly into

its place.

She stepped back and stared up at the statue. Uneasiness washed over her. She remembered that in the starry realm, change—a transformation, a next step, any kind of change at all—was often uncomfortable, even terrifying. It seemed so long since she had transformed. Hannah had begun to feel stagnant, stale. Perhaps this accomplishment would refresh her.

For a moment, the anxiety ebbed. Nothing was happening. Hannah turned to Piscis, but the fish-thing was nowhere to be seen.

When she looked again at the statue, Hannah found it liquifying before her eyes. Its noble form distorted into silent waves of rolling gray, flowing downward until they touched the water's surface, where they hissed and created a great cloud of steam. Hannah stepped back, driven away by the sudden heat. The water warmed around her legs; she retreated farther, and once again she slipped, falling backwards into the river.

The steam began to lift, revealing a new shape in place of Orion: blue and silver luminescence in the shape of a wheeled chariot. Even as it seemed anchored in the water, it moved; Hannah could not quite get a solid glimpse of it, yet along its side she recognized one of the same zodiac symbols that had been carved into the statue's armor: Leo, the lion. On the front of the chariot was engraved the symbol of the bull. Of the statue, nothing was left except for Orion's head, which looked onward from the prow. The rest of the chariot shimmered strangely, as though it was made of light.

Hannah approached with caution. As she came closer, the vehicle seemed more substantial; she trusted that she could climb inside of it without falling through. The nearest wheel, on closer observance, was an immovable plate that depicted the zodiac—and, strangely, in its center was the word "Saiph" above the image of a foot. Hoisting herself up, Hannah saw that the chariot was inlaid with wood; it seemed to have shaped itself around Aquarius' rowboat. The sack full of tokens and the ragged fleece nightgown were still lying on the bottom. Hannah seated herself on the rear bench and wondered what to do next.

Nothing needed to be done; the chariot moved on its own. Hannah clutched its sides as the vehicle rose above the river. A thrill overtook her; surely, she was close to freedom! The chariot would take her to Ophiuchus, and there she would solve the next puzzle. And then . . . .

She found it difficult to imagine what would happen then.

The chariot ascended in one smooth, soundless movement. Its silence was all-consuming; Hannah no longer heard the rush of water below, or the air whipping around her. She felt as though she was in an invisible bubble, cut off somehow from her surroundings.

The view, however, was not obscured in the least. As the chariot passed from the realm of Orion, Hannah clearly saw the giant bull that lumbered towards her from Taurus. Its head was at level with her, so that she could look directly into its fierce, fiery eyes, and see the pair of horns protruding dangerously in her direction. Hannah gasped in fear, but the chariot rose higher, a safe distance above.

As the bull came closer, though, the vehicle seemed to falter. Its light sputtered, and Hannah felt it dip beneath her. There was a moment of stillness, of uncertainty, and then the chariot dipped again.

With a loud crack, Orion's neck was pierced through by the tip of the bull's horn. The stone head broke from its bearings and plummeted downward. The whole chariot tipped forward on impact, and the horn continued to drive through it, splintering wood and penetrating the ethereal bubble. The tokens came loose from the sack, rolling through cracks to the ground far below.

Hannah screamed as she clung to the wooden bench. Just before the chariot spun out of control, she witnessed a seemingly impossible sight: Surina and Wibben, sitting below, looking up at her from the back of the bull.

From there on, the ride was a confused jumble. The whirling and jarring of the chariot made Hannah nauseous, and she slumped down in the boat, her fingers sliding from the bench. Somehow, she stayed inside the boat as it hurled back toward the ground. She felt the chariot falling, and then jarring, and then falling again, until finally its luminescent frame hurtled away and the wooden boat dropped straight down, landing with a loud splash. Hannah lurched forward, falling onto her hands and knees as foul-smelling water surged up around her. She pulled back, but the remnants of the boat sank beneath her, leaving her submerged.

Yellow water steamed around her. It was hot, but not scalding, and smelled like rotten eggs. Hannah hoped that the smell was sulfur and not something worse. She splashed toward shore and reached it in a matter of seconds; the pool she'd landed in was a small one, easy to swim across. On its bank was a wooden sign that read: *Crater*. Hannah grabbed the signpost and heaved herself out of the water.

For some time she sat there, catching her breath and trying to squeeze the stinking water from her clothes and hair. Aside from the smell, the water seemed not to have affected her.

To Hannah's left, a waterfall spilled down from a small, rocky hill, trailing into the yellow pool. She stood up and scanned the area, trying to get her bearings. She must have flown back over Gemini and Cancer before being dumped into the Crater constellation. A river flowed nearby—probably Hydra rather than Eridanus. Hannah thought it best to stay away; Wibben had warned her about Hydra.

She turned back to the hill. Just a few yards past the sulfur pool, a cave led into the rocky earth, its passage blocked by a metal gate. Hannah went to it and peered through the bars. If she was in Crater, and Hydra was behind her, then surely this passage led to Virgo—the queen of the underworld and master of transformation.

She leaned on the gate. It swung open easily.

Hannah hesitated. The dizziness and the shock of the crash were starting to wear off, and new realizations and feelings were swimming up into her consciousness: failure, confusion, helplessness. She knew that the underworld had been an unpleasant place, but its queen had been a source of comfort and hope. Perhaps she could provide guidance once again. How long had it been since that first visit to Virgo's chamber? Try as she might, Hannah found herself unable to remember any specifics from their conversations. Surina had said that only days had passed, but time surely ran a longer course in the stars.

Hannah shuddered. The air had become cold; unwelcome breezes blew through her tunic and sent her into a shiver. She hurried through the entrance and into the cave.

The cave was small and quiet, an unremarkable tunnel of gray stone. As Hannah retreated farther in, she began to remember the frightening things she had seen wandering around Virgo's chamber: animated corpses, half decomposed; other strange, inhuman figures. She shuddered again. When she noticed a figure coming toward her from the darkness of the tunnel, Hannah let out a yelp and jumped back in alarm.

A woman stepped from the shadows. She wore a

simple tunic and a delicate twelve-pointed crown; her hair was loose, hanging in dark, wavy locks past her shoulders. Hannah recognized Virgo immediately.

"You needn't come any farther, Hannah," the queen said gently. "The underworld dead will latch onto you. It isn't the most pleasant way to enter my realm."

Hannah looked into Virgo's eyes, saw wisdom and compassion there. A surge of emotion rose up within her, and suddenly she couldn't restrain her tears.

"I messed up," Hannah said. "I had the Orion tokens, and I put them in the statue, but . . . I must have done something wrong. It turned into a chariot, but it crashed."

"I see. And how did you get the Orion tokens?"

"By answering Aquarius' riddles. He gave them to me."

"Ah. You figured out all of his riddles?"

"Yes. Well . . . someone helped me."

"And where is that person now?"

Hannah wiped her eyes and lowered her head. "You already know where she is. You see everything. I left her behind."

"So you did. It's true, I know where Surina is. She is descending from the great bull; her work there is finished."

Hannah remembered seeing Surina on the giant bull as its horn drove through and destroyed the chariot. A new possibility formed in her mind. "Did Surina and Wibben make me crash?"

The queen chuckled softly. "Do Surina and Wibben control Taurus?"

Hannah interpreted the comment as an insult; she had asked a stupid question. She pursed her lips and lowered her eyes again.

"When you're back in your own realm," the queen said, "and you look up at the night sky, you will see

Auriga—the chariot—being pierced by Taurus' horn. You will understand and remember, then, why you crashed. You will never get back to your own realm unless you understand."

"I need you to explain it to me," Hannah said desperately. "I'm tired of puzzles. I can't *think* anymore."

"You can think well enough. Believe me, Hannah, I've been in your place. Once, in my youth, I also rode the starry chariot into the heavens, and I also crashed."

"Why?"

"Orion requires that you approach with deference to a higher purpose."

"Like what? I *do* have a higher purpose. I'm not just trying to get home; I'm trying to free other people, too."

"Who?"

Hannah hesitated. "Everyone."

"Free yourself first," Virgo replied. "Consider the realms around Orion and Taurus. Think of the places you've recently walked through. You traversed Cassiopeia and Perseus. Do you know the story of Perseus?"

"Yes. Kind of."

"What is he famous for?"

"Cutting off Medusa's head."

"Exactly," Virgo said softly. Her eyes, at that moment, seemed strangely dark. "The story has two versions. You've probably heard the one about Perseus the hero, who used Medusa's head to defeat his enemies and rescue Andromeda. Who was Medusa?"

"She was a gorgon who had snakes for hair."

"A being from the underworld realm. How did she come to have snakes instead of hair?"

"She was a priestess at Athena's temple," Hannah replied uncertainly. "She was attacked by . . . Zeus, I think. Zeus attacked her, and Athena accused her of polluting the temple."

"Why would Athena accuse Medusa, instead of Zeus?"

The questions had begun to stir a deep anger within Hannah. It seemed ages since she'd read the Greek myths—but she tried to keep her feelings in check. "I think it was because Medusa was vain. I'm not sure. Medusa had beautiful hair, or something, so Athena punished her by turning her hair into snakes."

"So here you have a story of jealous women who cut each other down," the queen said, "and a man not held accountable for his crime. In this version, serpents present that which is venomous and evil. In other stories, the serpent represents rebirth through the shedding of old 'skins.' It represents knowledge of the underworld. The snakes protrude from the head because the head represents learned wisdom. Let me tell you another story about Perseus: when our hero descended to the cave of the gorgons, he met a creature who had knowledge of the underworld. Rather than learn a lesson from it, he became frightened and cut off its head. He returned to Earth, wielding an unlearned power, and committed many murders with it. First he killed the demi-god Atlas, the scholar of the stars, because Atlas didn't support his quest to slay Medusa. Then he killed the sea-monster Cetus, and Phineas, and several of Phineas' friends, and Polydectes, and Proetus, and Acrisius. Perseus even poisoned the sea with Medusa's life-blood and killed many other people by accident."

"I don't care about myths!" Hannah burst out. "I'm sick of them! How should I know what happened thousands of years ago?"

"You should know what's happening now. Tell me, Hannah: What should you do when faced with a man who has abused the powers of the underworld and poisoned a whole village—who has stolen a people's life-blood to secure his own kingship?"

Hannah began to reply, but a sudden fear stole the words from her mouth. Virgo's face was changing; the skin bore a grayish-green pallor, and it seemed rough and leathery, as though from illness and exposure. Her eyes, too, seemed large and yellow with age. But what struck Hannah with fear was Virgo's hair. Instead of the neat waves cascading from her head, a dozen serpents trailed there, their heads gently probing her neck and shoulders. Hannah heard the faint sounds of slithering as they coiled and meandered. "Will you support him out of pity, and make excuses for him, and refuse to hold him accountable?" the queen asked.

Still stunned by the transformation, Hannah stopped breathing. She couldn't respond.

"When you came here," the queen continued, "Tagua persuaded you with stories of his own design. He told you that his people became trapped here because his village was attacked by the wizard Askha-Quyllur and her army."

Hannah nodded. Slowly, she released her breath.

"Askha-Quyllur isn't the name of a person. It's an ancient name for the celestial realm, including its queen. Tagua was dabbling in celestial magic and abusing it for his own gain. Who do you think trapped him here?"

Still, Hannah didn't respond—but a glimmer of realization formed in her mind.

"I trapped him with the help of every being who guards this realm," Virgo said, "but I can't decide his fate. When he was on Earth, he rose to power because humans refused to stop him. A human must take the next action. I won't do it for you. I have done too much already. It isn't my place to do humans' work for them."

"But why do *I* have to do it?"

"It's because of such thoughts that Tagua continues to ruin lives. How many people do you suppose have asked that same question?"

Hannah didn't answer, but various responses formed in her head: *It isn't fair. I was only eleven.*

"Stories like the tale about Medusa are important because they allow vicarious learning. Even now, Surina is telling a story that you could have learned from. Instead she's telling it to Wibben, who already knows the lesson well."

"I'm sorry," Hannah mumbled.

"Don't waste time feeling sorry. Go and correct your actions."

"I don't know what to do. The chariot broke."

Virgo nodded. The movement seemed to excite the serpents; they slithered restlessly against her scalp. Hannah noticed one snake that didn't have a head; it ended instead in a mass of red and pink flesh, a dark crimson ring of blood dried around its edges. It caught Virgo's attention, too, as it writhed in front of her forehead. She raised a hand and touched it delicately, avoiding the wounded area. "Ah . . . I had a bit of an incident with this one. It happens sometimes. My snakes sometimes peek into other realms; they surprise and scare people, and people panic and attack them. It will grow back, though. They always do." She lowered her hand. "You can recreate the chariot, too. Pick up the pieces and start over again."

"Pick up what pieces? The Orion tokens? I dropped them."

"They will call to you. The Orion tokens are the tablets of destiny. Whoever holds them rightly has power over this universe. You'll find them again when you're ready—but you're not ready yet, and neither is the realm. I will sculpt another Orion statue. In the meantime, go to Tagua and ask him for the fleece nightgown that he took from you. Go as a griffin; he will take you more seriously that way."

"He doesn't have the nightgown anymore," Hannah protested. "I dropped it in the river."

"I know you did. Nevertheless, Tagua has the nightgown," the queen assured her.

"He won't give it to me."

"You must insist. Tell him you need it to solve the next puzzle."

"I can't lie. He'll know."

"Will he?" the queen asked lightly. "Or do you simply dislike the idea of deceiving him? If you truly want to free 'everyone,' Hannah, you must stand up to him—or you can refuse to change, and linger here with the rest of the undead. You've seen the once-human spirits who wander my halls. Why do you suppose they stay?"

Hannah didn't look at her, didn't answer.

"When you have the gown, fly back to Fornax. There is a dreaming tree in the middle of the labyrinth, sculpted with the image of an underworld being. You must bring the fleece there. Rest in the tree's upper branches. Bathing in Crater has already begun to renew you from the outside. The dreaming tree will give you introspection; it purifies from the inside. A serpent guards the trunk, but if you enter the tree from above, the serpent won't harm you. The tree's roots are fed with underworld waters, and its branches are full of stars."

"But . . . didn't we already kill that snake?" Hannah asked.

"You will find the snake guarding the tree just as before. Make sure you cover yourself with the fleece while you're resting. It will help you gain enough strength to finish solving the enigmas of this realm. And while you're there, consider: while I am re-making the Orion puzzle, what are *you* going to make?"

"I can't transform into a griffin," Hannah said glumly.

"I've tried, but I can't."

"You're in the underworld," the queen reminded her, gently extending a hand. The dark yellow eyes, though still frightening and stern, suddenly seemed to have kindness in them. "You can't leave as the person you once were. The last time you were here, you became Griffin Princess. And you will still be a griffin—but now you shall start to become a queen."

9: Gemini

"How was Cetus?" Surina asked.

"Dark," Wibben replied. "Dark, lonely, introspective. A long time alone with my memories."

"A long time? You were hardly gone. You got here ahead of us."

"So it might seem to you," he replied, "but I was there a long time."

Surina gazed at the landscape ahead: a sandy, barren plain with a single column rising in the distance. Behind the column was a dark mass that Surina initially mistook for a mountain. Now, though, she could see its features; the mass appeared to be a metallic structure, molded in the figure of a giant bull. Two sand-colored horns curved forward from its head.

Wibben had explained that they were presently in Taurus, the realm of the bull. Eridanus flowed past Taurus and then past Gemini—but for the moment, it was impossible to follow Hannah downstream. A great wall separated Taurus from Gemini, right up to the riverbank. The only way to get around it was to enter the river and swim downstream, but Surina was wary of touching the water. Wibben had pointed to the tall stone column, suggesting: "Let's try that. It looks like it's trying to get our attention."

As they walked, though, Surina began to have doubts. "Maybe I should go back," she said. "I'm not sure I should be here."

"No, I think you're supposed to be here. I was told to travel with a companion, and there aren't any others. And there's no point in going back now. Do you know why Hannah went on without you?"

"Well . . . I get the feeling it has something to do with Tagua."

"It does."

Surina scrutinized him, waiting for an explanation, but Wibben offered nothing more. "Is she afraid of him, or is she protecting him?" she asked. "Hannah seems to have kind of a Stockholm Syndrome thing going on. I mean, it seems like she's making excuses for him. She's more concerned about helping him than she is about getting home."

"I would say that's accurate. Hannah cares about Tagua. She feels sorry for him." Wibben gave her a serious, sidelong glance. "I have no pity for Tagua. I want to feel compassion, but pity is a dangerous thing. Hannah's pity has eroded any boundary she should have kept with him. She lets him manipulate her."

Surina looked back toward the river, but it had vanished from sight. "I'm worried about her."

"There's nothing you can do for her at the moment. Worry about yourself for now." Wibben gestured ahead, at the stone column that rose from the dust. About four feet from the base was a small crossbar. Surina and Wibben could already see the etching on its surface. "We have a riddle to solve," he added.

Four distinct lines radiated from a square stone base; the column was otherwise featureless except for the crossbar. Wibben circled the column once, looking at its whole, before stopping to examine the riddle.

Claw your way up to Hadhyans,
imbued with an astral will.

Surina was weary of riddles. Surely, Wibben was better at them than she was. He'd had countless years of practice. She stood quietly and waited for him to find the solution.

After stepping back and gazing at the bull for some time, Wibben smiled wryly. "Have you heard of Hadhyans?"

"No."

"Hadhyans is a Zoroastrian figure—a bull so enormous that it can straddle a mountain," he explained.

"Zoro what?"

"Zoroastrianism. It's an ancient religion, but people still practice it today . . . at least, they still did in my day. Supposedly, Hadhyans carried humans on its back to transport them between regions." Wibben reached out, laying the flat of his palm on the bull's metal hide. "Perhaps this bull can straddle the wall, and transport us to the next realm."

Surina regarded the massive figure doubtfully. "How's it going to do that?"

Wibben raised his eyebrows. He tapped a finger against the riddle. "Both beginnings in alliance: *Climb*."

"What?"

"Look." He beckoned her, and together they approached the bull. Wibben stopped somewhere near the middle of the beast, where a long, thick rope ladder hung. It trailed all the way up the side of the bull, so high that the top seemed to vanish into the distance. "Do you think you can climb this?"

"Sure," Surina said, unconvincingly.

"It looks like it leads all the way up. If this thing really is imbued with an astral will, maybe it can take us over this heap of stone."

"You don't mind heights?" Surina asked.

"Not anymore. You?"

"No." She glanced up once again at the daunting height and placed her foot on the lowest rung. "I'll go first."

The rope felt thick and sturdy beneath her feet. Surina climbed deftly toward the bull's midsection, pausing once as she felt Wibben's movements below her. As she mounted the next step, her foot slipped; she clutched the sides of the ladder as her feet fumbled on the rungs.

"Carefully, please," Wibben said. "Without killing both of us."

"Sorry. I'll make sure I have a better footing before I put my weight on it."

"Maybe I should go first."

"No, it's fine," Surina replied, and kept climbing.

The climb was a long one. Despite the fact that she usually enjoyed a good climb, and didn't mind heights, Surina felt a growing queasiness in her belly as she moved farther and farther from the ground. The ladder curved up and over the back of the bull, making it difficult to grip the rungs. Surina slid her fingers behind the rope and against the warm metal, holding tight even after reaching a flat surface. The ladder ended at a small, square cavity in the bull's back: a sitting area with a metal bench on either side. Surina crawled inside and sat facing the bull's head, leaving Wibben to face the rear.

"I don't see any riddles," Surina said as Wibben settled in. "How do you think we get the bull to move?" She gripped the sides of the cavity as the bull made a sudden movement; it gave a slight lurch forward, and then Surina felt it rising. She felt a strange exhilaration mixed with anxiety. "Well . . . that was easy," she said.

The metal legs creaked and groaned as the bull stood

upright. A faint *boom* sounded on the ground below as it took its first step.

The bull had just started walking when Surina noticed something in the sky: a blazing orb of light, like a meteor trailing through the air. It flashed blue and white hues as it made a steady path into the realm of Taurus, appearing larger and larger as it neared the bull's head. "Look," Surina said, pointing.

As Wibben turned around, the ball of light made contact with the tip of the bull's horn. Its glow seemed to brighten for a moment, and then it careened away, sputtering back through Gemini.

"What was that?" Surina strained to peer past the bull's head. Its bulk obscured her view.

"No idea."

"It looked like it fell, but I can't see where it went." Surina gave up looking and settled back onto the metal bench. "This isn't bad. It reminds me of sitting at the top of a Ferris wheel."

"Hm."

"A Ferris wheel is a carnival ride. It's a—"

"Yes, I've seen one."

"Oh." Surina leaned over again, peering down at the river that meandered like a blue thread. She could see the length of river on the opposite side of the wall, and even caught a glimpse of its end, where it burst into a series of tiny rivulets—but the boat was nowhere to be seen. Surina felt a twinge of concern, mingled with lingering annoyance.

"Thanks for your help," she said to Wibben. "I'm not great with puzzles. I don't think I ever solved a riddle in my life before I met Dominic—or deciphered a code, or even tried a jigsaw puzzle. The closest thing I've done is an obstacle course. Whenever I do a 5k, or a 10k, I—"

"A what?"

"A race. There are foot races that you can go to, where instead of just running to the finish line, you have to do an obstacle course. You know, you have to climb a tower or a net, or swing across a river, without breaking the rules. Most of them I've done alone, but I did a partner course last year with a friend. All of the obstacles required two people, and we had to figure out how to get both of us through without breaking the rules. I had to carry her on my back, and she had to tell me where to walk while I was blindfolded . . . stuff like that." Surina gazed at Wibben's blue-tinged face and pale eyes. She found it difficult to imagine him as a human. He looked like a phantom, some other-worldly apparition. "What did you do when you were on Earth?"

"I studied music and philosophy," he replied. "Well, I suppose it's more correct to say I studied music and mythology."

"That must've been a great help here."

Wibben averted his eyes. His tone became dry. "That's how I ended up here. I was chasing a myth."

"Which myth was that?"

"The myth of my noble origins. I was part of a . . . secret society. We were trying to recover mystical rites from the past."

"Oh, yeah—you mentioned that."

"Do you know much about Indo-European language?"

"Nope."

"The early Germans, Celts, Indians, and Iranians shared a common language and mythology. Indians and Iranians referred to a group of noble ancestors, the Aryans, who knew the magic arts and could pass between dimensions. We read a lot about Aryan heroes—but I was mostly interested in Celtic lore. The Celts named Ireland Ériu after the Aryan goddess, and they also referred to an ancient supernatural race called the Tuatha Dé Danaan, people of the goddess Danu; they were spirits who lived in another dimension, who helped human beings."

"Like the beings here," Surina said.

Wibben nodded. "Yes, exactly. The Tuatha Dé Danaan gave four magical instruments to humanity: a sword, a spear, a cauldron, and a stone. Our society believed that if we possessed all four instruments, we could rule the world and prove our theory of Aryan superiority. Some of us thought that the stone was the Lia Fáil pillar in Ireland or the Stone of Scone in Scotland, but I believed that the Germans had our own stone of destiny at the Externsteine. I thought the Externsteine was an astronomical observatory and a shrine to the goddess. I had a firm belief that one of the great Germanic heroes was raised in the forest there, and that he had slayed a giant serpent at the rocks."

Surina looked at him stonily. "Aryan superiority? Were you a Nazi?"

He wouldn't meet her gaze. "I'm not that way anymore."

"But . . . you were?"

"It's something I would like to forget, but this place doesn't let me."

"You were," she said. "That's what you did with your life back on Earth? You played violin and supported the Nazis?"

"I'm sorry," he said. "I know what they did. I'm glad you're offended."

Surina clenched her teeth before answering. "I'm not sure 'offended' is the right word, but, okay."

Wibben was unfazed. He continued calmly: "When I first came here, and realized that I was in another dimension, I thought I'd made it to the world of the Tuatha Dé Danaan. I found a riddle about one of the magical instruments, and then another, and another. This place has been forcing me to spend eternity looking for those instruments and learning other things along the way . . . things that made me see myself as a self-aggrandizing fool. One of the first things I did when I arrived here was seek an Aryan goddess. I found one, but she didn't look the way I wanted her to; she was made of light. The riddles led me to another one, but she was a brown-and-white cow. The next one was a silver fish. The next was a snake." He paused, his eyes vacant for a moment as he delved into memory. "I've walked through this realm with all kinds of people, and they all have their own Tuatha Dé Danaan. I don't doubt that you have something like them."

"Sure. My mom's family has the Orixas, and my dad's has the Malakhim. Have you heard of the Malakhim?"

He regarded her with mild apprehension. "You're a Jew?"

"Half Jewish. And mixed-race, to boot. That must get under your skin."

"I haven't been that way in a long time."

"What year was it when you came here?"

Wibben paused. "I don't remember. Why do you want to know?" He waited, but Surina was silent. "You want to know if I was still a Nazi during the war."

"They did more than go to war," Surina replied.

"I know. I was there, but I didn't care. I cared about finding the sacred instruments and tracing the lineage of the gods." He paused again, looking introspective rather than anxious. "For a long time, I did the same thing here—especially in this region. Hadhyans and the Hyades led me in a maddening circle, and Perseus and Andromeda snared me for some time. Back on Earth, we thought that Perseus and his mother Danae, and other key figures around the Mediterranean and North Africa, were descendants of the goddess Danu. We searched for traces of their civilizations so we could find their objects of power." Wibben was about to say more, but he seemed to choke on the words. He was quiet for some time before continuing. "That's all I remember about my life. I don't remember my family, though I know I had one. I don't know who they were, or why it upsets me so much that I can't remember them anymore. I suppose I loved them." Wibben gazed at the floor as he spoke, then at the landscape, anywhere but Surina—but abruptly he faced her. "I know these are just words, but I truly am sorry for the person I was. I'm not that man anymore."

Surina felt a sudden sensation of falling. She realized that the bull was sitting; it had cleared the wall, and now descended to the ground.

"This place . . . forces us to know things that we desperately don't want to know," Wibben continued. "It keeps forcing us until we're finally glad of what we learned."

The bull's descent was quick. With a sudden lurch it set upon its knees, and Surina crumpled forward in her seat.

Wibben reached out to steady her, but Surina shrank from his hand. "I'm fine," she said.

The climb down was far more daunting than the ascent. Surina gripped the edge of the seating console with both hands and placed her feet in the rope ladder, but found herself unable to let go of that upper edge. The metal was smooth and slick; she was afraid of sliding over the side. She looked at Wibben and grudgingly asked: "Could you do me a favor, and just hold onto one of my wrists, in case I slip?"

He obliged without a word. He clasped her left wrist, and slowly she moved her right hand until she gripped the ladder. Wibben didn't let go until both of her hands were secure on the rungs.

Quietly the two made the descent back to Earth.

Gemini was a vast, bare, red realm. The soil was crumbly and dry beneath their feet, and it dusted their shoes with a deep crimson hue as they walked. The monotony of the landscape was interrupted only by some low, dark hills in the distance and a sandy, beige-hued path that led into the heart of the realm. Near the border wall, a crude wooden sign greeted the travelers: *Welcome to Gemini. Population: 2.*

As they followed the path, their mutual silence began to weigh on Surina—yet she couldn't think of anything to say to this strange, otherworldly man who was now diminished in her eyes. So they crossed Gemini in a quiet and somber manner, until at last the path separated into five branches, each marked with a signpost. Two of the paths were roped off; the way to Cancer bore a sign that read "Closed: Follow Detour," while Auriga read "Under Repair."

The two remaining paths bore signs for Monoceros, Canis Minor, and Lynx.

Another placard stood at the point where the path branched off. Its inscription read:

My first is sixth in firstly;
My second, last in thirdly;
My third is first in ninety;
My fourth is x + nullity;
My sum will lead you rightly.

"What the hell," Surina muttered. "I'm really starting to hate riddles. Can you solve this one?"

"Try it," Wibben suggested. "You should practice, in case we get separated."

"I'm terrible at math. That first line makes my mind go blank."

Wibben didn't respond, so Surina stood with her chin in her hand, considering the first couple of lines. "My first," she said slowly, "is sixth . . . in firstly. . . . My first is sixth of something." She paused for some time. "Okay, I tried. I don't get it."

"I'll give you a hint," Wibben said.

"Do you know it? Just tell me. I'm in a hurry; you said yourself that I have to get back before the water gets low at . . . wherever I came in. And I'm sure Hannah is getting herself into trouble."

Wibben replied coolly: "The first letter is probably also the sixth letter in the word 'firstly.'"

Surina looked at the riddle again. "My first letter is the sixth letter . . . in firstly? F-I-R, S-T-L. My first is the letter L?" Her gaze moved to the next line. "My second . . . is Y."

"Good."

"My third . . . is N. My fourth is x plus nullity. What is a nullity?"

"Nothing."

"It's nothing? So . . . x plus nothing." Surina paused. "So it's just X, right? My fourth is X. My sum . . . what were the letters again?"

"L-Y-N-X."

"My sum will lead you rightly. Let's follow Lynx."

"Let's."

Now they walked at a slight incline. The path veered to the left, winding between two of the dark hills that stood out against the crimson plain, all the way to the edge of a precipice. The view from its edge revealed a wide, parched valley riddled with cracks and craters and a few steaming fissures. Within one of these cracks Surina could see some movement, as though the soil was meandering along the bottom—a lava flow, perhaps.

The barren red landscape with its hot, shadowy

abysses recalled images of a descent into hell.

"I think we made a mistake," she said.

"The path will lead us through it," Wibben replied.

"Yeah, I can see that. Look." Surina pointed at the path, following its descent with her fingertip, stopping where the path bridged over a stream of flowing red mud. "It goes there, over that little land bridge."

"Let's get to it. You're in a hurry."

Carefully, they followed the path downward. It zig-zagged along the cliff and trailed to the bridge, where a large placard warned the travelers to take caution.

Obstacle 10 Ursae Majoris
Two rules to keep the bridge intact:

Rule #1:
Only one may walk across; only one dare touch the beam;
Only one can't cross at all; only two cross as a team.

Rule #2:
Acting as the one's Hadhya, seeing as the blind one's eye,
Only one who rides may look; only one may act as guide.

"Only two may as a team," Surina murmured. "Only one may walk across, but only one can't cross at all?"

"I think it's saying that one person can walk across, but not alone," Wibben said. "So how can two people cross while only one walks?"

"Huh?"

Wibben read through the riddle again. "Isn't this like the obstacle you talked about? When your friend had to ride on your back while you were blindfolded? Look at the second rule."

Surina finished reading quietly. She swore under her breath.

"I'll carry you across," Wibben offered. "Only the one who rides can look, so I'll keep my eyes closed."

Surina didn't move. She looked at the sign with distaste—and a touch of anxiety. "What happens if we cheat?"

"Well, the sign does say 'Two rules to keep the bridge *intact*.'"

"Damn."

"It's a short distance," Wibben assured her. "I think you can bear it."

"You're skinnier than I am. Maybe I should carry you."

Wibben shrugged. "Whichever."

"Here." Surina crouched. "Hop on."

Wibben's pale hands crept over her shoulders. He was heavier than he looked. Surina stood easily enough, but his weight made it impossible for her to walk normally. She took tiny steps forward, hunched over, head bent back, shuffling unsteadily toward the bridge.

"We won't make it like this," Wibben said.

"Fine." Surina let him slide to the ground. "I'm not as buff as I thought."

Wibben crouched, and Surina pulled herself onto his back, draping her arms lightly around his neck. He stood with difficulty; Surina began to heave to one side, but she steadied herself.

"You're heavy," he said.

"So are you. At least you can walk," she replied as he started forward.

"I can feel my leg bones grinding into my hips."

"Oh, what a pity. You must really be suffering down there. I feel really bad for you."

"Yes, I know where your sarcasm is coming from."

Wibben huffed a few times, and his voice sounded strained. "I'm not like that anymore, Surina. I have nothing but the deepest shame for the person I was."

"You *sound* ashamed."

"I've already been apologizing for it for centuries. You'll have to forgive me if it doesn't sound genuine anymore."

"It hasn't been centuries. It's been decades."

"Not here, it hasn't." Wibben hesitated at the bridge and hefted Surina higher on his back. "I'm going to close my eyes now. I'll walk forward slowly. Tell me if I'm drifting."

Surina tried to focus on the bridge, but her attention was pulled over and over again to the sights below. She felt at once fascinated and terrified by what she saw: a dark red river of flowing earth, pebbled with dark, rolling stones, its heat wafting up around Surina's limbs and warming her face. Surely it presented a fatal drop, yet there was something pretty about that moving red earth. It reminded Surina of something, though she couldn't remember what—perhaps it was the sight of campfire cinders, or a lava flow she'd seen on TV.

"Stop," she said. "You're drifting right. Turn to the left, just a little. That's good. Keep going straight. . . . Go to the right a little bit. No, more to the right. Good. . . . Slow down here, okay? The bridge is narrow. . . ."

Together they made it across. The distance was not long; even with Wibben's painstakingly slow creep across the beam, they had passed it in a few minutes. When Wibben was several feet past the drop, he released Surina's legs.

"Okay," she said. "That was scary as hell, but we made it."

The trail led them safely past a few more steaming pools of mud. Surina caught sight of a large archway ahead. Beyond it the landscape was markedly different, with hues of green and brown and a splotch of deep blue—colors that seemed more natural than the blood-red dust of Gemini. "I think we're coming to the next constellation," she said, with a note of relief. "Doesn't that say 'Leo'?"

As they came closer, Surina was dismayed to see another steep decline in the ground.

"Looks like we have to cross another bridge," Wibben said.

Surina stopped short of the crossing and stared. "That isn't a bridge."

There was, indeed, a steep drop between the travelers and the archway, and a beam leading across the chasm— but the beam didn't invite walking. It had a triangular surface that came to a sharp peak at the top, with two sides angling downward, so that trying to walk along either side of the peak would mean an easy slip into the depths below. Surina stood at the edge of the precipice and looked into the pit. Red mud moved below, swirling with black rocks and orange-yellow bits that looked like cinders; it flowed far below the ledge, yet its heat warmed Surina's face.

The sign read: *Obstacle 38 Lyncis. A slippery path is not feared by two people who help each other.*

"No way," Surina said. "I've done something like this—at one of the obstacle courses. The partner one. Except . . . ." She crouched down, examining the apex of the beam. She reached out to touch it. "This looks sharp. I think this could actually cut our—ow!" Surina's hand snapped back. "It's hot."

She straightened up and glanced around, then looked down at Wibben's tunic. "It's too hot to hold onto. Maybe there's something we can put over our hands. If I tear some pieces off of your clothes . . . ."

"I can't imagine we'll get a good grip that way. How did you get across before?"

"Well . . . that was different. We had to stand on either side and reach across, and hold hands."

"Ah. And that helped both of you keep your balance?"

She hesitated. "It kept us from falling. It's harder than it sounds, though. I couldn't get my balance at first. I kept falling forward."

"It might be our best option. Feel free to think of an alternative, but this place responds to our thoughts and experiences. I think you called up this obstacle, and you called up its solution as well."

"But . . . what about our feet? We still have to walk on it." Surina eyed Wibben's flimsy-looking shoes, which consisted of soles tied to his feet by linen wraps.

Wibben went to the beam and pressed the flat of one shoe against the hot metal. Surina did the same on the opposite side.

"We'll make it if we keep moving," he said, and reached out to Surina. "Like you said, you're in a hurry. Are we going to do this?"

Surina looked down at his hands. She didn't move.

"If you don't hold my hand," he said evenly, "we're going to die."

She pondered that for a moment. "Can you really die in this place?"

"You can. And then your soul gets reincarnated through Hydra or some other port, or it gets stuck in the underworld. I've seen it happen."

"Okay. Well, I'd like to live *this* life a little longer."

"Good. Let's make that happen."

"Let's practice first." Surina beckoned him away from the beam and extended her hands to him. "All right, make sure you've got a good grip. Lean back and test it. Lean more. Okay? Good. We'll step sideways, starting with the leading foot—my right foot and your left foot. Do what I'm doing, like you're my mirror image." She raised her right foot and made a short step, then followed with her left. "We'll get a rhythm going, so we're at the same pace. The leading foot will step once every second, like this: *One* one-thousand, *two* one-thousand . . . ."

They practiced stepping until they both felt comfortable. Once they stood at the cliff, though, Surina's confidence vanished.

"Take my hands," Wibben said.

She wrapped her fingers securely around his wrists. She took a breath, tried to exhale her fears. "Let's start by putting the lead foot on the beam. We'll find our balance, and then follow with the second foot. Ready? Go."

He complied, and the two stood half on the scalding beam, half on the crimson soil. Surina felt the heat beginning to seep through her shoes. "All right. When I say go, let's move the other foot. Move carefully, though. Don't make a big step. Just sort of drag your foot. When we're both on, I'll start the count."

She felt the pull of Wibben's weight as his other foot began to glide onto the beam. "No big movements," Surina said anxiously. She leaned back a little, trying to compensate for Wibben's weight—but she caught sight of the vastness below and felt herself beginning to fall backwards into it. Her legs folded beneath her, seeking the safety of the beam; she landed with her hip against the metal, the heat searing along the side of her leg— bearable, but intensifying.

"Surina, I need you to stand up," Wibben said. He was still on his feet, but in a low crouch. "Carefully, please. Come on. Balance yourself."

"Okay. Okay, I'm trying to stand." She hoisted herself onto the balls of her feet, then made a slow attempt at straightening her legs.

"That's it," Wibben said. "Take your time."

She gasped, feeling herself pulled forward. Surina threw herself back onto the metal slope, felt the heat burning into her knees.

"It's all right. Try again," Wibben coaxed her.

She got back onto her feet, leaning back slightly as she rose to a standing position. "Okay," she said shakily. "Just wait a minute. I can't move yet."

"All right."

"Wibben, I'm really scared."

"That's okay. You've done this before, right?"

"Yes, but I fell!"

"Of course you did. That's how you learn to stay balanced—right? When you're ready, we'll start stepping."

"Okay . . . hold still. You're throwing me off."

"I need to move my feet. They're starting to burn."

Surina tried to steady herself, but her gaze moved along the length of the beam, which suddenly looked as though it was a mile long. "We're screwed," she said.

"I think we've done the most difficult part: getting onto the beam and finding our balance. We've got that now. Let's count—a slow count to start, okay? Don't do anything yet. I'm going to count like this: A, B, C; and then I'm going to start counting *one* one-thousand, *two* one-thousand. *One* one-thousand will be our first step. Are you ready?"

"Yeah."

"Here we go. A. B. C. *One* one-thousand . . . ."

Together they moved, and then Surina stood still, trying to muster her courage. "Let's start again," she said. "I just needed a minute."

"Understood. I'll start counting now. A. B. C. *One* one-thousand . . . ."

They stepped again, and kept on stepping in a rhythm

Surina focused on the count, on Wibben, on anything but the drop below—but after a couple of minutes she felt her palms sweating. "My hands are starting to slip," she said.

"Don't worry. Keep your grip tight, and they won't slip past my wrists."

"Okay," she replied, but felt her arms trembling even more. Her circulation seemed to slow; her fingers felt as though they were going numb. She fought off the urge to let go of Wibben and cling to the scalding metal beam instead.

He seemed to sense her growing panic. "We've got a good rhythm going," he said calmly. "I'm going to stop counting. Is that all right?"

"Yeah."

"Tell me about your family. Do you have siblings?"

"No, it's just me."

"Where did you grow up?"

"Florida and Arizona. I'm in Arizona now. My dad lives overseas, so it's pretty much just me and my mom. My mom's sister used to live with us, too, but she stayed in Florida when we moved. . . ."

Surina rambled on for some time, keeping her mind from the fiery doom that lurked below. "What about you?" she asked. "Do you have siblings?"

"I had a sister. I may have had other siblings, too. I don't really remember. There was some urgent reason that I was trying to get back to my sister . . . like she was in danger without me." He was quiet for a moment. Surina heard his breath quickening, as if the treacherous journey was finally wearing on him. "She may have been disabled. Maybe I'm remembering it wrong, but . . . I felt that if I was important to the Nazis, then I wouldn't have to be afraid for my sister. They would have spared her."

A twinge of disdain surfaced through Surina's fear. "Is that supposed to be your excuse? You became a Nazi to save your sister?"

"No. I became a Nazi because I was ignorant and vain, and angry."

"Angry at what?"

"Whatever it is that ignorant and vain men become angry about. I really don't remember what offended me so much about my life on Earth. I was well off, I think. I wasn't suffering, or poor."

As they reached the end of the beam, Surina realized with a small shock that her own sudden anger had chased away her fear. "Keep going," Wibben said. "When we get to the end we're just going to keep stepping, right onto the grass. Just keep going until we're a few feet from the cliff."

"Okay."

They stepped onto solid ground and went a few paces farther—and then Surina fell, trembling, to the ground. She stayed on her hands and knees for some time, trying to steady herself—but as she looked back at the beam, she was overcome with sudden emotion. Tears sprang to her eyes and pooled on her eyelids. She quickly wiped them away—again, and again.

Wibben started to offer his hand, but let it fall when he saw Surina's tears. "What's the matter?"

"I don't know," she said.

The path zig-zagged back up to the plateau. It was a long walk, but wide enough for the travelers to walk side by side, and so they talked along the way. Surina spoke freely now, still rambling on about her family. The words seemed to release some pent-up anxiety—or perhaps her passage over the potentially fatal drop made her want to review her life. She talked about her childhood and what she knew of her grandparents and great-grandparents. Her great-grandmother, Rivka, had lived in Hungary when the

Nazis came to power. She escaped with her younger sisters to British Palestine before deportation to the camps began; others were sent to Auschwitz. When Surina was born, the only remaining survivor was Rivka's older sister, Perl. Surina visited her several times at her home in Tennessee, and occasionally tried to question her about the tattoo on her left forearm. Perl never talked about that part of her past. She simply told Surina that "You will learn about it in school someday." Oppression was also a prevailing theme in the stories of her mother's childhood in the poverty-ridden favelas of Brazil.

Surina had told these stories before. Now, though, she heard a tremor in her voice, and her eyes kept watering, though she wasn't sure she was crying.

"I wanted to make sure I wouldn't live like that," she said. "So I did a lot of community work, like . . . those community programs that try to help people get along, meet one another, and have the resources they need. That kind of work doesn't pay, though. It pays a little or not at all. I worked like a dog for—I mean, I worked a lot of hours so I could pay the bills and save a little bit of money. And then my jackass husband stole my savings. I had to spend the little bit I had left on the divorce and a new apartment, and I had to drop the community work and get a higher-paying job so I could stay in college." She glanced at Wibben. "I'm not sure if you know what I mean."

"Sure. You worked hard, you were poor, your husband stole the money you saved."

"I meant about the community work."

"Are you still mad at your husband?"

"Obviously. Why, do you think I should forgive him?"

Wibben shrugged. "That depends on the effect it has on you. You look young; it must have been recent. And I suppose he hasn't changed."

"Why would he? His family doesn't hold him accountable. They brush it under the rug and make excuses. I sometimes did that too, so it's not like I don't understand." Surina paused. "And now, I guess I'm thinking about whether I should forgive you, even though you did something unforgivable." She added tonelessly: "I know you were still there when they tortured people and slaughtered them in death camps. You didn't ask questions when I talked about it. You already know."

"I've walked these realms with a thousand people. They told me about it."

"I know because of what you said about your sister. You knew they would kill her. That's why you wanted to get back to her so badly."

They had reached the plateau. A short distance remained between them and the archway, and Surina was dismayed to see yet another signpost at the entrance. Near its base was a plastic laundry basket, looking well out of place in a realm so devoid of humanity and its inventions.

Surina approached and nudged the basket with her foot. "Are we doing laundry?"

Wibben read the riddle aloud:

If two have two feet each for this last test,
one of each pair must in the basket rest;
If one takes one step, in two it must go:
From floor to basket, from basket to floor.
If one takes one step, the court will expect
one's counterpart's foot to accomplish the next.

They re-read it carefully a few times, though Surina thought she already knew how to solve it. "I know what it is," she said finally. "It's the basket walk. These are all from the partner obstacle course that I did with Felisita. Each of us has to keep one foot in the basket, and drag the basket across the ground with us while we walk, and we have to take turns stepping forward." She looked again at the riddle and made a sound of distaste. "Can't they just say it in simple language? The obstacle is hard enough."

"It doesn't sound that bad," Wibben said.

"It's hard. You can't just step forward with your outside foot; you have to put it inside the basket first, and step out again. 'If one takes one step, in two it must go: from floor to basket, from basket to floor.' That's when people lose their balance."

"From floor to basket . . . I see." Wibben nodded. "Let's practice."

"I know it's a little late to say this," Surina said, looking back at the crimson landscape, "but I really think this was a mistake. Where are we *going*? I feel like this place is trapping me—like I'm just going deeper and deeper into it, and . . . it's a trap. Every one of these stupid riddles leads to another stupid riddle. What's the point?"

"There is a point," Wibben said. "It may take a while to realize it." He gestured to the arch. "The next realm is a small one. It looks like it's taking us to Virgo, the queen of the underworld. You can see her realm from here."

Surina peered through the archway. On the opposite side was a small courtyard of cobbled stones, the darker-colored stones arranged in the shape of a lion. Beyond it was a dome with a single door set in the side—a deep blue structure streaked here and there with gold, and beyond that, grassy hills and trees in the distance. Surina's gaze was fixed on the dome. A memory nagged at her: a dark hallway of the same blue stone, its speckles and streaks of gold like stardust in a deep blue universe. "What does she look like?" Surina asked.

"The queen? She usually looks . . . like a human. A modest human. Not very fancy for a queen."

Surina frowned. A strange unease gripped her, but she

leaned over and grabbed the basket. "All right. Let's practice over here."

She directed him to stand so that his right foot was in the basket beside her left foot. "Go slow," Surina said. "It's easy to get mixed up, or to lose your balance."

As they started forward, he did lose his balance—not once, but several times.

"Hold my arm when you take a step," Surina said.

"I don't want to pull on you."

"You're bumping into me anyway. I'm anchored when you're not, so you'll keep your balance better if you hold onto me."

The practice session didn't give Surina much confidence. She went to examine the riddle again, and said with a note of relief: "Well, it doesn't say we're going to die if we mess up. Should we give it a shot?"

"Might as well."

They placed the laundry basket at the threshold and each set a foot inside. Surina slid her hand around Wibben's arm. She hadn't really noticed it while holding his hand, but his skin felt strangely dry and leathery, the bone beneath his flesh hard and pronounced. Holding his arm felt like grasping the limb of a mummy—but she clung to him anyway. "Let's drag it forward first," she suggested. "Ready?"

The plastic basin scraped against the stone floor as they pushed it into the court. "Okay, stop," Surina said. "Short steps are better. Do you want to go first?"

"Sure."

"Get a better grip on my arm."

Wibben clasped her bicep in both hands and took a step.

"No," Surina started to say, but was startled into silence by a sudden commotion: a loud cracking, a frightening scraping and groaning. Wibben gasped and jumped back, stumbling onto the safe ground before the archway. Surina followed, grabbing the basket and pulling it back with her.

One of the stones had given way beneath Wibben's foot. Surina stared into the gap where the rock had been. She saw nothing but infinite darkness.

"I forgot to put my foot in the basket first," Wibben said breathlessly.

"Yeah."

"Well . . . at least we know what happens if we mess up. I won't make the same mistake again."

"Good. I'll count on that."

They moved the basket to the right, well out of the way of the void, and re-positioned their feet. "Okay, wait," Surina said, gazing anxiously across the court. "Let's make a plan. It's more dangerous to cross over the bigger stones, right? Some of these are big enough that we could fall through. We should try to go around those. Like . . . that big beige one right there." She pointed to the misshapen stone not far ahead of them.

"Yes, let's not risk stepping there," Wibben agreed.

"Let's go to the left of it. And make sure that when you step, you're only stepping on one stone at a time— not on the mortar lines. Try to step on the smallest ones."

"Right."

"Ready?"

"Yes. Don't worry, I won't forget again," he reassured her.

They started the slow creep across the court. Surina muttered to herself as she moved: "In . . . out. Okay, let's drag." Wibben followed her example, voicing his steps out loud: "In, out . . . drag."

The court was silent except for the murmur of their voices and the scraping of plastic against stone. The sounds became rhythmic, predictable—and then, as

Wibben began to draw his foot toward the basket, Surina felt him pulling away, felt the panicked tensing of muscle in his arm. She tried to steady him, but his foot ended up back on the floor. The cracking sounded again; Wibben's foot jerked and landed on another stone.

Surina tightened her grip, pulling him closer as another chunk of floor gave way. "Get your foot back inside," she commanded.

He obeyed, using Surina's solid stance to help balance himself. When he had both feet safely in the basket, he stood for a while, catching his breath and looking at the path ahead. Surina glanced up at his strange blue eyes— light blue irises, surrounded by a shade nearly as blue where they should have been white.

Wibben's breath slowed. He carefully stretched out his leg, placing his foot on the nearest unbroken stone.

They went on—on and on, it seemed, one short segment at a time. Though the court was relatively small, Surina felt a pained dejection every time she looked up to see how much distance they still had to cover—but focus and a slow pace got them safely across. When they stepped from the last of the cobbled stones and onto the deep blue platform, Surina let out a relieved sigh and let herself fall from the basket onto solid ground.

"That was unpleasant," Wibben remarked. "I wouldn't mind a rest, either, but there is still a time limit for you to get home."

She nodded and pushed herself to her feet, facing the doorway into the dome.

"All right," she said, her voice resounding with weary determination. "I'm ready for whatever's next."

10: Virgo

Flight lifted Hannah into a quiet simplicity. As she soared over the Eridanus with her newly feathered wings, she heard nothing but the rush of air around her ears—no riddles being muttered aloud, no strange fish-creatures threatening to topple her into dangerous waters, no lectures from a know-it-all queen. Hannah thought of the queen's transformative powers and remembered the exhilaration of her first flight—her feelings of amazement, excitement, empowerment. None of those feelings graced her now. Flying was just another thing she was doing, another tedious chore to get her free from this universe. She gazed down at the blue curve of the river and the realms along its borders. Those realms seemed so small and simple from this perspective. If only she'd been able to fly all the way to Orion; how easy it would have been! Why, instead, did everything have to be so difficult, so seemingly endless?

Clutched in her talons was the fleece nightgown. Hannah had already been to Tagua's realm in Lepus—that strange, cave-like place with its wide plaza and open high-rise at the far end, its perpetually rising and descending platform moving among the different floors. Hannah had boarded the platform and let it take her up to Tagua's rooms, while around her milled the realm's ghoulish inhabitants: a multitude of child-like creatures with deep blue flesh and solid black eyes. Those eyes had once struck Hannah with fear, then unease, then pity.

Now, though, they provoked little feeling in her at all. She had barely noticed the creatures as they brushed and bumped against her on the platform, their movements clumsy and inattentive.

The wings, claws, and knobby fur-covered legs of Hannah's griffin-like body didn't seem to faze Tagua at all. He had addressed her without really looking at her. Instead he gave a brief, disinterested glance, and then made a point of turning away. It had become his customary way with her. She had learned to appreciate it. If Tagua did look into her eyes now, it was usually to express a quiet but scathing disappointment.

He stood there in his usual guise: clad in a deep violet robe, with an air of mingled irritation and nonchalance. Tagua was profiled so that Hannah could still see part of his face, along with one of his eyes. Though Tagua's eyes were dark, she could still see the vague impression of his brown irises; they were not as featureless as the eyes of others in this realm. Hannah could exchange a glance with Tagua and still detect a soul, could still see feelings and persona.

When she asked for the nightgown, he'd replied dryly: "Why?"

"I need it for the next riddle," she'd said. In her own voice she heard a now-familiar tone, a kind of strained emotionlessness—as if she was trying not to sound sad.

He ordered one of the child-creatures to retrieve the garment; the creature fetched it; Tagua gestured for it to be given to Hannah. She took the nightgown in her hands and felt a small shock at the sight of her extended arms. They were already strange, with their fine layer of fur and soft feathers, and long taloned fingers—but Hannah saw another, unprecedented change. Her skin, visible on her wrists and the back of her hands, was turning blue. Blue like the skin of the people around her, who had faded into hollow shells of themselves.

Hannah clenched her teeth. She didn't want Tagua to notice her feeling of dread. If he noticed that she was fading, he would only become more disappointed, more disgusted.

Back on the platform, Hannah was no longer unaware of the child-things that bustled aimlessly around her. She was keenly focused on them, on their disturbed mannerisms and the voids of their eyes. As she descended toward the plaza, a sense of horror rose within her. *I might become like them. I* am *becoming like them.*

Though she promised herself she would not let that happen, and that she would do whatever she could to fix her mistakes, Hannah feared that she had already failed. A muted despair hung over her as she approached the tan-hued stone formation of Fornax. Below her, the tops of the labyrinth walls were bare. Hannah felt disappointed; when she and Surina had flown above the stone walls on the wooden bird, they had seen not just one family of owls, but dozens of great horned owls resting on top of the maze of rocks. Now, as she looked down at the empty surfaces, Hannah felt rather lonely.

In the center of the misshapen labyrinth was a splotch of gray—a splotch that, on closer observance, turned out to be the twisted tree. Hannah had half expected to see a ruined mass of branches and a shattered trunk, but she was surprised to find the tree still intact, the branches once again spread out in thick, curving forms. Hannah tried to land gracefully as she settled on the thickest upper branch, but she landed with a hard thud, gripping the trunk for support. Her gaze fell on the blue-tinted skin peeking through the tufts of fur on her paw. Once again she felt a sickening fear.

"I won't become like that," she whispered.

She was situating herself against the branch, trying to

find a comfortable position, when she noticed two large, golden eyes staring up at her. Hannah froze, startled, and then saw the rest of the face: the short, dark beak, the feathered tufts. The owl was safely nested on a branch not far from her, surrounded by its sleeping chicks.

"You came back," Hannah said softly. She opened her mouth to speak again, but worried about scaring the owls. In a near whisper, she added: "I won't bother you. I'm just here to rest."

She moved quietly, leaning against the trunk and putting her feet on the branch below. This was a dreaming tree, or so Virgo had said—but Hannah didn't feel like sleeping or dreaming. Her mind buzzed with questions. What was supposed to happen here? And how had the tree come back together again, so that even the nest with its owls was back in place? The realms were always changing, always re-making themselves, but it seemed strange to Hannah that the destruction of the snake and tree could have undone itself.

She leaned forward, peering through gaps in the branches to see if she could spot the snake. From her perspective, all she saw was a mass of gray—and then she noticed a depression in the sandstone base, a shallow pit where the thick gray coil of the snake was wrapped around the trunk. When she looked closely, Hannah could see the head with its black eyes and tapered snout. Something else on the sandstone floor caught her eye: a circular strip of wood, perhaps a piece of bark that had curled off and fallen. The strip was curved so that it made a near perfect circle. Beside it was a small branch, straight and thick. They looked like the drum stick and frame that Hannah had seen on her first visit to the tree. Quietly Hannah climbed downward, keeping her wings folded close to her body. She reached down and grabbed the stick, and then the other piece of wood, and crept back to her perch.

As she climbed, Hannah noticed the lines curving along the bark—the figure of the underworld being. Its form was hard to distinguish up close, but as Hannah settled against the tree, she recognized the details of small snake heads just where her own head would be resting, and numerous spirals on the branches above.

She covered herself with the fleece gown and cradled the stick and frame in her lap. The patterns in the tree had given her an idea: she would do her own sculpting, perhaps make a carved drumstick like she one she'd seen earlier. The queen's words echoed in Hannah's memory: *What are you going to make*? Perhaps a carved stick was a little thing, but Hannah could make it into something of significance. She worked on the drum frame first, whittling down the too-thick sections with her sharp claws. As she worked, she thought back to the instruments that Dominic had helped make from the ram's body: the hide drum, the hoof-rattles, the horn flutes. A drum from the shedding parts of the dreaming tree seemed a good thing to make, too—and perhaps the tree had even offered these pieces up to Hannah, gifting pieces of itself like the ram had gifted its whole body.

Hannah turned her attention to the stick. She would carve that first, and then decide what designs to make on the frame. But which images should she choose?

A warped sense of time, along with the effects of the sun gate, had begun to fog Hannah's mind—not much, but enough to frighten her. She tried to think of the lessons and ideas she needed to remember most. She would start by engraving them into the wood in her hands. The memory care residents at the veteran's home, where her dad lived, looked at photos to help them remember things; one man even had something that he called a "memory map," a huge poster illustrated with images that helped him recall important people and events. Hannah, too, had things she needed to remember, such as what it really meant to be a griffin. She thought back to the first time. The queen had said something about having claws like a crab—and Hannah saw that the talons of her over-sized thumb and index finger did, indeed, look like crab claws. Virgo had told Hannah to grip securely, but without piercing, because the points and edges were sharp enough to cause serious harm.

Or to do something good, she thought, *depending on what I use them for.*

With the point of her index claw, Hannah scratched an image into the soft wood: the outline of a crab, a rough oval with six tiny legs and two thick pincers. She thought back over her adventures and carved more images of the memories that were important to her. She made stick figures of herself and Dominic as the Gemini twins, to remind herself that she was not alone; Dominic had even come all the way to a mountain in Peru to try to find her. Hannah carved spiral waves with two fish to remember her ordeal in the ocean, and then a griffin whose wings spanned half the length of the stick.

As she worked, Hannah felt herself beginning to drift into slumber. She let the stick fall into her lap as her eyelids became heavy and her head leaned against the hard surface of the tree. In her half-sleep, Hannah was left alone with her fear and loneliness—and as she reached into her memories for comfort, she found that her greatest comforts could be found in her life on Earth: her father, her foster parents, the few friends she'd had. Her grandmother Sofia, who had died when Hannah was only six years old, but of whom Hannah still had a few precious memories. On her last trip back to Earth, Hannah had been able to visit a library in New Mexico. She went there to try to research the sun gate riddle, but in that library she had come across a book of fairy tales written by her grandmother.

Once, not long before she died, Sofia told Hannah that she had written those tales for her—and the book itself was dedicated to her. Sofia's stories were often dark; they were laced with suffering, greed, and betrayal, though they also contained magic and magnificence. Hannah had taken the book from the library shelf and opened to a random page, where a small gray snake was illustrated against the backdrop of a dark forest. The story was about a man who found his grandson lying ill on the ground, seemingly being attacked by a snake and an owl. The man chased down the snake to kill it, but discovered later that its venom had stopped the boy's blood from clotting in his lungs; the owl had slashed the boy's shoulder open to remove a deadly parasite, which the owl promptly chewed up and swallowed.

Hannah's own thoughts whispered to her that her hardships in this realm, too, must have some hidden benefit. The gray snake below her, like the one in the story, perhaps used its bite to protect and heal—or not at all. And Hannah's own claws were like that of the owl: capable of help and relief.

Gently, Hannah clasped her hands in her lap, careful not to scratch herself with the long claws. The fine layer of fur felt surprisingly soft. Another memory surfaced: holding hands with Lama-Zu, the griffin lady she'd met in Leo. Lama-Zu's words of comfort came back to her: *I've known what it's like to be alone, and to be afraid. Whenever you feel that way, like you don't have the courage and you need someone to hold your hand, remember how I held your hand like this. Remember that my grip was strong . . . and that my sharp claws never hurt you.* It seemed an important message, somehow. Virgo had mentioned it too. *The griffin has flight, it has knowledge . . . and it has claws. They can be used to grab or repel, to cut or hold together.*

Though it wasn't a memory, Virgo's voice suddenly cut into Hannah's thoughts: *How will you hold Tagua?*

The question was like a new riddle forming in Hannah's mind. Slowly, as she thought back over her time in the starry realms, she began to realize how Tagua had affected her.

It struck her, then, that she had asked Surina for help—and even after Surina had answered by traveling across the world and risking her own safety, Hannah had resented and abandoned her. When she thought over her trip down the river, it was no wonder to Hannah that the Orion chariot had crashed. Perhaps she hadn't placed the tokens correctly, or had chosen the wrong ones, and Surina could have helped her—but more importantly, Hannah had approached Orion with deceit and jealousy. She didn't want Surina to be the one who solved the puzzles, or who helped Tagua. How, after the mistakes she'd made, could Hannah try again? How could she pick up the pieces from the mess she'd made? She still had to find the Orion tokens and try again.

In Hannah's half-sleep, she heard the murmur of the queen's voice: *The Orion tokens are the tablets of destiny. Whoever holds them rightly has power over this universe. You'll find them when you're ready . . . .*

Hannah's eyelids fluttered. The memory startled her, nearly woke her from her half-slumber.

She sensed, then, that the words were more than just memory. She sensed Virgo's presence; the queen wanted her to remember those words, was prodding Hannah with them just as if she was whispering in Hannah's ear. Virgo's essence seemed to be traveling up through the tree by some strange energy—up from the roots, up through the serpent coiled below, the serpent whose body trailed deep into the tunnels of the underworld. Hannah could almost see the queen sitting in her chamber, eyes closed, communicating through invisible vines that snaked beneath the realms and emerged from portals such as this one. The words had a comforting tone. Virgo's very presence, even as it pulled Hannah into slumber, seemed to be waking her from a confused and lethargic sleep. Yet the queen's words also provoked anxiety in Hannah; they only hinted at more riddles, and provided no solutions. *And yet, like the snake venom in your grandmother's story*, the queen's voice whispered, *perhaps these hardships are meant to heal you.*

The comment about the Orion tokens nagged at Hannah. Someone else had said those same words, here in this labyrinth. *The Tablets of Destiny . . . whoever holds the tablets has power over the universe.* The sculptor had been looking for the Tablets of Destiny. Was it possible that he was seeking the Orion keys?

Other words came to mind, other snippets of his stories. *The tree supposedly holds the golden fleece of Chrysomallos.* The tree did, indeed, hold a golden fleece—both now, and when Hannah had first come to the tree. *I don't know much about the ram itself, except that it was created to rescue Phrixos and Helle, two children who were about to be devoured by the celestial guardians. The ram carried the boy, Phrixos, to safety—and then the ram was sacrificed, and its fleece removed. I'm not sure what happened to the girl. I think she fell into the sea and was swallowed by Cetus.*

"It's . . . us," she whispered out loud. "*I* was swallowed by Cetus." And Dominic—he and the ram had helped each other walk into Aries, where the ram was killed; its fleece was removed and made into Hannah's nightgown. She and Dominic were chased from Aries by the celestial guardians: the hounds of Orion.

Hannah felt her fingers tightening around the soft fabric in her hands. Taloned fingers, the claws of a bird-woman. Again, the sculptor's words echoed in her mind: *The anzu? It's a creature who stole the Tablets of Destiny—a frightening half-bird, half-human thing . . . really more of a demon than anything. It took the tablets from Aquarius and nested somewhere in the labyrinth, where no one can find it.*

"It's *me*," she whispered.

Despite her lingering misery, Hannah let out a small, sardonic laugh. This universe was vast and intelligent, in command of infinite things she knew nothing about. She had no power here. The universe had power over her; it was drawing her toward a lesson. The more she avoided it, the stronger the pull.

Before Hannah could become steeped in this realization, a voice began pulling her back toward consciousness: "That is the anzu! It has the body of a lion and the wings of a bird!"

The words were familiar, but they didn't come from inside her mind. Someone was in the court with her. Another person spoke—a female voice, just as familiar. Hannah struggled to wake as the murmurs continued. She felt the hard surface of the tree's trunk and branches, the rough bark against her feet, but it wasn't enough to fully rouse her. The words of the intruders rose in volume, became panicked.

A sudden commotion jolted her fully into consciousness.

The tree shook, as though its roots had been jolted beneath the ground. Hannah opened her eyes. She saw the labyrinth wall in front of her. A loud cracking sounded below, over and over again, and in between the clashing she heard the soft, distressed peeps of the owl chicks.

Hannah grabbed the tree trunk and peered around it.

Looking down, she saw the sculptor standing there with his hatchet, his face red and his eyes wild with fear, his clothes splashed with blood.

The serpent was in pieces. Its blood streamed across the stone floor. Hannah saw the tapered head lying below, its mouth open in a lingering expression of agony.

"No!" she cried.

The owl cried out below her, echoing her distress. It flapped its wings, readying for flight, and tried to nudge its chicks from the nest.

"Catch it!" Sculptor shouted. Hannah saw him reaching for the nest, trying to jump past the lower branches. The owls flew up and out of the tree, safely out of his reach.

The comforting voice had ceased. Hannah's sense of recovery and renewal had stopped as well. Looking down at the sculptor, at his excited eyes and blood-stained pants, Hannah felt a sense of sudden resentment and rage. Beyond him, Surina stood open-mouthed—and beside Surina stood another Hannah. For one startled moment Hannah wondered if she had left her own body behind when she became a griffin, but she quickly realized what was happening: she was seeing her old self, the one that had first come here looking for help.

And Hannah resented her old self, too.

"Idiots!" she shouted. She spread her wings and shot upward from the branches, still glaring down at the intruders. *The old me doesn't deserve to make it to Orion*, she thought bitterly. *She doesn't deserve this tree, or anything else in this realm*. With one leg she lashed out and struck the tree, and it cracked under the blow.

Hannah was high in the air, fleeing the labyrinth, before she realized that she didn't know where to go. She simply wanted to leave her old self behind.

With no other plans, and no comforting voice to guide

her, Hannah began the flight back to Orion.

Surina had hardly finished speaking when the door to the blue dome opened. A woman stood just beyond it. She wore a simple sleeveless tunic that hung to her ankles. Her dark eyes gazed calmly at Surina, but Surina looked back at her without the same air of serenity. Instead, she felt a prickle of angry recognition.

Surina leaned close to Wibben. In a low voice she asked: "The queen of the underworld?"

He nodded and addressed the queen: "My lady. I wonder if you could direct us. I want to take Surina back to Hydrus . . . as I'm sure you already know. She needs to get back home before the water drops below the flutes."

"Indeed," the queen said softly, her gaze still fixed on Surina. "And did you accomplish what you came here for?"

Surina hesitated. "I don't think so."

"Hannah called her here to help with the sun gate riddle," Wibben said. "But . . . ."

"Of course," Virgo replied. "Both Dominic and Surina have visited this realm before. Those who have been to this realm remain connected, and have a window into it. That is how they were able to receive Hannah's transmissions."

"Surina has never been here," Wibben corrected her. "She has."

Wibben glanced uncertainly at Surina.

"I have, actually," Surina said dryly. "This isn't my first time meeting this person."

Virgo replied with a small, wry smile. "I'm not a person."

Surina stared haughtily, as though trying to bore through the queen with the intensity of her gaze. "I have a bone to pick with you."

"Most people do." Virgo leaned against the door frame, folding her arms across her chest. "The bone you want to pick, I suppose, is attached to the skeleton of your marriage."

"Yes, my marriage to Victor, who you went out of your way to recommend to me," Surina said. "Who you praised to the sky."

"I didn't praise him."

"You told me to give him a chance!" Surina's rose steadily in volume. "I wasted a year and a half with that crook while he drained my savings and sucked the life out of me, like a freaking vampire!"

"I didn't tell you to marry him."

"Fine, but you *insinuated* it. You insinuated things, and put ideas in my head that wouldn't have been there otherwise—and now you're going to say, 'Well, it's not *my* fault. I didn't specifically say to do this, or that.'"

With unchanging calm, the queen asked: "Is that what I'm going to do?"

Surina ignored the question, continuing in a fury: "I thought he was a narcissistic scumbag, and you were like, 'Oh, *no*, Surina, this man is different! Give him a chance!' And then you gave that speech about the progression of the cosmos, and made it seem like we were meant to be together!"

"And so you were, for a time."

"And a lot of good it did me!"

"Tell me this, Surina: Which person do you prefer? The person you were before marrying Victor, or the person you've become? If you could go back to being that woman who was so easily stepped on, and who constantly stifled her own voice, would you do it? Or would you stay as you are now: a woman who draws the line, and who speaks up for herself?"

Surina felt her anger abating. The queen's words

stirred uncomfortable realizations. Her experiences with Victor had exposed some of her greatest weaknesses, and made her determined to change them.

"I won't humor that with an answer," Surina muttered.

"I think you already have." The queen's gaze rested on Wibben. "And you, do you have a question?"

He asked bluntly: "Am I dead?"

The queen gazed at him for some time. "You haven't asked that before."

"I was afraid," Wibben replied. "Even though I have wished for death in this place. I even thought of making Tagua kill me, but . . . ."

"There is no death here," the queen replied, "only transformation."

"Did I die at Externsteine?"

"If you returned to your body, you would be returning to a corpse. You drowned in the pond."

It seemed a harsh way to convey such final news. Surina felt a small shock, another surge of anger at the queen.

Wibben's face was impassive, but his voice had a sudden frailty to it. "And my sister?"

"You needn't worry about her. Your sister is in my hands."

"That doesn't comfort me," he replied bitterly.

"Your sister was killed at Hadamar." The queen gave Wibben a slight nod. "But you've known that for a long time, haven't you?"

His words came out softly; the bitterness disappeared. "I don't remember what Hadamar is. But . . . I suppose I knew."

She turned away as a figure approached her from behind: a strange, looming figure, humanoid but not human, with flesh like lustrous metal and two blank ovals for eyes. In its thick arms it carried a pair of boots set upon folded fleece garment.

"Surina, give Wibben his tunic," Virgo said. "Wear these instead." She took the boots from the creature and set them in front of Surina. "These belonged to Dominic, but they're of the celestial realm. Wear them, and Tagua's servants won't be able to distinguish you from those who belong here."

Surina slipped off Wibben's cloak and handed to him, and pulled the fleece sweater over her head.

"Take this, too." Virgo held a curved horn in her hand. She extended it to Wibben. "Sometimes, a difficult journey is helped by music."

Wibben took the horn—a ram's horn with holes bored along one side, modified into a flute—and Surina pulled the woolen boots onto her feet. They were a little too long in the toes, but the fit wasn't bad.

"What about Hannah?" Surina asked. "I don't think I helped her at all."

"Hannah is beginning to move away from Tagua," Virgo replied.

"What do you mean?"

"I mean that even as we speak, Hannah is looking for you, Surina, to apologize for how she behaved. She's beginning to realize how Tagua is playing her—but she's only *just* beginning to realize. She will need a little more help, and she may be more willing to accept it from you now, but your safest choice at this point is to go home."

"Go home? But . . . ."

"Hydrus is open to you now," the queen told Hannah. "You can return through it at any time, but don't take these garments with you. Remove them when you arrive at Hydrus. And don't worry about Hannah. You can help her when you come back."

Surina raised her eyebrows. "When I come back *here*?"

"If you're willing. Hannah's own prejudices may have prevented her from taking you seriously, but she will learn. In the same way, you may have failed to see the importance of the water-lord's advice—but you will learn as well."

Surina thought back over her lengthy visit to Aquarius' temple. "What advice?"

"There are three physical conditions necessary to return to the starry realm. Aquarius divulged them to you."

"Three conditions?" Surina searched her memories, but didn't remember any such claim. "He did talk about the places where people can cross over. He said that Wupatki and Chavín have similar features. They have . . . ." She hesitated. "They were built with two contrasting types of stone. And he said something about . . . blowholes?" Surina looked questioningly at the queen. "Do we need to be underground?"

Virgo replied coolly: "Give a woman all the answers, and she will learn lethargy. Teach a woman how to think, and . . . ." The queen imitated Surina's questioning look.

"Never mind," Surina muttered. "I'll figure it out."

"Do you know what your goal should be, when you come back?" Virgo asked.

Surina exchanged an uneasy look with Wibben.

"You both play chess, do you not?" the queen asked them. "Tagua thinks the underworld very much like a game of chess. His goal is to take out the king, but first he will get rid of whoever stands in his way—whether it's a well-placed pawn or a knight, or even a queen. He collects and controls his pieces; he subdues knights and rooks who fall into this realm by persuading them to slay the guardians of the underworld. Those he sees as pawns, he persuades to solve a riddle. Tagua sees Hannah as a mere pawn—but even a pawn, if she moves all the way across the board, will become a queen."

Virgo unfolded her arms and took a step forward. As she moved from the shadow of the dome, her eyes seemed to glow with a subtle fierceness. "Tagua keeps Hannah in a position where she can be easily drained. He wants her to solve a riddle, but if she gains too much ground while she's solving it, he will knock her down." Virgo raised a hand, making a slashing motion. "To me, the journey through this realm is more like a game of Aasha: you must move through it safely, and accept its gifts, before returning to your own world. It isn't at all like chess. Tagua doesn't realize that he can't capture our king because our king is already dead." The queen gestured to Surina. "These garments are made from his flesh."

Surina looked down at the soft sweater. "Didn't these come from a ram?"

"So they did. This is a place of transformation. The king can be a ram as easily as he can be a man or any other thing, and he can live as easily as he dies. He gave up his body to protect Dominic and Hannah, and you as well. He gave it up again to teach Dominic a lesson. Any death, for a king of the underworld, is just a little death—and because there is no such thing as time for him or for me, he is always alive and always dead. Tagua isn't capable of understanding that because he fears death. It's the same reason he can't conquer the netherworld, but can easily conquer humans: humans tend to live in fear. They cling to their mortality even when it means losing something more vital."

Virgo stepped forward again, facing Surina. Her voice lowered as if to speak in confidence with her. "Tagua desires immortality and power. He is afraid to die, or even to change. That's why he has never dared to enter my domain: anyone who goes below must leave a part of themselves behind and become something new. Those who fear death become trapped and walk the underworld as the living dead. Tagua's plan is to finish learning the magic arts of the celestial realm and use them to re-establish his power on Earth. If he is set loose there, no one in your world will be able to meet the level of sorcery he has attained. Knowing that, what will you do? Will you risk what you have to stop him from leaving, or will you cling to what you have and flee back to your old life, and watch your world crumble?"

At those words, Surina felt a quiver of alarm. "What do you mean?" She studied the queen's face, but the woman's expression was calm, unreadable. "What do you want me to risk?"

"Nothing. You can't risk what you have, because you don't really have it. You just think you do."

The sense of alarm subsided. Surina felt, instead, a twinge of annoyance. Her tone became weary. "I'm a little tired of riddles. I prefer straightforwardness."

"If I had been straightforward with you about Victor, would you have learned the same lesson, in the same depth?"

Surina felt her eyes narrowing in another expression of tired irritation.

"A superficial understanding can't compare to one that is necessary for survival," Virgo continued. "Your involvement with Victor forced you to change. Furthermore, if you hadn't entangled yourself with Victor, you wouldn't be fit to help Hannah."

"Hannah won't listen to me."

"Even now, Hannah is meditating on your words. She will listen when she's ready. Transformation is often slow enough as to go unnoticed." Virgo turned to Wibben, her expression still tranquil, but with a visible fervor in her eyes. "Transformation is terrifying, yet inevitable. This world will keep pushing you toward whatever you need to become. The harder you resist, the harder the push."

"I haven't been resisting," Wibben replied. "I believe I have been trudging along patiently. Wouldn't you agree?"

"You may not trudge along patiently with your next task."

"Which is . . . ?"

"I am in need of a new scribe."

Surina looked at Wibben, saw caution in his face. "A scribe," he repeated. "In the underworld?"

"Any figure of the underworld must know transformation: what it is to rise from ignorance, fear, and hate; what it is to suffer a deserved punishment, and to acknowledge that it was deserved. What good is a scribe who has never made mistakes, or learned to overcome oneself? How would that scribe record the deeds of humans, write judgments, and resolve disputes? I would rather employ a scribe who can teach others to move from cowardice to bravery, and from selfishness to compassion, and to cultivate patience and trust. You are well suited for such a position, but it isn't one that can be filled by the ghost of a human. The scribe of the underworld must be a true phoenix."

Wibben paused, lowering his eyes. "The phoenix riddle," he murmured. "What do I need to do?"

"Go next to Ursa Major. A task awaits you there. You will find the vessel with which to transform, and Surina will find the vessel to bring her home." The queen moved back into the dome. She reached for the door, but addressed Surina and Wibben again before closing it. "Ursa Major and Ursa Minor are places in which to contemplate the center of this realm. From your perspectives on Earth, the heavens appear to revolve around Polaris in Ursa Minor."

Surina felt a small shock as she realized that the queen's face had changed. At first she thought it was the shadow of the doorway, but now she saw that the woman's skin had taken on a strange, grayish hue, and the flesh itself seemed rough and mottled—and where her hair had hung loose behind her shoulders, there now moved at least a dozen snakes. Surina stepped back, but remembered the perilous court behind her and stopped.

"Polaris is almost like the Lanzón at the center of the labyrinth," the queen continued, in the same gentle but serious voice. "What do you see, Surina, when you look at the Lanzón? What do the serpents represent?"

Surina didn't respond, but stood staring. As she watched, the queen changed again, ever so subtly. The mottled skin became more clearly defined, with dark lines and forms that Surina recognized as the carvings on the Lanzón. The queen now wore those same markings on her skin like a tattoo: snake figures arcing over her eyes, spirals across her forehead, a clownish outline curving around her lips. "To humans," Virgo said, "serpents often represent the underworld: challenges, fears, and death. The great birds represent flight toward the heavens and eternal life. When humans seek the center of the labyrinth, they often look only for birds and the heavens, but the underworld is inevitably there as well. When the figure on the Lanzón looks up at the cosmos, it must also look past the serpent." Virgo touched the space above her eye, where the figure of a snake trailed across. "The Lanzón, in fact, bears several snakes between its upward gaze and the stars that crown its head. Remember that as you go. All humans meet with challenges. Don't lose heart when you meet them, no matter how cruel. You must do the best you can in spite of them. Remember that on your journey."

The door closed abruptly. Surina stood there and stared, perplexed by the queen's strange and sudden departure.

"Well," Wibben began.

"Was that supposed to be helpful?" Surina muttered, picking up her shoes. She gave Wibben a weary look. "Do you know where to go?"

"Yes. Back through Leo . . . ." Wibben turned, and fell silent again. "Ah. That makes things less complicated."

Behind them, the court was once again in one piece. The stones were in place, as though they had never broken, and the plastic laundry basket was nowhere to be seen.

"So we don't have to basket-walk again?" Surina asked.

"I imagine not." Wibben gingerly placed a foot on the closest stone, testing his weight on it. "It seems solid. I'll go first."

"No, let's just go together. I'll feel like a jerk if I make you go first."

Surina and Wibben made a slow start, testing each stone before applying their full weight; but once they had crossed, Surina hurried her pace, once again feeling the press of time. Wibben directed her down the left-hand path, assuring her that the next realm was a short trek from Virgo.

"I feel like I just got cheated," Surina said as they walked. "She didn't even admit that she tricked me. I feel like I should have gotten an 'I'm sorry,' at least."

Wibben shrugged. "I'm not sure she has something to be sorry for."

"Is she too proud to apologize?"

"Too practical, I'd say."

"Honesty isn't practical? She *did* trick me. And now she's like, 'Well, I didn't lie; I didn't say you should marry him.' But she did mislead me. That's such a Victor thing to do: intentionally misleading someone, and then being like, 'Oh, I didn't lie. I just withheld some information.'"

"I think she acknowledged that, but she doesn't think it was wrong," Wibben replied.

"Well, whatever. Let's just get this over with." Surina peered at the landscape ahead. "I hope that was the last obstacle. I wouldn't mind another riddle at this point. If there are any more, though, they shouldn't be that dangerous. The other partner obstacles I did were pretty boring. Like, we had to carry a box of firewood up a hill, and then we had to bring it all the way back down."

"Careful what you say," Wibben cautioned her. "The things you're thinking about can manifest as obstacles in this place."

Ursa Major was a mostly empty realm, flat and featureless and solemn. Surina and Wibben had just crossed the threshold when they saw a lone object in the distance. On closer observance they saw that it was a gilded table, several feet in length. Winged figures comprised the legs, each with blank eyes, serene faces, and cat-like paws that reached up to support the platform. Surina was at once reminded of the stone table at Phoenix. This platform also stood low, so that she could see writing engraved into the top—but the message was obscured by a large wooden box.

"Should we move this?" she asked. "It looks like there's a riddle underneath."

Wibben stood on one end and pulled on the corners. "Push it to your left. It's heavy," he warned, as the box began to edge from the table.

They maneuvered the box onto the ground. Surina scrutinized the interior and found it unremarkable, no more than an empty crate, except for a few small details. A short wooden tube, about two inches in length, extended from one end of the box; there were other tubes, too, fixed along the along the sides of the box near the bottom, with the openings facing upright rather than outward.

The other detail was a small canvas sheet, rolled up and lying in a corner of the box. Wibben picked it up and unrolled it.

"It's a map," he said. "Nothing to solve. It just shows us where to go next: back to Eridanus." He pointed at the figure of a lion on the map. A dotted trail led from Ursa Major back to the lion, into its belly and curving out through its mouth, and then making a straight route to the river.

Surina turned her attention to the riddle on the table:

Mizar and Alcor move together;
hero twins work side by side,
gain new life through transformation,
slain by the great star who guides.
Strive to heave the ark afloat,
through River Styx to funeral pyre;
quake no more at fear of death,
but live through a euphonic fire.

"Mizar and Alcor," Surina murmured.

Wibben came to stand beside her. "They're stars in the constellation—a double star, from our perspective on Earth. There's an Arab myth in which the constellation's quadrangle is a coffin, and the trailing stars represent a funeral procession. Mizar and Alcor are part of the procession." Wibben studied the words again and spoke quietly: "Quake no more at fear of death . . . ."

Surina walked around the base, leaning closer to scrutinize the inscriptions. "This is almost the same table we saw at Phoenix. It's just missing the bird."

He nodded. "It's a bier for a coffin."

"Is this a coffin? I thought maybe we were supposed

to use it as our boat." She ran her fingers lightly along the wood. "It's too small and angular for a boat, but the riddle says we have to bring an ark to the River Styx."

"Right. To the funeral pyre. We'll have to float it upriver to the pyre at Phoenix."

Surina hesitated, looking at Wibben over the top of the bier. "You think so?"

"Oh, I know so," he replied dryly. "Every riddle I've seen so far has been leading up to this."

She looked past him, at the distant bank. "Upriver, on the same river?"

"Yes, the same."

"How, when there aren't any oars?"

Wibben didn't seem to hear the question. "I'm afraid that when we get there, I will actually have to burn on the pyre," he said. He spoke in a flat tone, without looking at Surina.

"You mean, you think it's *your* coffin? It can't be. It's too short."

"It seems that way now," he replied, "but when we get there, it will fit and make sense. It always does. There was a woman who came through here before you, and walked some distance with me. When she found out I was exploring for the Nazis, she warned me that I was going to burn in hell. Maybe this is what she meant."

The route from Ursa Major to Eridanus provided an easy stretch of terrain. Instead of steep drops, molten streams, and perplexing riddles, Surina and Wibben passed over flat ground and gained ready entrance into the adjoining realms. At Leo, they found an open gate at the left-hand end of the court, near the mouth of the cobbled-stone lion. They passed through it without incident. A well-worn path led them through another gate and between the realms of Gemini and Canis Minor, and then to Eridanus, by itself presenting no challenge—but it was a difficult trek for two people carrying a coffin between them.

Halfway past Canis Minor they switched places, Surina picking up the front end of the box, and Wibben taking the rear. She had hardly begun walking when she noticed something on the ground ahead. A small, crumpled object stood out against the empty landscape. As she drew close, she came to a sudden stop.

A small thump sounded behind her; Wibben had likely run into the coffin.

"What's the matter?" he asked.

"I think I just found Hannah's fleece thing. Let's put the box down."

Slowly, Surina bent her knees and lowered the coffin. Wibben came around to her side and helped her ease the burden onto the ground.

"Look." Hannah picked up the dusty nightgown, giving it a light shake. "I'm sure this is it. What is it doing out here?"

Wibben looked out at the landscape ahead of them. "Let's keep going. We're close to the river."

Surina looked down at the fleece gown, at its stains and worn spots, at the embedded grains of dirt from the path below, and remembered the sense of wonder she'd felt when the broken owlet revived and took flight. The tattered gown didn't seem capable of magic now. In fact, the coffin seemed a fitting place for it. Surina folded the garment and lowered it into the casket, laying it on top of her shoes.

As they resumed walking, a movement caught her eye: a figure standing alone on the plains to her right, presumably a small dog, but hairless and with a strange purple sheen. The creature looked in Surina's direction and stood still. "Do you see that?" she asked. "Over in

Canis Minor. It looks like a dog.”

"Don’t worry,” Wibben replied. "It won’t bother us.”

The horizon broke up ahead, interrupted by the sight of the river; the water meandered in their direction and then seemed to vanish. "We’re almost there, Wibben,” Surina said. "I can see the Eridanus.”

The gently flowing water made almost no sound, but as she came closer, Surina heard soothing trickles and gurgles where it rushed up against solid ground. The river did, indeed, disappear into a rocky chasm below, and Surina eyed it with caution. "Let’s go upstream a little,” she said. "The river goes underground right here. I don’t want to get sucked in.”

As she short-stepped along the river, Surina listened to the serene sounds of the flowing water and assured herself that she was one step closer to going home—and then remembered that she still didn’t know what to do next. Her fingers had begun to ache from gripping the box, and she was about to call out to Wibben when a strange, pillar-like object rose up from the middle of the river, and the gentle soundscape was interrupted by a familiar voice.

"My lady Hannah’s servant!”

Surina came to an abrupt halt. The wooden box slammed into her back, jostling her another step forward. A matching thump sounded on Wibben’s end.

Piscis floated in the water, lightly bobbing as it swam against the slow current. "Greetings!” it called.

Surina swore under her breath. Then she yelled: "I don’t have the Orion tokens. I don’t have the boat, either.”

"I am aware of it!” the creature replied cheerfully.

At the back of the coffin, Wibben asked: "Who is it?”

Surina turned her head, answering in a low voice. "It’s some kind of fish creature from Aquarius.”

"The boat of the heavens, I’m afraid, has been severely damaged,” Piscis informed Surina. "It lies scattered across the celestial realms." The creature raised its hands, holding aloft an oar and a large, curved section of wood. "These two fragments fell into the Eridanus."

Wibben and Surina finished lowering the box to the ground. "What do you mean," Surina said, keeping her gaze fixed on the merman. "What happened to Hannah? Wasn't she in the boat?"

"My lady Hannah is resting safely in another realm. She will recover with the nourishment of sleep, but only the fleece of Aries can revive the boat of the heavens."

Surina approached the bank. She stood with her hands on her hips, looking at the items in Piscis' hands. "Tell you what: I'll trade you the fleece for that oar."

Piscis glanced at the oar, then at the box that lay at Wibben's feet. "And what are you going to do with one oar?" the creature asked, with the slightest hint of mockery. "Are you planning to row that wooden box upriver?"

"Yes."

"Have you any idea how long that will take? You wouldn't make it back to Beta Hydri in time to get through the portal. You'll be trapped here for the next two hundred and sixty years."

"Two hundred and . . . are you serious?"

"Quite."

Surina was silent for a moment, overcome with a strange sensation of unreality—a sensation laced with panic and regret. "Do you have a better suggestion?" she asked.

"My suggestion is that you use the fleece to fix the boat, and place your box inside of the boat, and place yourselves inside of the box. In taking the boat back to Aquarius, my assistants and I will also be transporting you and your box. Do we have an arrangement?"

Surina looked back at Wibben, who nodded silently.

"Deal," she said. "As long as you don't go back on your word this time."

"I didn't go back on my word. Aquarius—"

"I'm not interested," Surina interrupted, beckoning the merman closer. "Bring the wood over here."

Piscis moved toward the bank, dragging the debris with him. Surina and Wibben pulled the section of wood onto the bank, turning it with the outside facing up. Surina hoped to see the image of the bird there, but she only saw what looked like a section of the bird's wing. "I think we got the side of the boat," she said, as she draped the nightgown across the wood. "How is this going to work, when . . . ."

She trailed off as the ground began to tremble under her feet. Surina stepped back a few paces, and then a few more, as the river bank heaved. Some strange object began to push up through the soil—a long, dark, mottled object, and then a shard of something white, and then a multitude of objects of varying form and color, all melding together around the broken wood. The shapes rose, merged, and fused until they had formed the shape of a boat, with the darker objects fused to the wood, and the lighter-colored objects forming the rim and oars.

Surina and Wibben waited until the mutation had stopped, and then approached with trepidation.

"Hurry," Piscis advised them. "You don't have much time."

The two worked together to flip the boat over, and then maneuvered the wooden box into it. They found that it fit perfectly between the seats. When they had shoved the craft back into the water, Wibben climbed inside first, testing it to make sure it would stay afloat; then he turned and extended a hand to help Surina.

"Leave the fleece," Piscis said, as Surina bent to pick up the nightgown.

She hesitated. "Leave it? But . . . we might need it."

"Perhaps," Piscis replied coolly, "what you need is to stop taking things that don't belong to you."

Surina restrained a sigh and left the gown on the river bank. She stepped carefully into the boat, one hand holding Wibben's, and the other gripping the edge of the boat. "What is this?" she asked. "The stuff that came from out of the ground—what is it?"

"Volcanic rock," Piscis replied, "on the bottom."

Surina looked at the white and cream-colored material beneath her fingers. "And what about the rest of it?"

"Mostly bones."

She withdrew her hand. "Oh . . . lovely. We get to ride in a coffin made of skeletons."

It was only after the boat was far upstream, and docked in its original place at Acamar, that Hannah found the fleece nightgown beside the Eridanus. It caught her eye just as she landed on the bank. She picked it up and examined it, rubbed her fingers against the soft fabric, and puzzled over how it had gotten there.

The gown was a welcome sight, but it was not what she had hoped to find. Virgo had promised to create another statue. There was no such statue to be seen, and so Hannah sat down at the river's end with the fleece draped across her knees and tried to solve the puzzle of what she had done wrong. She had found most of the Orion tokens scattered along the ground between Leo and Hydra, mixed in with debris from the chariot, but after scouring the land, she had been unable to locate Alnitak and Saiph—so she did the best she could with what she had.

Hannah arranged the tokens with Betelgeuse at the top, and below that, Bellatrix. Where Orion's belt would be, she placed Mintaka and Alnilam, and below that was

Rigel. It was the same arrangement she'd used before, and it looked right, but she supposed she'd made some small mistake, like switching the token for Orion's right foot with the left.

Hannah was still puzzling over her mistake when she realized she wasn't alone. A streak of white flashed in the corner of her eye, and she looked up to see Virgo standing beside her, dressed in a simple white drape and watching her silently.

"You scared me," Hannah said, though she didn't feel particularly startled. Though her respite in Fornax had refreshed her, she still maintained a weighty gloom that seemed to mute her other feelings.

"Have you solved the imbalance?" Virgo asked.

"I can't find Alnitak and Saiph," Hannah replied. "But I'm trying to figure out what I did wrong." She gave Virgo a hesitant but hopeful look. "Are you making another statue?"

"I am making another Orion even as we speak."

"I really want to do it right this time," Hannah said. "I need to, in order to solve the sun gate."

The queen looked at her with a touch of pity. "You will never solve the sun gate riddle, Hannah."

Hannah sat and stared up at the queen, at her simple but regal form, at her serious brown eyes, and tried to reconcile the queen's promises with what she had just said. *You will never solve the sun gate riddle.* Never solving the riddle—that meant death. No, it meant a fate worse than death: an eternity wandering the celestial realms as an enslaved demon-child, aimless and miserable, like all the others who served Tagua. "But . . . what about all the things you said to me?"

"You don't need to solve that riddle. Someone else has already solved it. Other people know the solution."

Again, Hannah took a moment to process the queen's

words. *Someone can open the gate—it just isn't going to be me.* "What other people?" she asked.

"Would it surprise you to know that Surina can open the sun gate?"

This time, Hannah's silence wasn't introspective. She was too surprised for that, and simply looked at the queen in confused astonishment—and then the unfairness of it began to sink in. Why should Surina be the one to open the sun gate, when she had hardly made any effort?

"What upsets you the most?" the queen asked, sensing her thoughts. "That you can't free Tagua, or that you yourself can't solve the riddle? Or maybe that Surina is the one who knows it?"

Hannah lowered her eyes, as if by shielding her gaze, she could hide her thoughts from the queen.

"Tagua uses and stomps on you," the queen said gently. "Surina encourages and helps you. Why, then, do you resent Surina and seek Tagua's approval?"

Hannah thought she felt her face flushing. "I know what I did was wrong. I tried to find her so I could set things right, but . . . ."

"You can set things right with her later. Surina has just left the celestial realm, so don't seek her now. Finish this puzzle first." The queen gestured to the tokens that lay on the ground in front of Hannah.

"But even if I figure it out," Hannah said, "I still don't have two of the pieces. I don't know where to look for them."

"Whenever I have a need for something," the queen said, "I create it." She stepped forward, to the edge of the river bank, and knelt there. With one hand she reached over the edge of the bank and scooped up a handful of soil, and then came and sat beside Hannah. "The river bank is rich in clay," she said. "It's a perfect sculpting material." Virgo shaped the soil into a cake and placed it on the ground, and then pounded it flat with her fist. She took the Rigel token and placed in on the clay, and with a fingertip she traced around the token, and then plunged her finger in to remove the extra clay from around the edges.

"There," Virgo said, removing the Rigel token. With her fingertip, she drew a figure in the middle of the clay: a rough-looking foot, complete with an ankle and a big toe. "That's supposed to be a foot," she explained.

Hannah looked at the sand-mottled clay disc with an air of disbelief and a twinge of annoyance. "You're saying I can just use this, instead of the pieces I got from Aquarius?"

"The object that you place into Orion isn't important," the queen replied. "It only matters how you place it. The actual pieces are inside of you, and you are the puzzle. What is more important: putting a puzzle piece into a slot, or striving to achieve your own Meissa, the crown star of the human soul? The missing pieces are calling to you from within. Sit here and contemplate these symbols, and think about what it is inside of you that made you leave Surina behind and continue to Orion alone. Figure yourself out first, and those things I promised you will come to pass."

11: Phoenix

Surina shifted closer to the right side of the boat. She faced the rear, and from where she sat, she had caught frequent glimpses of Piscis' unblinking eyes and perpetually smiling mouth as the creature helped propel the boat upstream. Surina tried to position herself so that Wibben sat between her and the merman, but no matter where she moved, Piscis kept sidling back into view.

The journey back toward Aquarius had been easy thus far. The gates, to Surina's surprise, opened on their own as the boat approached. Even the clashing gates had stopped slamming together, and the boat glided through unassailed; the underwater creatures no longer threatened to topple the boat, but instead seemed to be helping it along. Surina couldn't see them in the dark waters, but she felt their movements beneath the boat and saw an occasional splash when some underwater creature began to break the surface.

Wibben talked for much of the journey, detailing some of his experiences in constellations that Surina hadn't visited—places like Draco, Lyra, and Ophiuchus, where Hannah was supposedly heading next. Surina listened inattentively. As the river led them into the dark caverns near the Aquarius realm, she finally blurted out the question that kept nagging at her: "Wibben, why did you do those things?"

He gave her a questioning look. "What things? Trying to solve the puzzles?"

"No. Why did you go exploring for the Nazis? I want
to know why. You don't seem like an evil person, and
maybe it's because you've changed since then, but I want
to know how you could have supported a group that
hunted and killed people. *Innocent* people."

Wibben lowered his eyes. He stared for some time at
the bottom of the boat, and then began to speak hesitantly.
"When I first came here, one of the things I was looking
for was the cauldron of Dagda."

"That's not what I'm asking," Surina replied.

"I know, but I will get around to it. Dagda is a
mythical king of the Aryans. He supposedly had a mace
that could destroy people with one end, and bring them
back to life with the other. He also had a pair of magic
swine; one was always being killed while the other was
always growing. He had a harp that played the harmonies
of the heavens; it could control the elements, the seasons,
and human emotions, and even the outcome of battles. A
battle-scarred harp—that was how I heard it described.
And he had a magic cauldron that never ran empty, and
that satisfied everyone who drank from it. The people in
my society believed in these things and looked for them,
especially the cauldron, because it was one of the four
gifts from the otherworld spirits." He cast Surina a grave,
probing look. "You understand what I mean? We thought
that we could find an actual harp that we could play
during a battle, to ensure our victory. We were looking for
a magic sword, and a magic wand, and a magic cauldron,
that would help us rule over humanity."

"Uh-huh." Surina's tone rang of boredom. "Am I
supposed to be surprised? It doesn't surprise me,
considering your other stupid beliefs."

"I found three of those instruments here in the
celestial realm: the stone, the sword, and the cauldron. I
found the mace and the swine, too. Of course, they

weren't what I expected." Wibben paused. "Neither are the people I would have persecuted, if I had lived. I know that now because this place has forced me to walk with so many of them."

"People you *did* persecute," Surina said. "Not 'would have.'"

"My cauldron of Dagda is Cetus' belly. When I was inside . . . well, it's a lot to explain. I've changed a lot since coming to this place, but I'm still changing. Cetus places you alone in the dark with nothing but a mirror; it forces you to face yourself. It destroyed parts of me and brought other parts to life. It killed off certain ideas and caused other ones to grow. It wasn't a magic cauldron that fed my ego and helped me conquer other people; it helped me conquer myself. So, what I'm saying is, I did those things because I was ignorant—and vain. I wanted to be special. I didn't think about the people being persecuted because I didn't need to. I was busy exploring and thinking about myself."

Surina's attention shifted to the back of the boat, where Piscis seemed to stare at her with one bulging eye. She shifted back toward the middle of the bench.

"I don't really remember everything from back then," Wibben continued, "but there are some things that stand out. I remember how it felt to be rejected. In Germany, there was a woman who I wanted to marry. I still remember what she looked like. She had light blond hair that was always done up in a stylish way, and red lips, and intense eyes. We went on a few dates, and I told my friends that I was going to marry her—but she broke it off. I asked why, and she said . . . I don't know her exact words, but she basically said that I was self-centered and condescending. I still remember the look on her face as she said it. I was hurt, but she was very calm and matter-of-fact, as though she didn't feel anything at all about breaking up with me. I was angry about it for a long time. It never occurred to me to think about what she said. At the time, I felt that if I wanted her, then I was entitled to her, and there was nothing about me that needed to change. But I was condescending toward women because I was the man, and I assumed I was more important. That's probably why I was always rejected by the women I liked. Afterwards, whenever I happened to see that woman, I was so angry that I sometimes imagined smashing her face in." He paused. "I still hated her when I died. I only knew her for a few weeks. I can't remember my own parents' names, but I never forgot how that woman made me feel."

Surina was silent.

"In this realm, I had to learn humility," Wibben said. "Some of the puzzles in this place perpetuate the idea that humans need to find a balance between humility and leadership. I think that's one of the ideas that Hannah is struggling with now. Hannah has also changed because of this place, but she's becoming lesser. When she first came here, she was outspoken and energetic. She never hesitated to confront me with her opinions. But then she started to follow Tagua, who doesn't deserve to be followed."

"Yeah, I got that," Surina said. "She cares about him. Intensely."

"I watched her become quieter and quieter. She started apologizing to him constantly. She *rushes* to apologize." Wibben's pale blue eyes were fixed on Surina, his tone one of grave concern. "He's keeping her prisoner, and draining the life from her, but she's apologizing. When I came here, I had to learn humility and compassion—but Hannah needs the opposite lesson. She was already humble. Now she's letting Tagua, who has no humility or compassion, grind her down into nothing." He looked past

Surina and added: "We're here."

Surina turned to look at the riverbank. The dock was nowhere in sight, but Surina saw the broken edges of the bank and remembered how she had destroyed the dock with the sonic cannon. That moment seemed so long ago. It made her wonder, with some anxiety, how much time had passed on Earth.

Piscis and his underwater crew didn't stop, but continued on until the boat had passed beyond the temple of Aquarius, to a spot where Surina and Wibben would have a wide section of dry bank to walk on. "I will part ways with you here," Piscis said.

Surina climbed out first and tried to help lift the wooden casket from its place. She managed to drag the box onto land, and then helped Wibben out of the boat. He had hardly set foot on dry ground when Piscis bid them good-bye. "The boat of the heavens is soon to be back in its proper place," the creature announced, and turned the calm side of its face toward Surina. "If you should need it again, don't hesitate to ask. I'm certain the water-lord Aquarius would enjoy another round of games."

Surina had nothing but sarcastic comments to make in response, but didn't want to say such things aloud—so she nodded and said, "So long," and then she and Wibben picked up the wooden box and began the trek to Phoenix.

Conversation, while carrying the box, was difficult. The two had to focus on keeping a secure grip and a steady pace, and so they walked mostly in silence, though Surina heard Wibben humming from time to time. At Phoenix they slid the casket onto the bier, and then Wibben climbed up onto the far end of the platform. He tossed Surina's shoes to her and stood looking down into the coffin. "I think I know what to do," he said.

He reached beneath his tunic and pulled out the horn

flute. Surina hadn't realized until then that he'd had the flute tucked into his underwear. She was about to make a comment about the hygienic quandaries of such a maneuver, but Wibben surprised her by climbing into the coffin and fitting the flute into the hole at the far end.

"Euphonic fire," he said with a wry grin, and put his lips to the flute.

"Wait," Surina said.

"Don't worry. I won't play yet." Wibben climbed back out of the coffin and down from the bier. "Let's get you safely home first."

Surina's gaze fell to the bier. Though the inscription was now hidden from view, she could still see part of the bird that had been carved into the surface; its head peeked out from beneath the casket, pointing toward the dark river. Surina assured herself that the image wasn't one of death, but of transformation.

She pulled off the boots and put her own shoes back on, and folded the wool sweater on top of the boots. "There," she said, and reluctantly added: "I better go."

"It's possible that I'll see you again," Wibben said, gazing toward Hydrus. From where they stood, they could see the massive sculpture that made up the fanged, snake-tongued gate. With its enormous facade and dripping stalactites, it struck Surina as a majestic sight. "But it's unlikely," Wibben continued. "I don't really know what I'll become, but I will be in the underworld, with Virgo. So, this is good-bye. I hope that you have better luck when you return."

Surina was trying to think of something to say when he added: "You know . . . the sun disc looks a lot like the chromatic scale. A ring within a ring."

"The sun disc? The one Hannah is trying to figure out?"

"Yes. The one that can release Tagua." Wibben turned

to Surina, his eyes serious and sad. "Tagua must never be released into our world," he said quietly. "We don't have the means to deal with an evil like him. You understand that, don't you?"

"I'll take your word for it."

"You must." Wibben took a step closer, his voice nearing a whisper. "Hannah pities him. She cares for him, and she'll release him out of desperation. You mustn't let that happen. Even Dominic, I'm afraid, would risk releasing Tagua in order to save Hannah."

"So how do we get her out without releasing him?"

"I don't know the answer to that," he admitted. "Keep solving the puzzles of this realm, and you might find the answer—though I think Hannah is meant to discover that answer. In the meantime, you mustn't open the gate when there is any chance of Tagua passing through it. Can you promise me that?"

Surina gazed into Wibben's pale eyes, seeing some secret burden there.

"It would be better for Hannah to waste away here than to unleash Tagua," Wibben insisted. "He has been imprisoned here for a reason. Can you promise you won't risk releasing him?"

"Yes," Surina said.

"Promise it."

"I promise."

He looked away, thoughtfully, and nodded. "One more thing: Please forgive me."

Surina hesitated.

"I understand if you can't," Wibben said.

"I'll try. Wibben . . . ."

"What?"

Surina faltered. At a loss for words, she stepped forward and hugged him instead—gently, sensing the frailty of his thin body.

"That's good enough," he said. "Surina . . . before I go, there's something you need to know."

Wibben's lips were close to her ear. Almost inaudibly, he began to whisper. She stood still and listened.

When he was finished, Wibben backed away. "Don't forget your promise," he said.

"Wait," she said.

He shook his head. "There's no time. Can you hear it?" He gestured to Hydrus. "Only two notes left. You need to go now, before Hydrus wakes up. If you don't make it, I'll play the flute, and hope that the music keeps Hydrus asleep just long enough."

"But, what about you? We need you. What if I can't—"

Wibben shook his head more fervently. "Don't say anything," he interrupted in a low voice, looking toward the river. "Go now. You're in danger."

Surina followed his gaze. She saw nothing out of place. "But . . . ."

"You need to go *now*, Surina." He leaned closer and whispered: "Tagua's spies are coming for you."

As if to lend urgency to his warnings, one of the remaining tones dropped out. Only one prolonged note continued to drone from the water flutes, and Surina backed away from Wibben—reluctantly, but hurriedly.

Wibben climbed onto the bier. He sat down inside the coffin and placed his lips to the flute.

Surina turned away before he began to play. She ran toward Hydrus as the first note mingled with the sound of the water flute.

A movement at the riverbank caught her attention. Something was emerging from the water: a human head, and then shoulders and a skinny body, the body of a young boy. He climbed onto the bank, first one knee, and then the other, his hands splayed in front of him. The boy's skin was a dark blue, vaguely luminescent. His dark hair dripped river water into his eyes, and those eyes were dark and featureless, two empty voids that stared directly at Surina.

Another figure began to climb onto the bank beside him. Surina ran faster.

At Hydrus she glanced back at Wibben. She saw more of them, then: blue children, some dressed in tunics, some hardly dressed at all. They were coming not just for her, but for the bier where Wibben sat in a burst of blue and gold fire. The flames spurted upward from the tubes in the coffin, leaping high above Wibben's head and igniting the casket in which he sat. It seemed a horrifying contrast: the soothing, beautiful sound of the music resounding through the box, and the sight of Wibben's gaunt face disappearing behind a curtain of flame.

A sudden, warm wind blew onto the side of Surina's face. She looked at Hydrus, at the serpent-like cavern that supposedly would lead her home. The snake's mouth seemed to move; it almost seemed to be closing.

The last water flute dropped into silence.

Surina put on another burst of speed, slipping once on a wet stone, but catching herself and hurtling through the opening. Another glance back showed her how close she had come to the strange creatures behind her. Two of them stood just at the threshold, staring in at her, but seemingly unwilling to enter—and then a loud hiss filled the tunnel, and the serpent's mouth snapped shut.

After Surina disappeared from their view, the child-like beings lurked around the charred ruins, sniffing at the coals and shielding their eyes from the lingering haze of smoke. A heap of fine ash sat in the center of the bier. Nothing remained that had any semblance of a man, and the creatures quickly gave up, wandering into other realms as Hydrus woke from its long sleep, retreating far from its fierce eyes and enormous fanged mouth—but if they had looked more closely, within those ashes they would have found an egg.

12: Chavín

Surina scrambled through the dark, her arms stretched at her sides to keep track of the stone walls. She avoided running into them, but she crashed anyway, falling to her hands and knees as her foot caught on a jutting rock. She hesitated there, with her hands splayed on the cool ground, and chanced a look behind her. A vague light glowed in the distance, but nothing more; no shadow pursued her, and the growling, wakening sounds of Hydrus had ceased.

She got to her feet, slowly making her way forward. As another light appeared ahead, Surina breathed a sigh of deeply felt relief. A closer look assured her that the light streamed from an opening above the tunnel. The ceiling angled downward as Surina approached, so that she had to walk at a low stoop—and then she seemed to be crouching at the edge of Earth, gazing up through the opening. She was greeted by at a glimpse of sunset-streaked blue sky and the sound of Hank's voice: "They're not looking. You can come up now."

Surina reached up, felt green grass under her fingers as she clutched the edge of the pit. Her arms trembled as she heaved herself up and onto the ground.

Light was all around her—light, grass, the setting sun, and so many other things she'd missed about this world.

Hank was entreating her to hurry, beckoning her back to the tourist path. She stood shakily and went to the temple steps, leaning against the dark pillar.

"Hey, hey, no touching," Hank reminded her.

Surina quickly withdrew. "Sorry." She lowered herself onto the stone step, tilting her head back and closing her eyes.

"You all right?" Hank asked. "It looks like you fell down."

Surina waited a few seconds before responding. She opened her eyes to see Hank peering down at her. A faint line of concern showed in his brow, and the same look was written in his pale blue eyes. Surina studied the details of his face, the sun-worn skin and the crinkles at the edges of his eyes. She had missed that, she realized: The faces of people she knew.

"I'm fine," she said. "Where's Dominic?"

"He's at the Lanzón. Nemcio went in too. See anything interesting down there?"

"Uh . . . no. But I'm not feeling that great. I think it's something I ate. I'm going to get Dominic and head back." She got to her feet again with an air of weariness. "We can see the temple again tomorrow."

Surina tried to hurry, but every part of her wanted to slow down. She was vaguely aware of a strange, heavy feeling that meandered through her like a thick mist, collecting in her chest and creating a pressure behind her eyes—and she realized that she wanted to weep.

Dominic and Nemcio were at the central chamber, looking through on the metal gate at the stone figure beyond. Surina stopped in the shadow of the tunnel and followed their gaze. She was already familiar with the Lanzón; she had studied its carvings countless times, its meandering serpents and spirals and stylized face, but the pillar no longer looked the way it once had. Where Surina had once seen snake hair, she now saw wisdom gleaned from the underworld. Where a serpent curved around the eye, an upward-looking eye that gazed up into spiral forms, she no longer saw a snake-eyebrow, but the symbol of one who can see the secrets of the underworld by looking up at the stars. Two small serpents falling from the eye looked suddenly like teardrops; they reminded Surina of Wibben weeping over his sister, and they called her focus back to her own inexplicable feeling of grief.

"Dominic," she said.

He half-turned, giving her the casual glance of someone who had just seen her a minute ago—but Surina felt the relief of a friend who had been estranged for months, and had to suppress the urge to hug him.

"Hi," he began, and started to say more, but Surina interrupted him.

"Let's go back to the hotel," she said.

He looked at her in puzzlement. "What? Why?"

She came closer, lowering her voice. "I already found her. I found Hannah."

Dominic stared. His gaze flicked to the tunnel behind Surina. "You already found her . . . just now?"

She nodded. "Yeah. I went in, and it's over. We have to go back—back home to Flagstaff. I'll explain everything at the hotel, okay?" She looked at Nemcio and forced a smile, explaining to him in Spanish that she didn't feel well and wanted to rest. As she spoke, she pulled on Dominic's arm, coaxing him through the tunnel.

"No need to drag me," he said.

"Sorry." She released him and tried to calm herself. Surina continued making excuses to Nemcio, and then to Hank, who both confirmed that she looked unwell.

"Probably that musty tunnel," Hank said. "Maybe some fumes that got trapped in there. That happens sometimes in places like that."

"So I've heard," Surina replied.

Dominic let her lead the way back to the hotel. "What happened?" he asked, when Hank was out of earshot.

"A lot," she said. "I'll tell you about it when we get to

the room. I need to sit down."

They went back to the little concrete-walled hotel and trudged up the stairs to their second-floor room. As soon as the door closed behind them, Surina's face became pained.

"What happened?" Dominic asked. "You really got in?"

"Wibben died."

"Wibben? Oh . . . ."

"Well, I think he's dead. Sort of." Surina wiped away a tear. "I think he might have become some kind of . . . celestial creature."

"What about Hannah?"

"Oh . . . ." Surina went to the bed and sat down, sighing deeply. "I think she was worried that Tagua would choose me to open the sun gate instead of her. She was supposed to solve a riddle at Orion, and then at Ophiuchus. I was helping her, but she ran off without me, and . . . I'm not sure what happened. She didn't make it to Ophiuchus. We can go back and help her," she added quickly, seeing Dominic's look of alarm. "The queen said so. But we have to go back to Wupatki in order to get back inside."

"What queen? The one at Virgo?"

"Yes, her."

Dominic leaned back against his own bed. His gaze dropped to the floor. He was quiet for a few moments, and then he looked at Surina sharply. "So we're done here. You're sure about that?"

Surina nodded. "Yeah."

"All right. If you're sure, we can leave in the morning." Dominic heaved himself onto the mattress and sat facing her. "You look tired. Can you stay awake for a while?"

"Sure."

"Tell me everything that happened."

In the morning, Surina and Dominic had a quick
breakfast with Nemcio and Pajarilla, and then packed
their things into the rental car. Surina yawned as she got
behind the wheel. She had stayed up late, telling Dominic
about her numerous adventures and trying to write down
every crucial detail that came to mind.

"Did you sleep at all?" Dominic asked her.

"A little," she said. "But I kept remembering things
that I needed to write down." She paused. "And . . . I kept
thinking about Wibben, and how much he bothered me."

"You mean, because of what he told you."

"Yeah." Surina had told Dominic all about Wibben's
revelation, and about her feelings of anger and revulsion.
"I don't really resent him that much now, but I feel like I
should. You know what I mean? When innocent people
are overpowered and abused, and even being killed, you
have a simple choice: You can help to harm them, or you
can choose not to. Some people choose harm. Even if it
was a long time ago, and even if they say, 'It was a
mistake and I know better now,' they're still the kind of
person who made that choice."

Dominic mulled over that. "Is he, though? If Wibben
was faced with the same situation now, and didn't know
what the outcome would be, do you think he would still
make the same choice?"

"I don't know. He doesn't seem like he would, but . . .
if he was back here, in this world . . . ." She hesitated,
remembering Wibben's last conversation with her. "No. I
guess he wouldn't." Surina pulled her seat belt into place
and grabbed the clutch. "I'm only going to drive for a
little while. We can stop at the lagoon, and I'll try to take
a nap. I don't want to doze off and drift over the cliff."

At the edge of town, they drove past a group of people

standing on the roadside. They were peering over the edge of the road, at the long drop that had frightened Dominic on the way into town. Surina stopped the car and rolled down the window, calling to one of the onlookers in Spanish.

After a minute of chatter she gave Dominic a grim look. "A car went over the cliff. They can't see it, but they're waiting to see if someone crawls up."

"Fat chance of that," Dominic replied.

"I know." Surina reached for the gear shift, but hesitated.

"Don't tell me," Dominic said. "You forgot how to drive downhill with a stick shift."

"No, it isn't that." She gazed out the window, her face still pained. Her voice was soft; Dominic could hear the sadness in it. "A few hours ago, even though I didn't bring Hannah home, everything still seemed to fit and make sense—but now I'm back in the real world, and everything seems so random. Nothing makes sense."

He followed her gaze for some time. "Well, not to sound like a jerk, but we're all going to die at some point."

Surina turned to look at him, but didn't respond.

"I just . . . I don't want you to dismiss everything that happened here," he added.

"I won't." She gazed toward the cliff again. "Anyway, I guess things don't need to make sense." She paused. "Do you know that passage from the book of Job . . . something like, do you know how to bring the constellations into place at the right time, and . . . there's something about the Pleideas, and Orion, and the bear constellation . . . ."

"I was never much of a Bible man."

"Well, I guess I don't know the verse either. But the point is, I don't try to figure out why things happen a certain way, because I can't comprehend the workings of the universe. I just do the best I can while I'm still here." She grabbed the gear shift and sighed. "Ready for another seven hours of Spanish polka?"

13: Wupatki

Back in Flagstaff, Surina racked her brain for the solution to one riddle: How to get back into the realm of constellations.

Her mind often drifted from the question as she remembered the words that Wibben had whispered in her ear. He hadn't clued her in on how to return; instead, he had given her a key to helping Hannah come home. Surina couldn't help fixating on his words, even though it seemed a waste to focus on them now, when Surina didn't know how to reach Hannah in the first place.

Both Aquarius and Virgo had given her hints; Virgo had mentioned three conditions necessary for entering the dimension, and Surina was sure that it had something to do with the water-lord's dissertation on the geology of Wupatki and Chavín. Two of the conditions surely lied in the properties of the stones he had talked about. Surina hadn't understood all of what he'd said, but it seemed to her that in order to ascend to the stars, she needed to know what was beneath the earth.

Surina gathered some information and brought it to the record shop where Dominic worked. She found him behind the cash register, ringing up an expensive vinyl album and an over-sized wall poster. She waited for the customer to leave, and then hurried over to Dominic, slapping a packet of paper on the counter in front of him.

"So," she said, forgetting to greet him, "there's a guy named Greg Yazzie who wrote a pretty extensive report on the geology of Wupatki, and I think he could help us. I looked him up, and he's local. Look—here's a photo of him. He was at the last city council meeting on land rights."

Dominic leaned forward, scrutinizing the first page. He pointed to the photo at the top. "This one? Shoulder-length hair, glasses?"

"That's him."

"He looks like a stoner."

Surina's shoulders slumped. She looked at Dominic without amusement.

"Not that it's a problem," Dominic added. "He looks like an *intellectual* smoker. Does he know what he's talking about?"

"He's a grad student, and he knows a ton about Wupatki and the surrounding areas. Look at this: he's saying some of the exact same things as Aquarius: The basic qualities of the subterranean landscape are changing."

Dominic reached for the packet. "Here, let me take a look."

"I already called him. He said he'll meet us Saturday at six. Can you be there?"

"Sure. Just tell me where to go."

She looked at him with impatience. "We'll go together. I'll drive."

When Saturday came around, Surina insisted on treating Dominic to dinner at a new Thai restaurant. They sat across from each other with curried dishes that turned cold long before the meal was finished; the two were deep in conversation, quickly straying from the subject of the constellations to the basic details of their personal lives. Though Dominic had just traveled with Surina partway across the globe, he had learned little about her. Now, she filled in some of the basic details about her background and her family, in particular her father, who had moved overseas to advocate for peace between Palestinians and Israelis.

A look of realization came over Dominic's face as she spoke. "Okay," he said, "I'm just now catching your meaning. Before, when you said your dad did peace work, I thought you said *piece work*--like when you make crafts or whatever, and you get paid for each piece that you finish."

"No, no. *Peace* work. He keeps trying to get me more involved, and I'm a *little* involved, but . . . I think I'm going to spend more time on that, or something like it. Some of the things I'm doing now don't seem that important."

"Like what? Going to school? Drawing comics? I like reading your comics, by the way. They're hilarious."

"Well, I'm not going to draw those comics anymore. It's too time-consuming. Anyway, I feel like it served its purpose." Surina gave Dominic a brief, knowing smile. "If it wasn't for that zine, we wouldn't have gone to Peru together."

"True."

"So, I probably won't be stopping by the record shop anymore. I don't really like going in there anyway. The owner gives me the creeps, and Chad is a jerk." Surina hesitated. "Are you two still not friends?"

"We're definitely not friends."

"That must be awkward."

Dominic shrugged. "It's getting easier, but Chad is spiteful to people who reject him. He was giving me hell, ridiculing me and playing pranks, but he's starting to lay off. It's true he's a jerk, but sometimes I do miss him. He's . . . adventurous. I like to travel, and get outdoors in summer, and in winter I go skiing at the Snowbowl, and none of my other friends like to do that stuff. Chad was the only one."

Surina leaned forward with sudden enthusiasm. "Dominic, I *love* to ski. I'll go with you. None of my other friends will ski, and I used to beg my husband to go with me, but he was always afraid of breaking his legs. What else do you like to do? Do you go kayaking, or hiking, or . . . ."

"I don't hike, but I love kayaking."

"We should go together. After we get Hannah." Surina reached for her water glass and hesitated, gazing at it thoughtfully. "We *will* get her out. It's not just wishful thinking. I feel like it's certain. As long as we do what we *should* do, we'll all get out together."

Dominic remained silent. He knew what he was likely to do, but wasn't at all sure that he would know what he *should* do. Especially not there, in that strange, frightening realm.

On the drive to Greg's house, Surina mused over her experiences in the starry realms. "I need water," she said suddenly, lifting a hand to her neck. "That food must have had a ton of MSG in it. My throat feels like it's swelling up."

"What?" A note of panic sounded in Dominic's voice. "Are you allergic?"

"No, I'm just thirsty."

"Want to stop somewhere?"

"Let's just wait until we get to Greg's."

"How sure are you about this Greg character?" he asked. "Shouldn't we look for someone more professional, like an actual geologist?"

"No, we need a grad student. If we get someone more professional, they'll ask too many questions, or they won't waste their time talking to us. Grad students just want someone to take an interest in their work. They're desperate."

"You've really thought this out," Dominic mused.

Greg lived in a trailer court about an hour north of downtown Flagstaff. Before either Dominic or Surina had a chance to knock on the door of his mobile home, he opened it with an air of excitement. His glasses reflected the porch light, veiling his eyes, but Dominic sensed the eagerness in his posture and tone. "Come on in," he said, waving them inside.

Surina smiled and thanked him with the same enthusiasm, but Dominic only felt his anxiety building. *What if we don't learn anything useful? What then?*

As they crowded into the entryway, Greg studied Dominic with curiosity. "Um . . . are you, by any chance, the same Dominic who fell into a blowhole at Wupatki?"

Dominic felt his throat constricting. "Yeah," he replied grudgingly. "That's me."

Greg ducked his head, shoved his hands in his pockets. "Cool. Well, I mean, it's not cool, because, you know . . . ."

"Yeah, I get it."

"Come in. We can sit in the kitchen, if that's all right."

He led them around the corner. The kitchen was low-lit and cramped, with a large dining booth taking up much of the space.

Surina slid onto one of the cushioned seats and started in right away. "I have kind of an odd question. A friend of mine is studying the geology of some temple grounds in the Andes. He pointed out that there's plenty of limestone in the area that's good for building, but the builders chose to travel deep into the mountains and haul huge chunks of limestone from hard-to-reach places. He said that the particular stone they used was a black stone that had special qualities. It was called dolomitic limestone, and—"

"Oh, sure," Greg said. He stood beside the table,

stuffing his hands into his pockets again. "Dolomitic limestone does have some special properties."

"So you know about it," Surina replied, surprised. "Have you studied Andean geology?"

"Well, dolomite isn't particular to the Andes. There are different types of dolomite—and technically, dolomite is different than limestone, but it is possible for limestone to become exposed to substances that give it dolomitic properties. When someone refers to dolomitic limestone, they're saying that the stone is transforming in a particular way. That's actually happening at Wupatki, but it's happening so slowly that the change has been in progress for hundreds of years."

"You mean, it's happening to the Kaibab limestone?"

"Yes. It's becoming dolomitic, probably from absorbing the upper volcanic layers."

"And what's the significance of that?"

"Well . . . hang on a second, and I'll show you." Greg started away, and then paused. "Can I get you anything to drink? Beer? Wine?"

"We could use some water," Dominic replied.

"Plain, or flavored water? I have this carbonated strawberry water . . . ." Greg opened the refrigerator and peered inside. "I don't have much in the way of food, but there's some leftover birthday cake. I turned thirty last week."

"Two waters, please," Surina replied. "I'll have the strawberry. Dominic likes plain. And happy birthday."

Greg set a can in front of her. The kitchen lights glinted across his glasses, so that Dominic couldn't see his eyes, but his voice sounded curious. "Are you two . . . together?"

Dominic exchanged a dumbfounded glance with Surina. "No," he said at last. "I'm together, but Surina is a mess."

She elbowed him.

Greg gave a slight nod and turned away. "I'll be right back."

Surina drummed her fingers on the table. Dominic leaned close to her, so close that he felt the warmth of her neck.

"I think he's high," he whispered.

Laughter erupted from her, though she tried to suppress it.

"There aren't a lot of windows in here, so I think he's into edibles. I saw gummy bears in the refrigerator."

"Dominic, stop."

"What? It's not a problem. Like I said, he's an intellectual smoker. Or whatever you call it when someone uses edibles. He can ride the gummies and explain complicated geological phenomena at the same time. You saw, it, right?" He waved his fingers in front of his face. "The vacant eyes?"

"Shut up," she whispered.

Greg returned with a warm beer and a printout of Wupatki's geology. The illustrated rock layers descended in shades of red, orange, yellow, brown, and black. He slapped the printout on the table and pointed at the darkest, topmost section. "Here's what Wupatki looks like under the surface. The top layer is basalt from the volcanic eruption. Basalt is less durable than it looks; it's harder than sandstone but much more vulnerable to environmental influences than, say, sandstone. Most of it has already eroded and seeped into the earth. Beneath that you have the Moenkopi sandstone, maybe a couple dozen feet or less, and under that you have a few hundred feet of Kaibab limestone. Sandstone is very porous, so when the basalt erodes, it's carried away in ground water and leaks through the sandstone, and settles in the limestone. Limestone is less vulnerable; it does change, but the

transformation will occur very slowly, so that we may not
be able to see it in a lifetime . . . ."

Dominic tried to focus on Greg's words, but he never
did well with long lectures on subjects he was unfamiliar
with. After a few minutes, all he heard was *Blah, blah,
erosion, blah, blah, millions of years*, and so on. He
watched as Greg downed one beer and then another. He
seemed to have beers stashed all over the place: a six-
pack of longnecks under the booth, two imperial stout
bombers within reaching distance in a small cabinet.
Surina helped herself to another strawberry water.

"Limestone is made from compressed skeletons, so
it's rich in calcium," Greg was saying. "When it becomes
dolomitic, it's slowly absorbing the basalt metals, so it
also becomes rich in magnesium and iron."

"But how might that change the capabilities of the
stone?" Surina asked. "I mean, for instance . . . since it's
absorbing metals, would it be more conductive to
electrical currents, or . . . ."

"Calcium is also a metal. It's generally more
conductive than magnesium and iron, but the actual level
of conductivity depends on other factors. Limestone, in
bulk form, would be a very poor conductor."

"Ah," Surina said. "Damn." She studied the graphic
with a frown. "So . . . the limestone is enveloped by
sandstone. Is there some significance to that? Because
there's a similar theme in the temple grounds we just
visited. It's made of dolomitic limestone and granite. Is
granite similar to sandstone in any way?"

"Yeah, they're both mostly quartz and feldspar, but
granite is made from lava, and sandstone is made from
bonded sand. It's usually bonded by calcite."

"My friend said it was significant that the builders
used stones that had contrasting properties—that when
you put those properties side by side, a kind of energy

builds between them," Surina said. "Does that make any sense?"

Surina's hopes diminished as Greg delved into a rambling speech about the crystalline properties of granite, the water-bearing ability of sandstone, and the organic wonders of calcium carbonate. The alcohol seemed to have affected him at last; his voice increased in volume, and his sentences became less scholarly. "The Great Pyramid—you know, the one in Egypt—that was made with dolomite and calcite too. Let's see . . . the inside was dolomite from Mokattam. And um . . . what was I saying? Oh yeah, the *outside* was white limestone that they brought all the way from Tura. Now, *that* limestone is full of calcite, which is the most stable form of calcium carbonate. So, like, it's like . . . see, calcium is important. Calcium is a key transmitter in humans; it reacts to hormonal and neurotransmitter signals to produce transformations within the body. Actually it's more like a converter. It initiates and controls our development when we're in the womb. Our whole growth as human beings is sparked by an intracellular calcium signal."

Surina glanced at Dominic and saw him slouching, resting his head on his arm as though taking a nap.

"So, when Khufu was overseeing the Great Pyramid," Greg continued, "maybe he *knew* this about calcium, and that's why he had giant stones hauled all the way from Tura. Calcium is just cool. There's a lot of it on the moon, and it kinda proves that the Earth and moon were once, like, one thing. I mean, they were one entity."

"Good Lord." Dominic raised his head to address Surina: "We should go."

Greg looked uncertainly at her. "You need to go?"

"Thanks so much," she replied, standing. "We really appreciate you taking the time to talk to us."

"Well . . . I hope I was of some help."

"You were."

He trailed behind Dominic and Surina as they headed for the front door. "Hey, if you have any more questions or want to talk, don't hesitate to contact me. You know, I'm kind of a buff for this subject. I could talk about it all day."

"We'll remember that," Dominic replied.

"I can't get enough of rocks." Greg gestured to a rack on the wall, where a rope hung with carabiners and a harness, and other items that Surina recognized as rock climbing equipment. "Do either of you climb?"

"No," Surina replied.

"All the best climbing areas are right around here. I just finished all the routes at The Pit—that's all Kaibab limestone, by the way. If you're ever looking for a new sport . . . ."

Dominic hurriedly opened the door. "Thanks. Bye, Greg."

Greg turned on the outside light and closed the door behind them. Surina hugged her arms across her chest; the evening had become unexpectedly cool. "This is why I didn't take any science classes in college," she said. "No science geek can stop at just one or two abstract concepts."

"Really? I was enrapt. Who knew that calcium was so fascinating? Calcium! It created the moon and powered the Great Pyramid! It sent embryonic signals through the King's Chamber! And then Khufu had a baby!"

Surina laughed. "He did get a little carried away."

"It was the edibles. No stoner can stop at just one or two mind-blowing ideas about the true meaning of, like, alkali earth metals."

"You're terrible. Why do you keep making fun of him? He's really smart, and he's helping us."

"It's your fault. You only laugh when I tease people, and I like making you smile. You look like every cell in your body is smiling."

Surina's smile vanished.

Dominic paused near the car, looking up at her. "What's the matter?"

She stopped and stood in silence, eyes lowered, and then met his gaze. "Did we learn anything that's going to help us?"

"I don't know. I'm going to take notes, sleep on it, and decide in the morning."

Both were quiet during the car ride. The silence began to seem a bit heavy to Dominic, and he was thinking of something to say when Surina blurted: "Don't tell me I have a nice smile. My ex-husband used to say that same thing to me."

"What, the same way I just said it?"

"Well, he'd say it like, 'Your whole being lights up when you smile.'"

Dominic shrugged. "It's true, though. Can't be helped."

"Fine, but you don't have to say it."

"All right. I'll keep it to myself."

Surina glanced at him. Seemingly against her own volition, she flashed a tiny, genuine smile.

Twenty minutes later they pulled up in front of his apartment complex. Dominic hesitated as he opened the passenger door. "Surina . . . you remember how you told me that when you were at Virgo, you found out that Wibben was already dead? That he had drowned in the pond?"

"Yes. Well, of course he's dead. He's been in there since the nineteen-forties."

Dominic was silent, brooding.

"Hannah could easily be alive," Surina said gently.

"There's likely to be water down there. Greg said the sandstone acts as a filter for the water that seeps down into the tunnels. Hannah could survive on that. And she has air to breathe, through the cracks and holes. But . . . the tunnel system is at least twenty-four miles wide. She could have wandered anywhere."

"It is that wide, but most of it isn't accessible. The tunnels are too small even for a child to crawl through."

"She can't be that far, then. We'll find her and bring her home . . . somehow."

After an evening of internet searches, note taking, and futile attempts at solving the riddles of the stars, Dominic and Surina found themselves seemingly at a dead end. They sat at Surina's kitchen table with their laptops open among a spread of books and papers, their silence reflecting their lack of ideas. Surina rested her chin in the palm of her hand, gazing helplessly at the notes and star charts strewn in front of her. "I've still got nothing," she murmured. "The only thing I've figured out is why some of the things that happened to me and Hannah seemed so familiar. Do you know much about Sumerian mythology?"

"Not really," Dominic replied, "but I read some things from The Epic of Gilgamesh. Chad talked about that story when we ended up in the zodiac together. He felt like he was living out the myth."

"Well, same here, except in my case, it was Inanna. She tricked a water-god out of some sacred doctrines—or tablets, or something—and she floated away with them in a boat, and he kept sending someone to stop her. I swear, it's almost exactly like what happened to me and Hannah." Surina sat back in her chair with a sigh. "But it's not helpful. Sorry."

"All right." Dominic stood up. "We'll keep trying. I'm

going to get going. Thanks, Surina.”

“No problem. I’ll let you know if . . . .”

She trailed off. Dominic paused, turning back to her expectantly, but she simply stared at the star chart. After some time she said, “You know what . . . maybe this is all simpler than I think. Like, it’s not a complicated riddle. It’s just something that’s right in front of me.”

“How so?”

She beckoned him toward the chair. “Sit back down.”

“What is it?”

Surina’s eyes lit with a new intensity as she studied the map. “Okay, okay . . . I’m an idiot. Look.” She pointed to the Orion figure. With a finger, she traced a line along the Eridanus constellation that splashed against the figure’s legs.

Dominic climbed back onto the chair, leaning close beside her with his elbows on the table.

“These web sites I went to, they say that the Eridanus springs from Orion’s leg,” Surina said. “But when I was on the river, Eridanus was flowing *toward* Orion—not away from it.”

“Okay.”

“Do you remember what Nemcio said about the Mosna River? He said that the labyrinth ceremony didn’t start on the temple grounds—it started on the opposite side of the river. People were expected to wade through it before climbing through the portal. You didn’t do that, but Hank insisted on showering me with water.”

“Because he wanted to see you in a wet T-shirt,” Dominic replied dryly.

“Nevertheless . . . .”

“You think it made a difference? For you, I mean?”

“It might have. Look: in the constellations, Orion is wading *into* the Eridanus River. Nemcio said that water from the river used to flow beneath the temple; it’s blocked now, but in the past, when people used the temple, it was important."

"Okay."

"I wonder . . . ." She paused. "Maybe the water isn't just symbolic of cleansing. Maybe it has a practical, scientific purpose. I'm just thinking . . . ." Abruptly she gathered the papers, flipping through them and pulling out the notes she'd taken on her trip through the starry realm. "Two types of stone," she said. "Limestone and sandstone. Aquarius kept talking about how there are those two types of stone at the labyrinth, the Great Pyramid, and Wupatki; he said that they have important chemical properties."

"So, what are you thinking?" Dominic asked.

"Water," she replied. "If there are three factors that need to be in place, and the first two are the types of stone, the third could be water. A lot of ancient temples in the Americas and India were built near confluences of rivers, or had canals built to irrigate water toward them. Nemcio said that a lot of the pyramids around the American have systems of water canals that flow beneath them—like King Pakal's and Kukulkan's temples . . . but I don't know if the canals were ceremonial, or if they were just irrigation systems." Surina gave Dominic a weary look. "I looked up some research on the Great Pyramid, too, but it just led to a billion unsubstantiated theories—so let's forget that one."

"It can't be water," Dominic replied. "There isn't a river at Wupatki. It's desert, it's dry . . . most of the time."

Surina raised an eyebrow at him. "*Most* of the time."

It hit him suddenly: "There was a rainstorm at Wupatki just as we fell in. We were crawling around in water. I was soaked."

"Exactly."

"But . . . ." Dominic thought back. "What about Chad?

He got in, too."

"But he was close by, and he was standing in the rain. Maybe all it took was for you to call him in. And it's not just that. Wibben told me that before he fell in at Externsteine, he was hiding from security guards in the artificial pond. And there's one more thing. Hang on."

She pulled the laptop close and clicked a few times, first on a photo folder, then on another labeled "Peru." Dominic waited while she scrolled through the thumbnails.

"Look," she said, clicking on an image.

Dominic peered at the screen. The photo showed Surina standing in front of the stone labyrinth, wearing a woolen poncho, clutching the sides and spreading it wide like a pair of wings. She stood in the rain, smiling, while a few people lingered in the sheltered area behind her. A water drop blurred part of the image; Dominic leaned closer, trying to get a better look.

Surina asked: "What's the difference between me and everyone else?"

"Is that Nemcio in the background?"

"What's the difference, Dominic?" she pressed him.

"Yes, I see it," he said. "You're soaked. Unless your llama cape kept you dry."

"No, I was already soaked before I put it on. I'm not going to find any solid evidence about how people did things thousands of years ago, so I'm relying on our evidence. This is a photo of my first trip to Chavín. I didn't want to tell you before, but . . . that first time, we bribed the guards and went into the temple after it closed, and I got lost. And somehow I ended up in the underworld—not for very long," she added. "Just for a few minutes. But I met Virgo. I thought I was . . . having a vision, or hallucinating. Well, it didn't feel like a hallucination. It seemed real. I found my way out, and I didn't tell anyone what happened."

Dominic stared at her, not comprehending. "What do you mean, you met Virgo?"

"I mean, that place I was just in, with Hannah—I've been there before."

"And you met Virgo? Were you in the underworld—the place with the zombie things?"

"No, but I must have gone to the edge of it. Virgo stopped me. And . . . we talked. I didn't tell you before because I didn't want to sound like a nut."

"You? *I* sounded like a nut."

Surina reached out and snapped the laptop shut. "Aquarius kept hinting that there were certain conditions that needed to be met in order to get into the celestial plane. And he kept talking about water. I thought he was just being arrogant, but thinking back, I think he was trying to tell me that there needs to be some kind of water element involved."

"Okay. Well, maybe this is something."

"I'm not *sure*, " Surina added hesitantly. "He was drunk . . . maybe. I don't know. He could have just been boosting his ego." She paused. "No, I *am* sure of it. He knew more than he was letting on. And now that I think about it . . . I'm sure he *told* me that the other factor was water, and then he said something like, 'I'm giving you that one for free.' I didn't take him seriously because I thought he was drunk."

"Then, let's go with it," Dominic said. "But please keep thinking of other solutions, just in case." He pulled his cell phone from his pocket. Surina waited while he swiped and clicked.

"Are you looking something up?" she asked.

"The weather." He held the phone out, giving her a view of the screen. "This is the forecast for the Wupatki area this week."

"Rain," Surina said, with excitement in her voice. "Two days from now." She gave Dominic a look of reluctant hope. "What do you think? We can get some things ready, and go to Wupatki during the rainstorm."

"Well, it doesn't say it's going to be a *storm*." Dominic scrutinized the screen again. "What do you mean, we can 'get some things ready'?"

"We'll get some climbing equipment. We can go back down the hole where Hannah got lost."

Dominic let out a slow sigh. "Okay, well . . . first of all, I know nothing about climbing or equipment. Secondly, if we go back to that hole, we'll have to sneak in. We will be breaking the law. And that's fine; it's worth it to save Hannah. I just want to make sure you're aware of that. And thirdly . . . no offense, but I'm not sure you can fit through the blowhole. I barely fit before. And I've gained a couple of pounds."

"So, go on a liquid diet for the next few days."

He scoffed. "Right. That's going to give me the energy I need."

"Well, we have to *try* to get in," Surina said. "Maybe there's a bigger hole somewhere. If you can get down there, maybe you can call me in somehow, the way you called Chad."

"But we still have a problem. Even if we get into the hole, we need a way to get out."

Surina mulled over that. Hesitantly, she said: "You know . . . we do know someone who has the equipment to get us down there and up again."

Dominic looked at her blankly.

"Greg," she said, and Dominic recoiled a little, his face set in a mild grimace.

"I'm sure he'd love to," Dominic said, "if it wasn't illegal. You know we'll be trespassing, right?"

"Yes, but when we talked to him, he was eager to do

anything to help Hannah," Surina reminded him.

"Sure he did, not knowing that 'anything' might involve a crime, an alternate dimension, and a soul-sucking demon."

"Okay, but listen: Are you broke?"

"Am I what?"

"Did you not just spend all of your money on a trip to Peru?"

"Ah," he said. "Right."

"Me too, and equipment rental costs money. I bet Greg would loan his out for free." Surina inched her chair closer to Dominic. "Let me see the weather forecast again. Click on the detailed view. We have to know what time it's supposed to rain, and for how long."

He showed her the display. "Evening. That's good. We can't go out there in the middle of the day, when the park is open."

Surina was nodding, her eyes fixed on the screen. "Right. This is good, Dominic. Two days. She's likely to still be alive." She paused, and added with determination: "I will make myself fit through that hole."

"Well . . . we'll figure that out when we get to it. But we need to plan this. We have to scope out the park at night, figure out how to get in, and we'll have to go and look at that hole. There's no way they left it uncovered after what happened. They might have a grate over it like the one in the tourist area. We'll probably have to go out there with tools and remove it. So there's that, there's getting the equipment, learning how to use it . . . ."

"I'll handle the climbing equipment," Surina said. "Just trust me to manage that, okay? Can you scope out the park?"

Dominic nodded. "I'll see if I can take the bus out there tomorrow morning, before the park opens, just to have a look. If the bus doesn't go that far, I might need you to drive me."

"Sure. Let me know."

Dominic started toward the door, and Surina watched him with subtle concern. "Don't get into any trouble, okay?"

"I don't intend to."

"All right. Good luck."

After he left, Surina paced the apartment for some time, thinking up various explanations to give to Greg about her sudden need for climbing gear. None of her rationales seemed plausible, and every lie seemed to lead into a larger network of lies. She decided on a partial truth: she and Dominic wanted to practice with the gear, Dominic already had an instructor lined up, and their rush to learn came from the hope of finding Hannah. If someone did end up detecting life somewhere in the belly of Wupatki, and broke the earth open to find her, Surina and Dominic wanted to have the skills to be part of the rescue team.

It was a lame story, but Surina told herself that there was truth in it. She knew that the local authorities had given up looking for Hannah. There would be no rescue team aside from her and Dominic.

At home, she called Greg and informed him of her newfound enthusiasm for rock climbing. It was a lengthy conversation, full of unfamiliar terms that Surina pretended to understand and questions that she tried her best to evade. Greg eagerly agreed to meet with her the following day.

After hanging up, Surina spent the rest of the night watching YouTube videos on climbing basics. She studied into the late hours. Long after she retired to bed, her mind was still busy with plans and with riddles that still needed solving. In the early hours of morning she gave up sleeping; she got up and opened the window to gaze at the night sky. The early night had shown her the constellations of familiar realms, of places she had traveled through: Cassiopeia, Ursa Major and Minor, and more. She had looked to them for remembrance, to help recall any clues she might need on the next part of her journey.

Summer was beginning the transition into fall, and the ever-moving wheel of stars was changing with it. As Surina looked to the horizon, she saw Orion, the warrior, emerging from behind the Earth, ascending once again into the night sky with its staff raised aloft and shield cast forward. From Surina's perspective, the constellation would rise earlier and earlier each night, becoming a beacon constellation throughout the cool winter months. She saw hope in the sight. She kept the image in her mind throughout the following days, and at night she continued to search for signs in the stars, and patiently waited for the clouds and the rains to come.